THE EMERALD PEACOCK

by

Katharine Gordon

BOOK CLUB ASSOCIATES LONDON

This edition published 1979 by
Book Club Associates by arrangement
with Hodder & Stoughton Ltd

First printed 1978

Printed in Great Britain by
Richard Clay (The Chaucer Press) Ltd.,
Bungay, Suffolk

1

A line of sunlight, sharp as a blade, shone between the drawn curtains of the carriage, and burned on Bianca's closed eyelids. She wakened slowly, reluctantly returning from the dreaming comfort of sleep, to the cramped reality of the brougham, where her mother slept beside her, too exhausted to be disturbed by anything—either the dust thickened air, or the heat and constant jolting.

Bianca, awake, felt that she could not breathe. She leaned forward and opened the chink in the curtains a little wider, peering out, to see dimly through the dust the uniforms of the mounted escort and her father riding slowly alongside, his horse picking its way carefully over the rough ground. Rocks and stunted thorn trees loomed beside the road, their size and shape hazed by the dust, but in the distance the air was clear, and she could see, far ahead, the red walls of the Madoremahal, shimmering in the heat of the afternoon.

Colonel O'Neil, riding beside the carriage, saw the distant red walls with relief, and the heat and the dust, which in fact he did not notice, had nothing to do with his desire to see the whole party inside the walls of the Madoremahal, the palace of the Ruler of Thinpahari. The holiday feeling, that usually made the journey so enjoyable, had begun to change very soon after they had left the foothills of Jindbagh State, and he knew that the escort were restless too. He watched their disturbed faces as they talked among themselves and wondered with anxiety what they were discussing, what was so secret and frightening that they could not speak with him about their worries, but lowered their voices, or fell silent whenever he came near. Whatever it was, it made them very uneasy and taciturn. Indeed, this year, the journey to Madore was not proving to be a happy one.

The annual Durbar, held in Madore city by the Maharaja of Thinpahari, the Ruler of the combined States of Jindbagh, Lambagh, and Diwarbagh, was the great event of the whole year, not only for the families of the Rajas of the three northern States, and their friends, but also for the Europeans attached to the royal households. Cut off all the year in the small isolated hill States, these people seldom met except on this visit to Madore city, and as a rule, for the O'Neil family, the travelling was one of the pleasures of the visit—a sort of splendid series of picnics before the more sophisticated pleasures of the Durbar.

Colonel O'Neil knew the journey well. He had been in India for nearly thirty years, and had served the Ruler for most of that time, commanding the State Forces of the three States known as Thinpahari. Terence O'Neil had helped the Ruler weld the three small hill States into one country, and to him it was his own country, the land of his heart. He loved and admired the Ruler, and was in his turn loved and trusted by the Ruler, and by the people of the hill States.

Terence had come out to India as a young man, having joined the army. India took his interest immediately and he soon felt that it was a country that he would never wish to leave. When he met the young Nawab of Lambagh who was staying in Madore City, in his palace, the Madoremahal, Terence found a kindred spirit. The two men liked each other at once, and the Nawab suggested that Terence might like to come up to his State of Lambagh for some shooting. Terence did this at the first opportunity and got more shooting than he bargained for. The two small States adjoining Lambagh, which were the States of Jindbagh and Diwarbagh, had joined together and were attempting to take Lambagh from Terence's new friend. He joined in the campaign with enthusiasm and his clever strategies and planning routed the marauders, defeating them so thoroughly that the Nawab found himself the conqueror of the two States. Terence helped him to bring them peacefully under his rule, and the Nawab took the title of Ruler of the new State thus formed, which he called Thinpahari. He offered the command of his army to Terence, who had already decided that these valleys were where he wished to live. He bought himself out of the army and took possession of the small palace in Jindbagh, and soon became famous for his ability to train and lead the Ruler's forces.

It was to the beautiful valley of Jindbagh that he brought a bride, after his first and only trip back to Ireland. He had met and fallen in love with the daughter of an old friend, and married her as soon as he could get her father's permission. Blanche O'Neil adored her husband, but, to his sorrow, never ceased to long for Ireland—India to her was a place of exile, where she lived willingly, because he was there, and for no other reason. She liked the hill people, who loved her for her gentleness and her gaiety. She never complained, but Terence, loving her as he did, was unhappily conscious that she always hoped that one day they would go away from the valleys and back to the green wet fields and cold winds of her own country. When they had had their first child, a son, he had hoped that she would become more reconciled to India, but the child had not lived—nor had the second baby. The daughter born to them at last was strong and healthy and they both adored her, but as she grew older, Blanche seemed to long more and more for what she still called 'Home' and Terence, watching her fade before his eyes, knew that the time was coming when he would have to give in, and leave.

On their yearly journeys down from the mountains, through the green foothills and over the dusty plains, he met many old friends, men who had fought beside him in his younger days. These men, retired now to their villages, would wait on the side of the road to greet him, and would take the family back to spend the night in small mud-walled whitewashed houses, where Mrs O'Neil and Bianca were made welcome in the women's quarters, while the men fought old battles over again, and the cry of the *koel*, the hot weather bird, punctuated the talk and laughter like a distant bell tolling among the trees.

But this year the talk around the evening fires had not been of past battles and old victories, but of the present unrest throughout the country. Jindbagh, high in the mountains, had been untouched by rumour. Protected by windswept passes, life went on, unchanged by any whisper of mutiny or murder; indeed British rule had not touched the lives of these distant hill people. They had their own rulers and their own laws, and in the case of the hill States of Thinpahari, they were content and peaceful. The only changes they knew were the changes of the seasons, when different labours and different crops came round in known rotation. The plains could be seen on clear days, lying like a

Persian carpet under the shimmering heat haze. A different place, a country so far away that it was like something imagined or dreamed, but completely unreal. Very few of the hill peasants went down through the passes, it was a long and dangerous journey to them, and no one had time to waste in travel without reason. The hill people got on with their lives, content to sit and listen to travellers' tales when the Ruler and his servants and soldiers returned from their yearly visit to the plains. They enjoyed hearing the stories, while the winter winds howled through the passes and snow lay thick over the fields and the paths, but they did not believe more than half of what they heard. Such doings were so far outside their experience and were therefore for entertainment only, for brief amazement, until spring broke the snows and life could go on in an orderly way again.

Terence O'Neil, living so long among these people, had absorbed the same easy attitude—indeed, it was his nature to be content and cheerful, seeing things as they appeared, and not looking for trouble. This feeling of unease, and of something happening beneath the surface of life, was like the symptom of an unpleasant illness, the first warning of a germ attacking a healthy body. O'Neil had heard nothing, and was shocked by the stories told in careful undertones of threatened mutiny, of sudden fires in the cantonment towns and of the spread of strange tales of the imminent overthrow of British rule in India. The men who spoke to him were confused by all the hurrying rumours, but of one thing they seemed sure. There was trouble everywhere and blood would flow.

Even the women were affected. 'You should not travel the roads this year, Lady Sahib—take your daughter, and go back, and stay in the hills. There is blood in the stars this year—stay a little with us here, and then go back—do not travel further—' Soft voices pleading, kind worried eyes in brown faces. Blanche O'Neil, already exhausted by the journey, somehow so much more tiring to her this year, paid very little attention to the warnings. She felt very ill for one thing and, for another, she had the Victorian woman's complete trust in her husband's judgment. Had there been any danger he would not have allowed his family to travel, she felt sure. She was far more worried by her own engulfing weakness, and by Bianca, who had at first been feverishly eager to start the journey to Madore, and who now seemed to live in a daze, her eyes veiled and secret, her mind far away. Blanche O'Neil watched this beloved daughter, born to her long after she had given up hope of bearing a living child, and wished that she was safely back in her quiet home in Ireland with this child who seemed to be so swiftly becoming a woman. Blanche loved her husband and would live where he lived, but she was homesick for her own country and could never love India as Terence did.

Bianca listened to the women talking but did not register anything that they said. She sat, rapt in dreams of the year before, and all that had happened at that last Durbar.

Sher Khan, the boy she had known all her life, the Ruler's nephew and his heir, had arrived for the Durbar as usual, and suddenly everything had begun to change for Bianca. Sher Khan, twelve years older than she was, had not played a very big part in her life until then. He was like a loved much older brother, dear to her because he was Khanzada's brother. Khanzada was Sher Khan's youngest sister and Bianca's dearest friend.

Then came last year's Durbar, after the lonely year in Jindbagh.

Things had started to be different, really, when Bianca and Khanzada had been lying under the trees in a corner of the garden. It was early enough in the morning for the air to be cool and fresh, with a breeze blowing the tree shadows over the girls while they lay and gossiped, or fell silent, listening to the doves' soothing croon.

Then a carriage, with outriders, rattled up the drive, and Khanzada said idly, 'They come to arrange the day for my marriage. I suppose the priests from Sagpur have found an auspicious day. What a fearful colour Sagpur puggarees are—that yellow!'

'Marriage—Zada, what are you talking about?'

'Marriage, my dearest Bianca. Come out of the clouds and listen. I am talking about my marriage. I was betrothed to Hardyal, Nawab of Sagpur when I was nine—you have forgotten?'

'No, of course not. But marriage! So soon? Zada, when is it to be?'

'This Durbar, while all our friends and relations are here.'

'It seems to soon. Khanzada, we are only fourteen—'

'You are only fourteen. I am fifteen, and in any case, age does not matter. We are both women now, you know that.'

'Yes—and how I hate this stupid uncomfortable business every month. It is not fair.'

'Well, it is not something that we alone have, Bianca. All women have it. And now that I am grown, I am ready for my husband's bed. Do not look like that, Bianca—it will make no difference! The palace of Sagpur, where we will live, is beautiful, right on the sea, and you will be my first visitor.'

Unconsoled, Bianca lay and looked at this suddenly grown up Khanzada. Presently she asked, frowning, 'Zada, do you love Hardyal?'

'Love? How do I know yet? I have not seen him for six years, but no doubt he will be a good husband, or my uncle would not have chosen him.'

Bianca was thinking this over, when two women servants came out of the Madoremahal, and called Khanzada's name.

'I shall have to go,' said Khanzada, getting up reluctantly. 'Bianca, Sher Khan is going to bring me a bridle for my horse Gila. Will you take it and keep it for me? God knows how long I shall be, being looked at and picked over like a chicken by those Sagpur relatives, making sure that I am a fit mate for their precious Nawab.'

Something in her voice made Bianca glad that she was not about to be a bride. Not like this, chosen and bargained over and going off with a man she did not know.

'Bianca—come back! Where have you wandered to in your mind?' Sher Khan was leaning on a tree beside her, laughing at her as she turned, startled from her thoughts, to look up at him. 'What were you dreaming about, Bianca?'

'I was thinking that I am glad I am not getting married.'

'I thought all girls wanted to get married.'

'Well—yes. I do, one day. But Khanzada is marrying—'

'Yes. I can see why you might be reluctant to have Hardyal as a bridegroom.' He frowned, twirling the rose he held in his hand as if something about it displeased him.

'But if you do not like him, and Khanzada does not know him, why is she marrying him?'

'Because his father is a very old friend of our uncle's. Because he is very rich. Because he is already betrothed. Oh I do not really know why this marriage is going to take place.'

'It seems silly to me. I shall not have my marriage arranged. I shall marry the man I love—'

Sher Khan laughed, the shadow gone from his face. 'Oho, will you indeed? And who is the fortunate man?'

'No one. There is no one.'

'That seems very sad. What about me?'

'You—?'

'Well, there is no need to appear so astonished! What is wrong with me?'

Bianca looked at him, her eyes moving from his thick tumbled black hair to grey eyes full of laughter, to broad shoulders and elegantly slim waist and hips. Sher Khan was very tall and she had a long way to look up as she examined him. The expression on his face changed as she looked, something came into his eyes, a look that was suddenly serious and intent.

'Well, do I please you? What is wrong with me as a husband?'

'Nothing—nothing. But you are my brother—' Bianca was stammering, looking away from those very compelling eyes. What had started as a joke, seemed very different now.

'Bianca. I am most certainly not your brother, most assuredly not. Look at me, Bianca.'

But when she looked at him, he said nothing more. He stood, staring down at her, as if he had never seen her before. A silence fell between them that was so full of meaning that Bianca could not sustain it.

'Zada said—she said that you would have a bridle—'

'A bridle—a golden chain to bind my white bird to my arm—'

'What are you talking about?'

'I do not know. Bianca, when did you become so beautiful? How dare you become a beauty without telling me, changing into such beauty while I was not here!'

'I am beautiful?' The upward, questioning look she gave him was without coquetry, and all the more telling for that reason.

'You are beautiful. So beautiful—Bianca, tell me, are you going to Sandala's party tonight?'

'My father and mother are going. I do not know if they will take me.'

'Wear this for me and do not change any more while my back is turned.'

He walked away, a tall striding young man with a splendid figure, and Bianca sat on the grass, her white dress dappled with green shadows as the breeze blew, her mind as disturbed as the leaves in the breeze.

When Khanzada came out, Bianca was still looking confused and had no bridle, nothing in her hand at all but a white rose. Khanzada gave her a sharp look, sighed, and said nothing, smiling a little to herself.

Bianca was not allowed to go the Raja of Sandala's party that night. Her pleading did no good.

'No my darling child, no indeed. It is a late party, and not for you. I am not going to let you go out after dinner until you are grown up. Not another word, Bianca, it is high time you were in bed already. There's my good girl—kiss me, and take yourself off.'

So Bianca had gone, reluctant, to her bed, had lain sleepless, and had finally got up and gone into the dark garden, trailing her muslin nightrobe and her peignoir ruffles over the dew-damp grass, her long hair heavy on her shoulders.

When she reached the trees where she had lain that morning, she stopped and stood looking around her as if she could see herself and Sher Khan there and hear again what he had said. Instead, he himself had stepped out from the trees, frightening her considerably. He was as startled as she was.

'What are you doing here at this time of night?'

'You sound like my mother—'

'My thanks—I have never been told that I sounded like anyone's mother before. But you have not answered my question. What are you doing here?'

'I couldn't sleep. So I came here to think—'

'A pretty story—you keep a rendezvous. You came here to meet that idiot Charles Morton, or that donkey Durrampore. I noticed they left the party early.'

'Why on earth should I meet two idiots? What would I do with them?'

'Oh, not both of them—one of them! Oh Bianca, you are driving me mad. Go away, with your trailing muslins and your hair like dark water, and your eyes. Girls are not supposed to go about alone in the night—you should have your woman with you. Where is she?'

'You *do* sound like my mother—'

'Do not keep saying that. Go *away*.'

'Very well. Now you know what you are doing here.'

'What do you mean?'

'*You* came here to meet one of your girls. Everyone knows how many girls you have.'

'Oh, do they. Well, I did not come here to meet any girl. I came here to think about one.'

For some reason Bianca's heart began to beat very fast.

'Which one?'

'A very aggravating one. Now, are you going?'

'Yes. But I would like to tell you something first—'

'What?'

'I wore your rose—even though they would not let me come to the party. Look—'

The rose rested precariously in the ruffles at her throat. Sher Khan saw only the white throat in the moonlight, and the innocently inviting eyes.

'Bianca—thank you. The rose is valuable to me now. May I have it?'

'I am afraid it is a little crushed—I must have lain on it, I think—'

Their hands touched, clung—the rose fell, forgotten, as Bianca accepted her first kiss.

That kiss burned on her mouth now, in memory, as the women spoke of omens and disasters, and Bianca smiled, remembering grey eyes, and ardent words and the smell of a crushed rose.

As the days of the journey went by, Colonel O'Neil heartily wished that he had left his family behind in Jindbagh. If his wife had not been so exhausted, he would have sent her back, but he feared the extra travelling for her, and also he was anxious to get to Madore and see for himself how things were. So he travelled on down the road over the plains, with a feeling of unease that grew deeper every day.

As they got further from the hills, the change in the temper of the country grew more marked. There were fewer old friends waiting to greet him, and less hospitality. The family camped out each night, drawing off the road into the shelter of the trees, sleeping round a great fire, the escort rolled in their blankets beside their tired horses. Several times they were disturbed by the horses whinnying, and had wakened to see riders galloping past, like shadows on the white road, and in the daytime, too, they met dusty men on tired horses, riding fast down the tree-shaded roads, men who did not draw rein for the customary greetings, but rode on with averted faces, as men who pass something they fear to see. All the travellers on the road seemed to avoid looking at the Europeans. 'As if we were lepers, or people condemned to death—' Terence shuddered at his own thoughts, and added this strange lack of interest in their movement to his other worries.

Now, crossing the great arid plain of Madore, they saw no one. The mud-walled villages of this district were built in hidden places, far from the road, behind the carven tumbling boulders and thick thorn scrub. A column of smoke, perhaps straight and motionless in the still hot air, or a brown shifting cloud of dust, marking where a restless herd of goats were feeding, or two or three carrion kites, hanging above, as still as pencil strokes in a drawing; these things showed that there was life in the vicinity, but that was all there was to see. No sign of another traveller. This was the hottest time of the day. People usually crossed this desert land before the sun was up, to avoid the burning heat and the constant blowing dust raised by the carriage wheels. But O'Neil decided to make a forced march of it and get to Madore a day early, and the escort made no complaint. They were, it seemed, as eager to reach the journey's end as he was.

Looking about him in the dusty no man's land of the plain, O'Neil glanced at the carriage lurching along beside him, and saw his daughter's face at the opening of the carriage curtains. He rode closer to speak to her. 'How is your mother?'

'Hush. She is asleep at last. Her head was troubling her, but she always feels better after she has slept.'

O'Neil frowned, trying to see his wife's face through the curtained dusty gloom of the carriage. His lowered voice was rough with anxiety.

'Bianca—I did not like her looks this morning. Perhaps we

should have stayed at Ranighar another night—'

Bianca, seeing his face, grey with dust and shadowed with tiredness, did her best to soothe him, for her father was the one person who must never be worried or upset. She had been trained by her mother to keep all domestic worries from the master of the house, who had his own life to lead, and responsibility for them as well.

'Please, father, don't fret. She is perfectly all right. She will be glad to get to Madore, and get out of this vehicle and have a proper bath and a rest. That is all she needs—she said so herself, if you remember, last night.' O'Neil, very little reassured by the forced cheerfulness of his daughter's voice, nodded, trying to be cheerful himself.

'Yes—so she did. Well then, my child, not so long now, another hour at the most, and the good God willing, we'll have her safely in the Madoremahal. Get your head in now, Bianca, and close those curtains together. You are letting in the dust all over your mother.'

Bianca withdrew her head obediently, and sank back into her seat, though the air was much fresher outside. The heat behind the canvas curtains was stifling and thick white dust lay on everything, creeping into every crevice, shifting a little with every turn of the wheels. Bianca could feel it gritting between her teeth, crawling over her skin and prickling in her eyes. She wished for the thousandth time that she could be riding with her father, but had made no bother about sharing the carriage with her mother, who had decided not to ride this year. Blanche O'Neil had been glad to have her daughter with her for more than one reason. Although Bianca had known the men of the escort all her life, and had ridden with them and her father and mother on all the treks back to Madore city, for the last two years Blanche had felt that Bianca was too old to ride astride like a boy with the men of the Native Escort. Blanche this year had an excellent excuse for taking to a carriage: she could not face the hours of riding, she felt too tired and ill, and her husband had decreed that Bianca should stay with her to keep an eye on her. So Bianca stifled in the dust and gloom and watched her mother with growing anxiety, lying so still and pale in her corner. She was more worried about her mother than she had admitted to her father. Blanche O'Neil looked terribly ill. Mixed with Bianca's genuine love and anxiety was the fear that if her mother became really ill they would not be able to attend the Durbar or the ball afterwards, and her meeting with Sher Khan would be delayed. This she could not bear to contemplate. She put a hand to the placket of her dress, which crackled faintly as she touched the hidden pocket beneath it. There was the precious note that had been smuggled to her in Jindbagh nearly four months earlier. It was, for a moment, as if she touched his hand and heard his voice saying the words that were scrawled on the coarse paper. 'I love only you, want only you, for the rest of my life. I wait with impatience to see you again, and I will never let you go. I will see you at the Durbar, our lives will be joined then, and until then, these words bring you all my heart.' Bianca drew a long breath, and it seemed to her that she breathed the scent of jasmine, and was back in the gardens of the Madoremahal on the night when for the first time a man had embraced her, and her mouth burned and throbbed again beneath the memory of her first kisses.

Her mother sighed, moved a little and, half waking, coughed rackingly, her handkerchief held to her mouth. When the spasm had passed she fell back into her corner again, as if she had never wakened. Bianca returned from the memory of love to see the stain on her mother's handkerchief, dark in the dusty light of the hot afternoon. There was no way in which she could make Blanche more comfortable in the cramped interior of the carriage, and the water they had was lukewarm. Bianca leaned forward and risking her father's displeasure, opened the curtains a little, so that the air might be fresher. Once again she looked towards Madore, as if by the strength of her desire to be safely there, she could pull the red walls closer, make the journey end.

2

The heat was burning at its height when they arrived at last at the great carved gates of the Madoremahal. The big house, and its walled gardens, covering about twenty acres, not including an artificial lake, was a few miles outside the city of Madore and made an oasis of shaded green in the dry plains surrounding the city. It had always seemed to Bianca that the Madoremahal lay behind double walls: first the desert, rock strewn, the thorn scrub building impenetrable thickets, and then the man-made walls of country bricks, baked to a rock hardness, plastered with cowdung and mud and washed with a red dye. She heard the big gates creak open, thinking, 'Ah— At last!' and began to rouse her mother and help her to straighten her dress and tidy the great coils of greying hair on Blanche's small head, as the carriage bumped over the causeway and into the drive.

Madoremahal was full of people. Two Rajas of the other hill States were staying there with their families, and their servants, and their European advisers, and *their* families and servants—quite apart from the Ruler of Thinpahari and all his entourage—but the house swallowed them all. There was room, and to spare. Now, in this afternoon hour, the whole place was silent, lying drugged under the press of the heat, seemingly deserted. But, as the carriage and the escort wheeled up the long drive to the entrance, servants appeared, led by an old woman, who shrilled greetings and orders in the same breath, her white head cloth dazzling in the sun. Terence O'Neil dismounted, stamping his feet to ease the stiffness of his long ride, and then hurried to help his wife down from the carriage, while the servants began to unload the baggage.

The garden, lying so quiet with its paint-bright flower beds and enamelled grass glittering in the sun, suddenly erupted into noise and movement. Clouds of dust rose from the baggage as the servants threw it down, and the dust dulled the grass and brought with it the acrid smell of the desert into the garden.

Mrs O'Neil climbed down from the carriage with difficulty, so stiff that she could hardly stand, and leaned heavily on her husband's arm. She was very pale under the film of dust on her face, and the old woman, Goki, came forward to her at once, exclaiming with disapproval at her looks. Blanche O'Neil, as always, thought first of her husband. 'Terence—dear man, how worried you look! It is nothing, only the fatigue of the journey. A bath and a rest, and I will be dancing your feet off tonight, in my fine new dress. Come later and take tea with me, and do not bring that long face with you—you will have me dead and in my shroud, the way you look! Dear heart, you are so tired yourself—there is not a thing in it between us, for looks. We are a pair of tired old people, so we are!' As she turned away, to take Goki's arm, she laughed back at her husband, and Bianca saw the look she exchanged with him, a glance full of love that had outlasted the years of loneliness, fevers, bad climates, and exile—for Blanche had not her husband's feeling for India. This year, Bianca had a new understanding of the love her parents had for each other, an understanding taught her by her own heart, which had been learning so much, so quickly.

Bianca remembered when fresh from her own sudden entry into the rainbow world of love, missing Sher Khan, and yet not daring to talk about him, she had asked her mother to tell her the story of how she had first met Bianca's father. Her mother had blushed like a girl, her pale face flashing into sudden beauty, and Bianca had realised that the need to talk about the beloved was universal, and that her mother was as much in love with her father as Bianca herself was with Sher Khan. So love, real love, lasted—

'We met in a garden—'

'In a garden—Mama, how wonderful—' Bianca was enchanted by the coincidence.

'Yes—it was wonderful. I was cutting roses for the table—your grandmother had people coming that evening, and while I was there, Terence rode up the drive to call on your grandparents, with a letter from a mutual friend. Do you know, Bianca, he saw me among the roses, and he didn't go near the house. Just dismounted, and left his horse straying about, and came straight over to me. I can never smell a rose, or indeed see one, without remembering everything about that afternoon. He said afterwards that he fell in love with me there and then, and he was determined to marry me.'

'And you? What did you feel?'

'I? I was lost, what with his blue eyes, and the look in them, and his black hair all tumbled over his brow, and him as brown as an Indian after his years out here—there we stood staring at each other like a pair of idiots, while his horse trampled the flower beds, until your grandmother saw us and sent a maid out. A fine scolding I got when I went in—and a cold welcome for poor Terence. But it didn't matter. I was in love, and I knew he was too, and within a month he was asking my father's permission to speak to me—as if he hadn't told me already. My father said no, of course—that I was far too young.'

'So what did you do? Elope?'

'*Elope?* No, indeed. I took to my bed, and my mother thought I was going into a decline, and persuaded my father, and we got married just before Terence's leave was up, in the church in the village, where my mother was married. It was a beautiful wedding, I can never forget a moment of it—the flowers and the friends, and my dear mother's face, and the rooks making a terrible noise in the trees, disturbed by all the talk and laughter when they saw us off, with children throwing roses into the carriage all the way down the drive. I have one of those roses still. No one had a happier wedding day, or could have enjoyed it more.' Blanche O'Neil had tears in her eyes, and Bianca rushed to put her arms round her mother.

'But Mama—you don't regret it?'

'Regret it—my darling girl, how could I? With your father as my husband, I regret nothing—not a single thing, it has all been worth it.'

With those words, the ghosts of two little dead brothers, and the loneliness of being for so long the only European woman in Jindbagh, and the constant ill health that was slowly growing worse, all these things stepped back and were lost behind Blanche's radiant smile, the smile of a girl in love shining on a face that was prematurely aged. She said to her beloved daughter, and meant every word, 'If you once meet the man you truly love, as I love your dear father, you will understand, you will know at once. You are only a child now, Bianca dear, but the time is coming when you will be a young woman. All I ask of life is that you find a man you can love as I love your father. Nothing else matters.'

'Nothing?'

'Nothing, my darling.'

Bianca opened her mouth to say, 'But I have met him, Mama—' when her mother had continued. 'That is why I am so anxious that we should go away home soon, so that you can meet some young people. There is no one here for you, and you are a good girl the way you never complain, when you must often be lonely—'

'But I love it here, Mama—I love it. This is home—'

'Ah, Bianca—you speak like your father—but you don't know what you are missing. But there—one of these days, we'll all go back, and you'll see it for yourself—the lovely land, and the lovely people. Oh sometimes, I wish I was a bird, so that I could just fly back, over the seas, and look at it all—just for a day, even.' Blanche looked at her daughter's worried face, and laughed. 'Darling child, I am only joking. What would I do, flapping about over the ocean, missing you and your father? Sure, I don't want to go anywhere at all, away from the pair of you. So stop looking like that, you'll make frown marks on your forehead—'

Bianca had laughed too, and smoothed her forehead, but she remembered her mother's words, and kept her love for Sher Khan to herself. There was no point in upsetting her mother yet.

Her eyes suddenly blurred with tears as she stood waiting, while her mother, leaning on Goki's arm, climbed slowly up the steps to the verandah. Her mother looked so frail. She blinked her tears away, and looked out over the garden, once more quiet under the burning sun. An orange grove, the trees full of blossom, sent a gust of heavy fragrance to her, as a wind, laden with heat from its journey over the plain, blew through the trees, disturbing questing bees, so that for a second or two the air was full of their sleepy humming. This garden had always been one of Bianca's favourite places, and after the month-long journey, and the crossing of the desert, it seemed to her to be the most beautiful place in the world, especially this year, when it was full of her memories, and of her hopes for the future. She drank in, with pleasure, the green restfulness around her, for, in spite of the heat, the garden gave the impression of coolness; there were so many trees, and the grass was so thick and green. The gardens were well kept. Even now, when the rest of the Madoremahal slept, there were gardeners working, squatting over the flower beds, weeding, their bare brown backs shining with sweat. Bianca turned to look towards the thick grove of trees that had a little shrine dedicated to Shiva. There, she thought with a sudden sweet shiver of delight, there was where we stood together that night, and there I shall meet him again, tonight—this very night!

Her mother called to her and Bianca looked about her, took a long breath of the orange blossom air, and regretfully turned to go into the house, but was stopped by her father's voice.

'Bianca—child, what in the name of the heavenly angels has got into you, you've no head left to think with, it's so full of dreams! Child of grace, will you look to your mother, I must go into the lines. Get her into bed at once, for she looks a bad colour—she is as white as a sheet. I will not be waking her for tea, but don't tell her. She'll sleep on, and it will do her good. Get along with you now, and get some sleep yourself—you look as dazed as a stunned mullet.'

Bianca went after her mother at once, found that there was no need to urge her to rest. Once she was in the cool high ceilinged bedroom, Blanche O'Neil allowed Goki to remove her dress, and sponge her face and arms, and was asleep before the old woman had finished, her breathing barely disturbing the light cover that Goki drew over her. Above, the punkah creaked softly as it moved backwards and forwards, throwing a shadow on everything, a moving shadow, a constant faint flicker, so that Blanche's face, white as her pillow, was one moment in clear sight, then dimmed with shadow. Old Goki had known her since before Bianca's birth—indeed, had helped to bring Bianca, living, from a difficult labour, and had attended the births of the two boys before Bianca. She looked down at the sleeping woman for a moment, noting the shadowed eyes and the hollowing of the pale cheeks, then adjusted the shawl over the thin body on the bed, and beckoned Bianca into the next room, where a wide low divan, heaped with cushions, made Bianca long to fling herself down and sleep, and a tin tub full of water stood ready in a corner, beside a big red jar.

'Thy mother is tired to death—did devils pursue you, that you travelled the roads like the wind, giving her no time to rest?' As Goki spoke, she was beginning to help the girl peel off her dusty sweat-soaked dress, and the many petticoats beneath it. Bianca felt herself settling back into an old habit; her earliest memories were of Goki bathing her, dressing her, scolding her, and comforting her when others scolded. The old woman was a beloved combination of grandmother, servant and trusted confidant. Bianca could talk to Goki as she could not to her gentle mother. She answered the old woman dreamily, stretching her body in relief as the constricting clothes dropped away.

'Nay—no devils. But the roads were hot and dusty and my father wished to get my mother to comfort as soon as he could. Truth to tell, Goki, we would have been better out of that sweat bath of a carriage. My mother has always ridden before—but now, partly because of me, and partly because of her health she torments herself in that carriage.'

'Because of thee?'

'Yes—now that I am a woman, she says it is not suitable for me to do the journey riding like a man with the escort, and I have no side saddle or habit yet—'

'A woman indeed! Thou art a scrubby child still!' Before Bianca could answer her, Goki spoke again. 'No devils on the road, you say—but did you hear talk of the troubles hereabouts?' There was anxiety in the old woman's voice, the same note had sounded in the voices of their hosts in the foothills.

Bianca shrugged. 'There was talk—there always is—'

'But this is true talk. There have been many burnings in the cities to the south, and the families of the other Europeans from the southern hill States have stayed in the hills—only the men have come. Now the people here are stirring, and the talk is that the English are going to force us all to worship their god. The army is disturbed also, it is said that they lose caste when they use these new rifles. Oh, child, I know not how this all came about—the stories are as thick as flies on a carcase—but my heart is troubled for you. I wish that like the Europeans from the south you and the Lady Sahib had stayed safe in the hills this season.'

'Oh Goki! "There is talk—" "It is said—"! Do not croak like a crow on my first day back. You sound like the women of old Sikunder Khan at Afritcote.'

'Why? What said they?' Goki was pouring clean water over Bianca as she stood in the tin tub, dipping it up with a small bowl from the big jar, and letting it pour, delicious in its coolness, over the girl's back and shoulders. Bianca shook the drops of water from her arms, shivering with delight.

'They said nothing that you have not said—Goki, do not be so glum. You know what I would hear from you—tell me. Is he here yet?'

Goki poured a great dipper of water over the girl, so that she emerged from the rush of water like a little seal, dark hair plastered down over her shoulders, eyelashes stuck together in points round her large blue eyes. The old woman looked at her, and suddenly sighed and smiled at the same time.

'Aye me—but you grow very beautiful, my child. Very beautiful. A pearl, a ruby, a very crown of loveliness.'

Bianca ignored the compliments. 'Goki—answer me. Is he here?'

Goki, wrapping the sleek young body in a towel, stopped and looked at her. 'Is it still as it was, with your heart?'

Bianca's eyes, clear as water, her thoughts and hopes plainly reflected in them, looked up at the old woman's face. 'How should I change? I love him. Of course it is as it was.'

Goki tightened her lips for a second, and then said quietly, 'Aye, he comes. He is not here yet, but he comes tonight, riding slowly, becase of the polo match tomorrow.'

Bianca made a little face—she would have rather he raced the wind to be with her. Goki nodded her head at her.

'I know how your thoughts run. But he is a man, and horseflesh is costly, and he wishes to win tomorrow.'

Bianca tossed her head, and turned away, but her joy triumphed, and she turned back, her eyes blazing with excitement.

'Oh Goki—tonight!'

'Child, I do not like this, I can see trouble—'

'Goki—I said, do not croak. I am so happy—let him come fast or slow, it does not matter so long as he is here, and I can see him—' Her words broke off on an indrawn breath, and she stood, eyes shining and lips apart, her towel falling forgotten to the floor, and before her joyously blatant young beauty, Goki was silent. She had seen Bianca grow from babyhood to this rich flowering, and she loved her as she loved no one else outside the Ruler's family. She had served the Ruler and his family since she was ten, a quiet little hill girl brought by her mother to assist the womenfolk of the old Raja, the father of the present Ruler. As she helped Bianca to dry herself, Goki felt memories of her own girlhood crowding into her mind, as if some of Bianca's burning youth was passing through her young flesh into the old woman's hands. Goki had shared the Ruler's bed on many nights when they had both been young, and she could remember how it felt to be beautiful, and passionately in love. But something here was wrong—there was a shadow on this love, Goki could feel the shadow, and yet did not know why she felt it. It was not the difference in race—Goki saw no handicap in Bianca, a European, being united to the ancient sacred House of Lambagh. No, the difference in race did not matter to her. But something—some event, yet to be, it seemed—was putting out a warning hand to touch her, and the hand was cold. Goki shuddered, and tried to throw off the shadow, turning to pick up a clean lace-edged bodice, stiff with whalebone. But Bianca pushed it away.

'Oh no, Goki, give me a *choli*, and a cotton sari. I cannot bear to be bound in any more petticoats and bones just now. I am too sore from all that jolting in the carriage, my ribs feel bruised.'

She turned, naked and slender, to look at herself in the gilt framed clouded mirror that stood against the wall, and her wavering reflection laughed back at her.

'Goki, see, I have grown. My bosom has come a little more, and I have a small—*very* small—waist—' She paused, eyeing herself, and then suddenly shy, looked away, blushing, and said in a small voice, 'My body has changed since I last looked in that mirror—Goki, will I please him?'

'Oh shameless one! Peacocking in front of the mirror!' Goki shook her head in reproof. Then, pride in her nursling drowned all other thoughts, and the old woman smiled. 'Nay, child, do not hang your head. You are a heart-taker, a queen of beauty. He was mad for you last year, when you were only half grown. Now, when he sees this year's blossoming, his heart will be yours for ever—and his body too, no doubt!'

'Goki!' Bianca put her hands up to her hot face, but her heart leapt at the old woman's words. Goki wagged her head warningly.

'I know not what to say. In this country you are a woman grown, ripe for marriage. But among your own people, you are still considered a child. Your mother thinks of you as her small daughter. Oh yes, she knows you are growing, but not so fast. If she knew what was in your heart, I do not think she would be happy. Also, my soul, do you know your own heart? Blood is hot when you are young, and speaks loudly, loud enough to deafen wisdom. This is no easy road you set your feet on.'

'I know my heart, and I know where I am going—'

The old woman looked at her. 'And your parents?'

'They must learn to understand and accept what is to be. Listen, old one. I was born here amongst your people. I have lived all my life with your people, knowing no other country. I am a child of your people in everything but blood. I know what I want. I want to live here for the rest of my life, with Sher Khan as my lord—and my love.'

The silence that fell when Bianca finished speaking, was long and full of meaning, as if all that lay before the girl, all that was to happen in the future was there in front of her for her contemplation, could she but clear her eyes and see.

Then this deep, growing silence was broken by a quiet tap at the door. Goki sighed, and blinked her eyes as if she was waking from sleep.

'That is the waiting woman from the Begum Sahiba, come to see if you sleep or wake. She came before, and I sent her away, because you were not then here.'

There was only one Begum Sahiba as far as Bianca was concerned—Khanzada, Sher Khan's sister, and her beloved friend.

'Oh Goki, evil one—why did you not tell me that Khanzada wanted me? I thought she would be sleeping! Tell the woman that I come at once.'

Goki turned to the door, leaving Bianca to wrap herself in a blue cotton sari. Bianca had worn native dress whenever she pleased, all her life. Now, suddenly, this year, her mother had forbidden it in public—like riding astride, it was no longer suitable. 'You are growing up, my dear, and must learn to dress and behave as a young lady.' Blanche put very few restrictions on her daughter, but when she said anything, she meant it, and Bianca obeyed her without question. But now, her mother safely asleep, she put on the blue sari with pleasure, enjoying its soft freedom after her constricting bodice and corset, and the many wide petticoats. Adjusting the folds of cool cotton, she thought of how she would always dress in such easy, becoming clothes when she married Sher Khan. She took up a comb, and pulled her hair smoothly back from her face, twisting it into a heavy knot, and then pulled a free fold of the sari over her head, and went to the door.

'Goki—I go. If my mother wakes, send for me—if not, I will return before sunset.'

Goki put out a restraining hand. 'Bianca—wait! there is something I should tell you—listen—'

But it was too late. The slender blue-clad figure had slipped quietly through the door, and was gone, and Goki turned back into the room to gather up the towels and tumbled clothing and to think—conscious again of the shadow in her mind, a depression, formless, but terrifying. She finished tidying the room, and then went to sit outside Blanche O'Neil's room, her back against the door, waiting until she should be needed.

3

The Madoremahal was very old. The original fortress had been added to over the years, until now it had become an enormous sprawling building, high-ceilinged rooms joined by twisting passageways and surrounded on all sides by deep verandahs. The passageways were confusing, because there were so many of them that ended either in a bricked-up window, or in open archways, leading to courtyards. The courtyards opened into other courtyards, which in turn led to more living quarters. In all, the building covered over two acres. Bianca had been born in one of the big marble-screened rooms of the Madoremahal, and could have found her way anywhere in the building alone, but it would not have been fitting for her to walk unattended through the palace, now that her childhood had been left behind. This, not a stricture of her mother's, but a custom of the Madore family. So, ruled by two habits of thought, two different sets of manners, Bianca, aged fifteen, followed the woman servant down the passages. Holding the blue sari decorously over her face, Bianca could easily have been mistaken for one of the graceful, delicately-boned princesses from the hill States.

The heat was more noticeable when they entered the open colonnaded passage between the palace, and the *bibighar*, the women's quarters. Although the open archways were hung with thick rush matting, dripping with water, the heat still found its way in. As Bianca passed, she heard water being thrown on to the matting from outside, and felt a gust of coolness, smelling of the rose scent of the wet kus-kus, the reeds that were woven into the matting.

The servant stopped in front of a high, carved cedarwood door, and tapped. An older woman, dark faced, a stranger to Bianca, opened it, and stood aside, salaaming. Walking down another long passage, Bianca had time to reflect that last year, before Khanzada married, the *bibighar* was not so carefully guarded, and then she was standing before a door hung with heavy embroidered curtains, and calling Khanzada's name softly, she went into a room closely shuttered against the light, so dim with shadows that she had to stop and blink to clear her sight after the glare of the passage.

A girl, lying on a pile of cushions in a corner of the room, rose with a soft sound of pleasure, and flung her arms round Bianca.

'Sister of my heart! I am so happy to see you! And you have grown—and how beautiful—like a goddess. You make me jealous. No one will have eyes for anyone but you!'

The two girls had been friends, closer than sisters, from the time they could walk and think. Khanzada had spent most of her life with Bianca, Bianca's mother had taken the place of her own mother, who had been killed with her father in the great earthquake in Madore soon after Khanzada was born. The two girls had seldom been parted until the last two years, when Khanzada's betrothal and marriage had separated them. Now that they were together again, they drew back to look at each other with considering eyes, two beautiful girls searching each other's faces to see what changes the year had brought. Bianca, looking at the other, caught her breath, and then said, 'Khanzada—Zada! No one told me! You did not tell me when you wrote—'

'About my big belly? But what is there to write? That I am with child, and hideous?'

'No, Zada, you are more beautiful.'

'*More* beautiful? With a monstrous figure, and swollen legs? Oh Bianca, sweet liar! My lord waits for his son with no more impatience that I want to be light again. I will not be running through the gardens with you, little sister, this year. But in any case, I do not think you will be interested in playing children's games any more.' Her eyes flicked up and down Bianca's slim body with envy as she said, 'Oh me—what beauty is here! We will have to put a veil on you to keep our husbands from straying!' She laughed as lightly and prettily as she had always laughed, and Bianca laughed with her, but suddenly she was depressed and ill at ease. This was not the welcome she had expected, and she was disappointed. There was a feeling of difference, of changed times, that she could not understand. First the strange woman guarding a door that had always been unguarded before, and then this brittle gaiety of Khanzada's, this half teasing, half genuine envy. This was not her Zada—this was the face that Zada wore for strangers. Could a year break such close ties, such a loving lifelong friendship? Last year, Bianca, dizzy with her first love affair, had found a sympathetic listener in Khanzada, who had said nothing of her feelings for her own bridegroom, but had acted gladly as go-between for her brother and Bianca, arranging the stolen, hurried meetings in distant forgotten rooms in the old part of Madoremahal. She had smuggled the love letters, and had smiled on the whole affair. After her marriage, before she left to go down to Sagpur, she had clasped a gold bracelet on Bianca's arm, saying, 'A charm for love and luck, little sister. Before the year is out, may I see you married to Sher Khan, and my sister in blood as well as in heart.'

The bangle still gleamed on Bianca's arm, the year had only a month to run, but Zada seemed ten years older, a stranger with Zada's face, her laughing eyes and beautiful mouth, though not with her body. Did marriage and coming motherhood change a girl so much? Did pregnancy change the spirit as well as the shape? Bianca's unease grew. Khanzada did not appear to notice anything. She called her waiting woman, and told her to bring tea, and sweetmeats, and Bianca, longing to be alone with her, and find out what was wrong, had to wait. She sank down on to the soft cushions beside Khanzada, and commented admiringly on the heavy gold ornaments and rich silks that she wore, thinking at the same time that this too was a change. For Khanzada hated silks in the hot weather, and had never worn anything but an ordinary cotton sari, or the dress of the hill women—a loose cotton shirt, over cotton trousers.

The dark-skinned waiting woman, Nila, prepared the tea on a charcoal stove in the corner of the room where the floor was bare of carpets. At last she brought the tall silver goblets of steaming hot lemon tea, and little plates of sweet sticky *jellabies* and *rasgoolas*, while Bianca chatted about nothing, and watched this new Khanzada, clinking with heavy gold ornaments, her swollen body swathed in brilliantly-coloured hot silk. Then, finally, the tea was finished, and the maid had gone, and they were alone. Now Bianca hoped for Sher Khan's name to be mentioned, here was her dear companion who had shared every moment of her romance, knew all her hopes. But Khanzada spoke only of her year of marriage to the Nawab of Sagpur, and of her life in the coastal city in the State so far to the south. But as she spoke of the wonders of her white palace on the edge of the sea, her voice suddenly changed. 'It is beautiful, I have everything—but I grow hungry for the hills, Bianca, for the high hills, and the cold hill winds. I feel ill all the time down there. The wind from the sea brings me fevers, and tangles my hair, and the green mould grows on the velvet slippers that your mother gave me—it is so damp and green down there. For aught I know there will be mould growing on my face as well soon.'

Her eyes were full of tears. Bianca had never, in all their life together seen her cry. Khanzada was always the one who comforted, who was gay and fearless. Here was terrible change indeed!

'Zada! Dearest—you are weeping—why? I thought you loved your husband, and were happy in your new life—'

Khanzada shook the tears from her eyes, laughing, but it was a strange laugh, shrill and high, without pleasure. 'Happy? Oh yes, I am happy enough. Why not? But I am a hill woman. I am homesick for the hills, for my own language and people. As for love— Ah! All you Westerners speak of this "Love"! What is love? Kisses, and touches, and glances, and the fire of the body? These things do not last, my little foolish sister. But *this* that I have—the honour of bearing a child—*that* lasts. I am the chosen one, the honoured—I who carry my lord's son.'

Bianca could not believe that this was Khanzada, that this harsh voice, speaking so bitterly, belonged to the gay, loving-hearted girl she had known. At odds with herself because of her confused feelings, more than a little angered at the tone Khanzada had used to her, she stammered, 'You are very sure it will be a boy you bear—it might be a girl, Zada—it cannot be known before birth, can it?'

Khanzada turned on her like a tigress, her face distorted. 'In the name of Allah! Do not ill wish me, fool! Of course my child is a boy—a fine strong son for Hardyal. Oh, in the name of Allah, the all powerful, let it be a son—'

Khanzada's sudden rage had vanished, her voice sank, and she stared before her with a look of such despair that Bianca put her arms round her, and held her tightly, as she would have held a child roused from sleep by a nightmare.

'But Zada—hush, do not tremble so! If it is not a son this time, if you have a daughter, it is not a fault! And there are other years, you will have many children. What are you afraid of, should you have a girl? What can happen to you?'

'I can die.'

'Die! Zada—what are you talking about?'

'If this child is a girl, I shall die, and the child with me. Down in the dark, down in the dark water, a death of cold struggle in the darkness in that sluggish water—oh, my life, my life, would I have died at my birth, rather than this death, holding my baby in my arms—'

Her voice did not rise, but the quiet terror in it made Bianca shudder, and look over her shoulder, even as she tried to calm Zada.

'Zada—don't. You are mad. Hardyal will not harm you! You are his wife—and your family are all round you—'

'Bianca, I tell you again. As surely as the sun will set tonight, as surely as the moon will rise—so sure am I that if I bear a daughter, I shall die in the Pool of the Women.'

'The Pool of the Women?' To Bianca, Khanzada sounded like a woman run mad.

'Yes—the Pool of the Women. Under the palace of Sagpur, in the deepest of the underground rooms—God knows how long the pool has been there, but it is so deep that all that is thrown in there is lost forever. Many a Begum in the history of Sagpur has gasped at the embrace of that water, for lesser crimes than presenting the Nawab with an unwanted daughter when he is without an heir. The family is run down. For the past two or three generations a son has been hard to find for the throne.' She shivered suddenly, like a sick animal. 'And Bianca—pray to your God for me too. Hardyal has had many women. Upwards of thirty, they say—and not one of them has given him a live son.'

'Do you mean he has killed thirty women?'

Khanzada laughed, a forlorn sound with no amusement in it. 'Nay—they were of no account. Only the highborn take that dark road to the pool. These others—they were palace women, dancing girls, servants—they live. But I am the Begum, I must bear the heir. And he cannot wait. I will have no second chance.' She paused, and then said, speaking with reluctance, 'Bianca, listen, and understand if you can. To my husband, I am only for child-bearing—to bear him a son for the throne. Do you understand? Only for bearing his son. He has to drink, and drug himself to the act. He cannot pleasure himself with me. His flesh responds to boys more easily than it does to me.'

Bianca, brought up in the freedom of native palaces, had little of Victorian girlhood's pruderies, but this was a repugnant subject, seldom spoken of even among the loose-tongued palace women. Her face twisting with distaste, she asked, 'But what of those other women?'

'To get a boy. What else? There are drugs he takes, and mixes with cognac, and then he can perform. He would have married the woman who gave him a son, brought the boy up as his heir, and would never have touched that woman again. He likes variety—a new face, a new body—and drugs.'

'But—but how do you *know*, Zada?'

'I found him. When I was first married, and thought myself loved and in love, like any silly girl. I went to his rooms, unasked, and found him there, in that great mirrored bed of his, with one of the palace guards. Oh, Bianca—I had looked forward to marriage, to my own man, and to love.'

She dropped her face into her hands, and Bianca sat beside her in stricken silence. She longed to sweep back the heavy curtains at the windows, and let in light and air, however hot, into this place of fear and shadows. Khanzada took her hand. 'One thing I must ask of you—tell no one. No one, I beg.'

'But Zada, your uncle can break the marriage—you are as his own daughter.'

'Oh *no*!' Zada's tone was full of horror. She put her hand on Bianca's arm. 'No, not my uncle. Not anyone of mine—for Hardyal will kill—'

'Oh Zada, now I am sure you are mad. How can Hardyal kill the Ruler, in his own palace, among his own people?'

Khanzada looked at her beseechingly. 'Bianca, listen to me. Of course the Ruler can be killed! A little pinch of poison, a snake within his bed, it only needs a weak man and a good bribe, or a jealous woman, or even a moment's forgetfulness. Never mind how, but I tell you this. Expose Hardyal's shame, and he will kill to keep face—'

The cushions on which they lay were of heavy silk, and filled with soft feathers. The carpets were rich Shiraz and Baluchi, with a velvet sheen. There were silver goblets on a carved, ivory-inlaid table, and sandalwood chests, and a great painted porcelain water filter, bought from Chinese traders. Khanzada's arms were laden with gold bracelets and gold and jewels glittered in her coiled hair. Everything spoke of rich comfort, except Khanzada's harsh whispering voice, her wide terror-filled eyes.

'Poison! Snakes! But Zada—'

'But Zada!' mimicked the other girl biting her lip, 'But Zada! My beloved Bianca, I have learned many things this year. There are poisons so virulent they can kill in seconds and leave no trace. There is that little snake, the krait, so small that it can be introduced into a shoe. Murder, I have learned, nay, I have *seen*—is easy. And you, my dearest sister, you too lie in that terrible shadow.' Khanzada brushed her hand over her eyes. 'Bianca—go to the door, and look out and tell me if that woman Nila is there. The windows are shuttered, and we have been speaking low, but that door is only curtained—Bianca, go and see.'

Bianca wished that she was outside in the bright clean heat of the afternoon, the change she had sensed was becoming a monstrous shadow, brooding in this luxurious room, and swallowing all the brightness of her happy dreaming. She got up, and moved silently to the curtained door, and with an effort pulled the curtain aside and looked out.

There was no one there, the passage was silent and deserted, and the heavy door at the far end was closed. Bianca had a sudden revulsion of feeling. What miasma, what nightmare was Zada living through, that she could be so afraid, so terrified by her own imaginings? She turned back to the figure huddled among the cushions.

'There is no one there. The passage is empty, and the door at the end is closed. Zada—I cannot speak, really, because this is something that I know little about, but I have heard that women have trouble sometimes when they are pregnant. Do you remember Rangadevi?'

Khanzada interrupted her, leaning forward to put a slender

hand over her mouth. 'Little sister. I remember Rangadevi very well. *She* was crazy before she started to bear a child. Bianca, I am not mad. Look into my eyes, and tell me that I am a mad woman.'

Bianca looked, and saw fear, and sorrow in the beautiful eyes, but no madness. Her heart sank, and she looked down at their clasped hands, and Khanzada nodded. 'Yes. I know what you are thinking. In some ways it would be better if I were mad, because the truth is so frightening. But I am not, though a great number of people in Hindustan seem to be going mad. Like dogs in the hot weather, they run about, snapping their jaws, and slavering to kill.'

She bent her head close to Bianca's, and the scent of sandalwood rose from her hair and body, reminding Bianca of many happy hours in the past, when she and Khanzada had sat talking through the long hot days. Those happy days were gone it seemed, and as Khanzada spoke, the shadow of fear that was in the room began to grow and come closer to the two girls, and Bianca knew that she was near to the very heart of the strangeness she had felt ever since she had come into Khanzada's room. She realised that this change had begun when she had sat in the women's quarters in the house of her father's old friends, and had seen the foothills fading into the heat haze of the plains.

'Bianca, did you hear anything of trouble in the plains, on your way down from Jindbagh?'

Always the same question, in the same tone of voice, as if the speaker held her breath. But this time Bianca listened, as she had not done to those others, and replied carefully to Khanzada's question.

'Old Sikunder's wife, and his sister-in-law at Afritcote spoke of trouble, and said that we should stay in the hills this year. But Zada, I was not listening.'

'Ah, if only you had turned back then! Bianca, the trouble that comes is death to you and all Europeans. The army is disaffected, the villages and towns to the south, and the Southern Rajas—all are speaking of death, and the freeing of the land from the yoke of the invaders.'

'What invaders?'

'Oh, Bianca—you! And your people—'

'But I was born here! The Ruler calls my father *bhaiya*—brother—and you learned to speak, and indeed to walk, with my mother. Zada, I do not understand.'

Khanzada's slim brown arm, put fiercely against her own, forced her to look down. 'There—see? Are we of one blood? One heart, one soul, one love—but different races, and perhaps for every good man of any race, there is one evil one. Arrogance there has been, and insults, and the wealth of the country leached away—'

Before Bianca's wide-eyed puzzled stare, Khanzada fell silent, and covered her face with her hands. 'Bianca, forgive me. You and your family—you are as our own people, and there are hundreds more like you. But you will pay for the others, the people of base instincts, who have indeed wronged our country. You will most certainly pay if I am not able to warn you.' Her voice sank even lower, and she said sadly, 'And I, shame on my head, I am so afraid for myself, I can hardly form the words for my warning.'

Khanzada, who had never admitted to being afraid in her life! This was terrifying for Bianca. But Bianca was angry as well as afraid. Khanzada had never spoken to her like this in all their life together. For the first time since she could remember, Bianca felt the difference in race. Sisters no more, the two looked at each other across a gulf, and on the far side of the gulf was everything that Bianca had loved. The gentle loving people of her childhood, Goki's warm arms, the laughing men of the State Cavalry teaching her to ride almost before she could walk. The smell of woodsmoke rising blue from the camp fires of their treks to and from the hills. Khanzada's companionship, the long confidences of a shared girlhood, the graceful dress, the soft sounds of flute and sitar and throbbing drum. The conch shell blowing at dusk, as the incense smell drifted out from temple doors, the cry of the Muezzin at dawn and at day's end. Blazing sunsets over the slow-moving rivers of the plains, pale dawns crowning the dreaming domes and minarets of the Taj Mahal, white spray and chill breezes, where the hill rivers tumbled down their rocky crags—and over all, above everything, Sher Khan. As she thought of him, her anger died, and was replaced by a dreadful desolation. Did Sher Khan desire to see her slaughtered? Her eyes filled with tears, and overflowed, and Khanzada, seeing her tears, sobbed herself, and then said firmly, 'No, no time now for tears. I must tell you these things, Bianca, for I think, through you, perhaps some can be saved. Listen carefully now, to what I tell you, for I have discovered plans—and no one knows that I have any knowledge of them.'

But Bianca could bear no more, could hold her question back no longer. 'Zada—does Sher Khan wish us all dead, or away?'

Khanzada put her arms about her and held her tightly. 'Dearest Bianca. I have not seen Sher Khan for eight months. He has been down in the Rann to buy horses. But whatever changes have taken place, I am sure that his heart has not changed. He would never wish you or your family any harm. I do not doubt but that he still loves you. I do not even know that he has heard of the troubles. Rumours, yes, but he will not have listened. My uncle knows that there is devil's work among the people to the south, but he does not worry. His people will hold firm, he thinks. But I know differently. Listen now, Bianca—'

Once again she leaned close to Bianca, and her voice dropped to a bare thread. 'This trouble started in the south, and is spreading fast. The army—the men are all, but *all* affected. Perhaps not all will mutiny, but I think that none of them will be very sure of their allegiance. Your father, and my uncle—their men will, I feel sure, stand firm—but this will not help us. Your father is to come down to Sagpur after the Durbar, to train our men in the use of the new rifle. Bianca—he must not come. He will be murdered, and your mother with him.'

She looked into Bianca's horrified eyes, and sighed. 'Bianca, this hate is not against you, or your family. You are beloved by all. But your race is hated, and hated more in the south than it is up here. Hardyal has always hated you. He will kill your parents for pleasure, and my uncle the Ruler, and Sher Khan because of what he stands to gain.'

'But what does he stand to gain? What does he want?'

Khanzada laughed harshly, and as if in answer, Bianca heard a peacock cry from the garden. 'What does he want, Bianca? He wants the Emerald Peacock, and all that it stands for. He wants the throne of the three States. He wants to add to his power and wealth. True, he is already a very rich man—but his State is small, and of no importance, he is a courtesy Raja, and soon Sagpur will be swallowed up by the larger Rissa State, and he will be nothing. This is why he married me, to be nearer to my uncle's power. And—listen well, Bianca—this is why Sher Khan is in great danger too. Sher Khan is my uncle's heir, and after him, if he is childless, or dies before my uncle—my child, Hardyal's child inherits. So—my child must be a son, Sher Khan must die, and then, when the Ruler dies, Hardyal will be Regent, in power over a helpless baby—for I do not think that the Ruler would live long after Sher Khan's death. He would not be allowed to. As for your father—'

It was as if her voice was spinning cobwebs in to the room, there was a greyness in front of Bianca's eyes, almost she put her hand up to brush the web away as she listened.

'But Zada—the Ruler will live for years. He is a strong man.' The fact of Sher Khan's danger she could not accept—she pushed it away into the back of her mind, so that by not thinking of it, the danger would not exist.

Khanzada's voice went on remorselessly. 'The Ruler could live for years—but he will not. He will be murdered, and the crime will be a hidden one—as I said, poison, a snake—oh, anything. Hardyal is clever, and now, with these mutterings of death and disaster running throughout Hindustan, any killing can be hidden. Bianca, I know what I am saying—and you must listen to me, for your life's sake, and for the sake of all that you love. Here is the beginning of the plot. As I told you, your father is coming down to Sagpur to demonstrate the new rifle to Hardyal's troops. When he appears on the parade ground, he is to be cut down, and his head and his hands are to be sent up here as a sign to certain friends of Hardyal's that the time is ripe—'

A sound in the doorway, no louder than a sigh—Bianca's heart stopped, and then raced, so that the blood thundered in her ears, but Khanzada's voice went smoothly on. 'This sign is that the fishers are returning. The lanterns hang high in the palm trees, so they are a double sign, the men see them, and know that they are in sight of harbour—'

Bianca stared petrified at Khanzada, her eyes begging for help. She knew who was standing just inside the door behind her. A strong smell of attar of roses filled the air, and a rich voice spoke.

'So! You two are together after your long separation! So much to talk about, so many months to cover!'

Khanzada climbed to her feet clumsily, her hands together in greeting, nothing in her bearing or her voice, but pleasure. 'My lord! I did not hear you come. Indeed it is good to have my sister with me again—see how she has grown in these months—'

'I see indeed. Very beautiful, a blossoming tree, a star of beauty!' His voice too held nothing but pleasure, and his hands were warm and softly gripping as he took Bianca's hands to pull her to her feet, and into his scented embrace. 'Welcome back, little sister—welcome to Madore. Soon I look forward to welcoming you to Sagpur. We will make your visit one you will never forget—parties all day on the sea, in our beautiful boats, and parties all night in the palace! You will need to sleep forever when you leave us.'

Somewhere within Bianca a stone had settled, big, and cold. His voice was so warm, his glance at Khanzada so loving—and yet. She fought down a strong shudder, and hoped that her trembling confusion would be taken for shyness. She had never liked Hardyal—when they had all been children, and the tall prince from the south had come to the festivals, much older than the other boys, and yet always with them, trying, it seemed, to ingratiate himself, always an outsider, in spite of all his efforts. Then, with a child's sure instincts, she had avoided him, and had often been very rude to him, playing a child's cruel trick, upsetting his precarious dignity, and laughing at his discomforting. He had always been the same—always polite, quiet, and friendly, seeming to notice none of the slights and the unkind tricks, ignoring the fact that he was kept outside the close alliance that there was between the other children of the Northern Royalties. Bianca, her eyes down, wondered now how much he recalled of the old days.

He stayed to speak to her of her journey, and of her mother's health. He spoke as a member of the family, an older brother, anxious and kindly, as if Khanzada was indeed her sister. Looking up to reply to him, Bianca saw his eyes cold, without expression, black as wet rocks. Fear is contagious, and because of her own sudden terror, Bianca knew that Khanzada was afraid. But no one else would have known. She was gay, gently teasing Bianca for being so quiet, begging Hardyal to stay with them, she had the wine he liked—pouting over her misshapen figure like a spoiled palace beauty when he said that he could not stay. In this guise, Bianca saw nothing of the Khanzada she knew—the beautiful stranger that Khanzada had become played her part, and presently Hardyal took his leave, telling his wife to rest, and embracing her tenderly. He smiled at them both, waved a slender hand at them with grace, and went as silently as he had come. The curtains parted and swayed and fell together again, and that was all.

Khanzada, her face suddenly all bones, sank back into her cushions. Bianca was horrified at her looks: her eyes were deep in their sockets, as if her face was slowly losing its flesh, the skull's grin coming through, and a grey shadow circled her mouth. She barely whispered, 'Bianca—see if he has gone—but do not let him see you.' Bianca slipped out of her heelless shoes, and moving silently up to the curtained door, looked through a crack. The passage was empty. She went back to Khanzada, and bent over her. 'He has gone. I cannot see that woman, either. Let me get you some wine?' Khanzada nodded, and Bianca filled a goblet from the silver jug, and brought it to her, holding it so that she could drink. Khanzada gulped thirstily, and then pushed away the glass, and struggled up.

'Bianca—! You have got to reach your father—now, at once! Bring him here if you can. Hardyal heard us, you know—I feel sure that he heard us, and so he will have to kill you and your family tonight, and start the troubles here earlier than he had planned, because he will know that you will warn your father. We have—if he heard us—only a little time—only the time it will take him to tell some of his creatures of the change of plans. Go, Bianca, go now and find your father, for all our sakes—I am so afraid!' Her face, her voice, implored. Terror shone in her eyes, showed itself in the sweat that was gathering on her forehead. Bianca was driven on the wind of that terror, to the curtained door. But Khanzada stopped her with a gasp. 'No—not that way, that woman Nila is not to be trusted. Here—the door to the privy leads to the courtyard—'

Bianca let herself out through the sweeper's door, into the brilliant afternoon light. The heat had been gathering itself all day—now, in these last hours before the sun set, it was a living remorseless enemy, striking with such burning force that she gasped, and sheltered her head with her hands. She crossed the paved courtyard quickly, and went out into the garden behind, a strip of cultivated ground that lay between the Women's quarters and the stables where she knew she would be most likely to find her father at this time. She felt conspicuous, hurrying through the garden, her bare feet wincing away from the hot ground, the blue sari blown against her body by her haste. Too late, she remembered that she had not worn her *choli*, the short-sleeved bodice that is worn with a sari. She had nothing over her bosom but a fold of the blue cotton. The thought of her father's reception of her, in the lines, dressed, or half dressed, as she was, made her hesitate—almost she turned back. But Khanzada's fear was still with her—she set her mind on that, and went on. Surely the news she carried would put everything else from her father's mind.

In the rich room Bianca had just left, Khanzada lay, sweating in sudden agony. At first she thought that the wine must have been poisoned. Then, as another pain gripped her in a clenching spasm, she knew that her time had come; she was in labour. The pains were sharp, but now that she knew what they meant she was not afraid. For her child's life, she would do anything, suffer anything, and she regretted only one thing, her terrible feeling of weakness. Each pain seemed to bring her one step nearer to the grey mist of unconsciousness that she dreaded. She prayed that help would come before the maid Nila returned from wherever she had gone.

Bianca passed two syces lying asleep in the shade of the wall, and a sepoy lying on a string bed, his arms over his face, his hooka forgotten beside him. She hurried past the stables, where inquisitive, satiny, large heads turned at her passing, and gentle whickering invited her attention, but gained none of it. The time when there were hours to spare, talking to the horses was gone—she found herself thinking of them as a means of escape—could her mother sit in a saddle and ride hard for her life, to the hills? Could Khanzada? With sinking heart she went through the door in the wall of the stables, and there, on the verandah of the guard room, she saw her father talking to Subedar Major Shaibani Khan, and another man, a stranger to her. Her resolution weakened. The enormity of what she was doing overcame her, here in the lines, barefoot and half naked—she could hear her father's very tones as he said the words. She forgot everything except the need to hide before her father saw her, and turned away, too late. Her father's voice, raised almost to parade-ground pitch, said, 'Subedar Major Sahib—who is that woman? I will not have families in the single quarters—and that one is a girl—'

'Colonel Sahib—the orders have been given, the men obey—but the girls! Daughters of shame, and their mothers as well. Hey, thou evil shameless one! What do you seek here?'

Paralysed, Bianca stood, her face turned away, and the three men, half laughing now, converged on her. Subedar Major Shaibani Khan, who had known her all her life, reached her first, and stood glowering down at her. She held a fold of the sari over her face, and stood, mindless, unable to do anything. She had forgotten Khanzada's gift, the gold bracelet, conspicuous on her arm. Shaibani Khan's drawn breath, and his whispered 'Miss Sahiba!' made her gasp, and drop the cloth from her face. Swiftly the old man moved his bulk between her, and the other two, and said below his breath, 'Something is wrong? You would speak with me? Wait in Raju's stable. I come. Now you go, running, afraid—' He raised his voice roaring 'Oh child of disgrace, wait, I will have the flesh beaten off thy body—' As he shouted, she ran, hearing her father's voice, laughing, saying 'Oh, be not too harsh Subedar Sahib. That one is a very beautiful little whore—'

The laughter and the voices faded behind her, and she ran through the stable gate, and into the cool darkness of one of the stables, where the great bay horse belonging to Shaibani Khan turned his head and whickered a welcome. She slipped round behind him, and stood close against the wall, her breath short. Presently she heard heavy footsteps. No one but Shaibani trod so firmly—or could move so quietly when he wished to—before she was aware that the footsteps had faded to nothing, he was beside her.

'Speak, Miss Sahiba—there is very little time.'

Quickly, in a whisper that strained her dry throat, she told him everything, including Khanzada's fears for herself should she bear a girl child—and watched his face with a sinking heart. As she finished her story, he swore a great round soldier oath, and for a moment his teeth showed in a snarl. 'That primping vileness of a Nawab! That we should have fallen so low that he has power over us! There has been talk, but our men have held steady—but now this serpent's poison will spread, he will use his gold to make sure it spreads! And God knows if we have enough loyal men with us. Never mind, that is not for you to worry about. Is the old woman Goki with you? Good. Now, listen, and do as I say—and child, your speed, and your obedience could save us all—' And may the Preserver forgive me for lying to you, he thought, as he began to tell Bianca what to do. 'Go back to the Begum Khanzada, and tell her the warning is given. Then, leave her and go to your own quarters, and wait. I will send you a message, and you must then do exactly as my messenger tells you, for by that time I will have made a plan. At present it is of importance that Hardyal suspects nothing.' Bianca, who had been listening to him with dawning hope, said, 'But Khanzada thinks he has heard us speaking—'

'He has not. If he had heard, you would have been killed immediately, because he would know that you would warn your father. That is one of his creatures with your father now. No, child. Do not stop to worry. Go and do as I say. You are a brave one to have come to give the warning—now leave it to me—and of course, to your father. And do as I say. Comfort the Begum, then leave her quickly, and go back and wait. Go now, and may Allah the Merciful guard you.'

Bianca went quickly, and was through the vegetable garden and back at the privy door in minutes. She had moved lightly, and it was as if her steps had been lightened by the raising of her spirits. Her fears were still there, but only now of making a mistake, and spoiling any plan the Subedar Major made. He had taken the weight of the afternoon's horrors off her shoulders. She knew that all would be well. Brought up in a country where it was naturally accepted that the man carried all responsibilities, aside from those of housekeeping and childbearing, Bianca had also been reared by a woman who believed implicitly that men were next to God, and that a man's strength and wisdom were always at the service of the weaker sex. It was easy for Bianca, trained thus, to lose her fears once she had told Shaibani everything.

She was smiling as she went into Khanzada's darkened room, and the other girl looked at her in amazement. Speaking as quickly as she could, Bianca told her what had happened, and Khanzada sat listening, her mind busy. Shaibani Khan was a man of Lambagh, the natural son of the second Raja, and had been brought up with the present Ruler. He was to be trusted to the death, and if there was anything to be done to save the family of the Ruler, Shaibani would do it. But Khanzada, as she waited for Bianca's return, had been thinking deeply, studying Hardyal's attitude, when he had been there with them, searching her memory for the tones of his voice—and she was filled with despair. She was fairly certain that Hardyal had indeed heard her speaking to Bianca. Even if he had not heard the words, he had heard the tone of voice. Fear would be easily recognised by a man who specialised in inducing it in others. She lay listening to Bianca's hopeful words, and felt an immeasurable despondency. But none of her feelings must she show and Bianca must not know that she was in labour. With a sure instinct she guessed what Shaibani Khan must be planning. Sher Khan could be saved, but only if Bianca played her part—and if Bianca lost hope, and saw certain death for her family and her friends, Khanzada doubted if she would do anything but attempt to die with her own people. So, her voice calm, her face smoothed of all her terror, Khanzada smiled and listened, and finally spoke cheerfully, and as if all her fears had been lifted away, as Bianca's had been.

'You did well, little one. I feel sure now that we are in time. Go, then, as you were told and I will wait here for news, for it is very sure that Shaibani will send tidings to me. No—I need nothing. I will sleep a little—' In the face of her previous terror, there was something most unnatural in this sudden calm. Bianca looked at her narrowly, and Khanzada looked back, and smiled. 'Ah, forgive me, Bianca—you think I recover too quickly from my fears? Do not blame me for my pendulum mind—I have that within me that makes me unbalanced, not only when I walk!' Bianca laughed with her in relief, and kissing her tenderly, got up to go. For a second, Khanzada's resolve faltered—she was in so much pain and death seemed close—but as her hand went out to stop Bianca, and her mouth opened, a steady sound of hoof beats came into the room. Sher Khan and his horses had arrived, and Khanzada's hand remained still, her cry stifled, as Bianca parted the curtain and went out.

The room was quiet, and suddenly very empty. Khanzada lay back, her eyes on the still moving curtain, and with a cold courage, bred in her by a long line of gallant princely ancestors, settled herself to wait for what would come. Before her eyes, in splendid, comforting array, moved scenes from her safe and happy childhood, and she saw the high hills, and smelled the hill smell of deodar and pine.

4

The heat of the day was declining, the sun was setting, and servants were about the passages, taking down the kus-kus matting, and opening shuttered doors and windows. No one paid Bianca any attention as she hurried past, a slender blue figure among so many hurrying serving women. She reached her room, and went in, and looked round at blessed normalcy. Had she really run barefoot through the lines, hidden in a stable, talked to Shaibani Khan? Had Khanzada's voice really trembled with terror, telling of unspeakable horrors? Her tidy cool room, the quiet face of her travelling clock, her small white bed, all gave the events of the last hours—only two hours!—the colours of a fevered dream. But a cut on her foot throbbed and burned, and louder than the ticking of her clock sounded Khanzada's voice saying, 'The Ruler—your father and mother—Sher Khan—they will all die.'

At once, in that peaceful room, terror fell on her again. All the relief of telling her story to Shaibani Khan and seeing him accept responsibility left her. A child alone in the darkness of her fears, she turned to run to her mother's room, but as she put her hand to the door it opened, and Goki came in. Bianca ran into the strong comfort of the old arms, and dropped her head to Goki's shoulder in a passion of tears.

'Oh, Goki—thank heaven you have come. We must go to my mother—has my father come back yet? Listen—'

Goki stroked the blue cloth back from her head with gentle hands, and led her to her bed, and even as Bianca began to pour out her story, she found that she was lying back comfortably on her bed, drinking a cold lime drink, while Goki's strong hands massaged the soreness from her feet.

'But wait—Goki, we must go now—there is no time—'

'Time—there is time. I will go shortly to the Begum Khanzada. Spare your voice child, and listen, and rest. I have seen Shaibani.'

Bianca searched her face and found nothing unusual. The seams and lines of the well known and loved face were as usual, the wise eyes were calm, and Goki's voice held nothing but steady purpose. Bianca felt her fears receding again, and in the relief of this was suddenly desperately sleepy. Goki, her eyes on the glass in the girl's hand, nodded her head approvingly.

'Good. Now rest, for this night you will not sleep. Rest without fears. Remember the Begum carries a child, therefore all her fears are doubled. It is true, there is danger—' The old voice was even, the eyes still calm, but inwardly Goki's whole being was shaking with the effort of hiding her fears, and her knowledge of how terrible the danger was. All that mattered to her now, as to Shaibani Khan, was the need to save Sher Khan. The fact that if all went well, Goki's beloved Bianca would be saved too, was incidental. At a time when danger threatened the Ruler and his family, everything but the bred in the blood and bones loyalty to the House of Lambagh, lost importance. 'True, there is danger,' said Goki to Bianca, 'but not so much now that you, oh lion heart, have given warning.'

'But my father—my mother—' Somewhere in the warm calm that was beginning to submerge Bianca, anxiety stirred.

'Do not fret. Your mother will not be told. Your father will know, but will say nothing to you, it is part of Shaibani's plan. Now, child, rest, and wait.' Her voice faded, grew strong, and faded—Bianca's hand relaxed on the glass she held, and Goki, her face inscrutable, caught it as it fell.

Sher Khan, watching the syces bustle about the horses that he had brought so slowly and carefully that their coats were satin smooth, and cool, in spite of the long days on the road, had three things on his mind. He was thinking with longing of a bath, a long cool drink, and Bianca, in that order. He had not seen Bianca for a year but was quite sure that she loved him, that he loved her, and that he wished to make her his wife. He knew that there would be very little opposition, and that it would all come from her family. Her mother would oppose the marriage, because it would tie her daughter to India, and Sher Khan, loving Blanche O'Neil as he would have loved his own mother had she lived, understood the woman's longing for her own land, and knew that although she loved him as a son, she would consider her daughter to be marrying beneath her station if she married him. But the Colonel would not care—his heart was in India, among his beloved State Troops anyway—and poor lady, his wife would need to conform with her husband, or appear to, for there was nothing she could do against her husband's wishes. Therefore, sure of Bianca, there was no urgency in his thoughts of her—the bath, and the cold drink were necessary to revive him, before he met his love again.

A horse jerked its head, a tired syce dropped a rope, and cursing, Sher Khan jumped forward to catch the shying horse, forgetting everything, as he gentled the beautiful nervous beast that was his hope for the next day's games.

He heard his name quietly spoken, and turned to find Shaibani Khan, almost unrecognisable in mufti, standing at his elbow.

The two men spoke for a long time, standing backs close to the wall where the light of the setting sun could not reach. There were questions and answers, but mostly Sher Khan listened in silence. When Shaibani had finished, it was full dark. The fires were being lit about the stableyard, and there was the good smell of woodsmoke, and the first pariah dogs were beginning to greet the evening jackal. Presently Sher Khan stirred, and spoke. 'Yes. It would be idle to waste time speaking of the rumours I have heard on the way up from the Rann. I did not listen. But this rat king that we are now tied to by marriage, may he die the death of all evil creatures. Have you spoken with my uncle?' Shaibani Khan nodded.

'Yes. He knows all, and is in agreement with my plans. You leave at moonrise with—with the lady. Without seeing the Ruler, for if you go to him, they will have eyes and ears on you.'

'Why cannot the Ruler go, taking the Rani, and the girl? I do not go. I stay here with Zada, and see to the Rat. There are some matters to see to, you will agree, and it is for me to deal with them.'

His tone was final, and Shaibani Khan's heart sank. 'Lord of the Hills—it is necessary for you to go. You are the heir. The Ruler cannot go. He must stay, and try to hold the other princes together. If he goes now, there will be disorder and dismay, and the evil that we fear will gain ground, and the bloodletting begin before time, before we are ready to combat it. And the girl—she will not leave without you.' Sher Khan shook his head.

'I do not think that she would wish to live, knowing that her parents, and the Ruler and his family lie in danger of death. Like me, she would prefer to die with them. What manner of man do you think me, that you ask me to slink away to the hills like one of those dogs—' he pointed to a cringing yellow cur beyond the circle of firelight '—like that yellow dog, my tail down, running before danger? Ah, speak not of flight. I *will* see the Ruler.'

Shaibani Khan straightened his shoulders, and his voice was so like the Ruler's voice when he spoke, that Sher Khan blinked and stared at him.

'Yes—you will argue, and you will waste time—and all the work of your grandfather and your uncle will go for nothing, when the sword drinks your blood—and your uncle will die, knowing that all is lost because you put your honour before his—and the girl you say you would take to wife—will she die, quickly, even if afraid, or will they take her and keep her alive—she is a woman grown now, and very beautiful. And Khanzada—the brave one! She will have died for nothing too. For I tell you, whatever you do, it is too late for Khanzada now.'

Sher Khan's teeth grated suddenly, and he took the other between his hands, holding him by the shoulders and staring through the shadows into his face. 'Do you speak the truth—is Khanzada dead?'

The other looked down before the angry questioning gaze. 'The lady is dying. The child is coming, and all is not going well. She has no strength.'

A moment longer the fierce grip held him, then Sher Khan turned away, releasing him, and said, 'Very well. But I will see my uncle before I go.' There was pain and anger in his voice, but there was acceptance too. Shaibani Khan stepped back. 'It is well. Stay, Lord. I bring him. Nay—' as the other started forward—'Nay. Be still. You cannot go to him, it would bring the hornets round us at once. By his order, I go to fetch him. He knew you would not go without seeing him, and he waits nearby.' He turned and was away, making no sound, and keeping close in the dark shadow of the wall, while Sher Khan stood, watching the firelight, one hand on his horse's neck, his thoughts slowly settling into a sad knowledge that he would lose the coming argument. It was necessary for him to go, for the sake of the line, and because of all the struggle that men of his family had fought through to make the safety of the three States. His cousin, the son of the Ruler, had died in one of those battles; now he was the heir and the Ruler's hope. A Ruler was also a slave, and the priest of his people, and their willing sacrifice. Sher Khan bowed his head for a second, then began to look about him. He found what he wanted, and when the Ruler came, dressed in the rough woollen robes of a hill man, with a heavy cotton scarf muffling his head, Sher Khan had already pulled a string bed into the empty stable next door, and salaaming deeply, led his uncle to it. The old man embraced him, and Sher Khan could have wept to feel the tremble in those arms. This had been a strong man, in the splendid strength of a healthy old age, suddenly laid low by treachery.

'Now, boy. You replaced my son, not only as my heir, but in my heart. I do not have to command you to go. I could have you drugged, and tied on a horse, and sent up to the hills like a bale of cloth. Do you go willingly?'

There was no argument really. The battle had been won by people of the past, speaking through Sher Khan's blood. All he asked, his voice breaking suddenly, was that his uncle would try to get to safety as soon as he could. 'And Khanzada—what of my sister, my Lord?'

'The Rani is with her. She is dying, boy. There is no strength in her, that accursed one has broken her heart. But at least she meets death in loving arms, and in peace, knowing her warning given. An evil hour, boy, and an evil year. This land will be riven by the earthquake of revolt. Keep our people steady in the north, and hold the passes, for it is now that those dogs from Russia will try to break in. They think the power of the British is broken, as do these fools down here. Get your men to the passes quickly—and keep all these renegades out as well.' The question that was on Sher Khan's lips was answered before it was asked.

'You will have tidings. If the Peacock flies, you will be told. Until then—' He put his hand to the neck of his robe, and for a moment Sher Khan saw, like green fire against his throat, the gleam of emeralds. Then his uncle raised his hands. 'Take the blessing, boy. Oh son of my heart, kneel.'

As he knelt, the strong old voice, caution forgotten, rose in the quiet stable, and he heard the horses stamping along the lines.

'Go in peace, and under the hands of Allah the merciful, the Preserver. Keep the people, guard the passes, fill the barns, and be wise in judgment. Be as the son of my body, and in time, put my ashes to rest beneath your throne—I doubt that you will ever see my body for burial. May Allah the merciful hold you until the fullness of your days be past, may he fill you with strength and give you sons, and may the guardians of the hills guide you.' Sher Khan, on his knees, felt the light pressure on his head lift, but did not look up until a subtle change of feeling in the stable told him that his uncle had gone. He found Shaibani beside him, and as he got up, the old soldier made a deep obeisance, touching his forehead to Sher Khan's feet, a salute reserved for the Ruler alone. Sher Khan felt the stab of cold certainty. He would never see his uncle again. He put the grief from his mind, and swiftly began to give orders. His syce, his eyes rolling in his head, came in and flung himself before him, to be rudely repulsed. 'Leave the mummery, Mansur. I would rather have service. Saddle Bedami for the Miss Sahiba, and Piyara for me. I shall need Lambaghi dress—'

'Lord of the Hills, it is done. The clothes are here, and the horses ready. The lady will be here as soon as you have dressed and eaten.'

Even in this time of strain and worry, Sher Khan bit back a smile. It appeared that Shaibani Khan no longer considered Miss Sahiba a suitable title for Bianca. As the old man outlined the best roads to the hills, Sher Khan changed swiftly, at the back of his mind, sternly held there, the incredible thought that, in all likelihood, he would never hear this slow deep voice again. For a second, the thought was too much.

'How can I go—' It was spoken half aloud, a groan of anguish, and Shaibani was swift to answer. 'You go because it is so ordered in the universe. You are Ruler, and ruled. You know that well. Your life is forfeit to your people, Lord.' Sher Khan made no answer, for there was none to give. Presently, eating the food that the Subedar had brought and served to him as if he were eating in his own room, he said 'And the lady—has she eaten? Do I have food suitable for her?'

'There is fruit and meat, and bread, in both your saddlebags. But the lady has eaten. Goki will have seen to that. You should go to Swaraja at Nathucota, and he will replenish your food. Are you ready, Lord? The moon is near to rise, and they are dressing for the Durbar.' He chuckled suddenly. 'I have a man in your room, laying out your ceremonial dress, and the jewels that are left—I have put most of the best in your saddlebags. There is another man splashing his humble body in your bathroom, so all sounds normal, should any be interested.'

'Ai, father of plotters! You have thought of everything. Be very sure I will never forget.' An idle promise from one not yet in safety to one about to die, but Shaibani's face lit with pleasure, and he salaamed deeply.

'My life for yours, Lord.' he said, and the conventional words said in the quiet dark stable, with danger and death standing close, took on a true, deep meaning. Sher Khan folded the old man in a close embrace and then stepped back, his eyes wet. He could remember when this man had seemed as tall as a tree, and like a tree to be swarmed up by a loving small boy, who found wisdom, love, and comfort in the Subedar's arms. Time was—time passes. Sher Khan said quietly, 'Go, father of my heart. Bring the lady,' and then turned quickly to his horse, his farewell wordless, but understood.

Bianca had wakened from a deep refreshing sleep to find Goki bending over her.

'Ah—you are awake. Child, you must move fast. The Prince waits for you in the stables, you ride to the hills with him tonight.'

The shock tactics planned by Goki worked on Bianca's sleep-drugged brain as Goki hoped they would. The girl sprang out of bed, fully awake, and babbling with questions. But Goki hustling her into the bathroom, and a cold sponge that made her shudder, would answer few of the questions.

'It is part of the plan,' was all she would say, and she rubbed Bianca dry and began to sort clothing from a bundle she had brought with her from a quick visit to her own quarters.

'But what—'

'Hush, child. You are to go to the hills with Sher Khan. To Lambagh. The Ruler has arranged it. Your mother and father—and mayhap the Ruler and the Rani, will follow later.'

'But Goki—I must see my mother before I go—I must say goodbye, and tell her—'

'—And bring the whole plan down? Nay, Bianca, see sense. If you go into your mother's room, and say farewell, and she, knowing nothing, starts to question and worry, time will be lost that we cannot afford. Your father and the Ruler want you to go with speed for Sher Khan's sake. For, before all others, he is in danger. He will be among the first to be killed.'

A cold finger touched Bianca. She had a flashing vision of Sher Khan's laughing face stilled by a sword, and she began to hurry without question into the rough clothes that Goki was holding out to her. Sher Khan's danger was a spur, for the others seemed safe now that the Ruler knew of the plot.

She looked down at herself, at the long tight black trousers and the black shirt, and then looked up into the mirror, to see herself transformed into a hill girl in every particular, as Goki pulled the black cloth over her plaited hair, and stepped back, leaving Bianca's reflection alone in the mirror. Indeed, she could not go into her mother's room dressed as she was!

'But how is my mother, Goki—is she better? Goki, tell her I wanted to see her,' begged Bianca, with tears in her eyes.

'She sleeps well, and will wake rested. Do not grieve, Bianca. You go to your lord, as you wished. Put all else from your mind. Now, eat, child, for there is much riding for you to do tonight—'
But Bianca could eat little. All her childhood seemed to rise and chide her with memories of her mother's kind love and understanding, her mother's voice sounded in her ears, comforting her, telling her stories all about her own childhood in the fabled land of Ireland, so green and beautiful, so far away. These stories had always ended, 'And one day, my little love, I'll show you the place where I was born myself. Ah, it is a fine beautiful country, full of lovely places, and we'll go there together, you and I—'
Alas for dreams doomed to failure! Bianca in her heart knew that there was no question of her ever wanting to go anywhere away from India—but the longing that sounded in her mother's remembered voice was a knife in her heart now, and she felt

treacherous, a deserter. Goki saw the trembling lips and filling eyes, and thanked her gods when there was a gentle scratching at the window. She got up at once, and took Bianca briefly into her arms.

'Come child. It is time.' She turned to the bathroom door, and Bianca was suddenly reminded—'How could I have forgotten?' she thought, angry with herself. 'Khanzada—Goki, what of Zada—?'

'All is well. The Rani is with her. Bianca! You think of so many things that I ask myself if your heart is firm. If you do not wish to go, tell me now, for Sher Khan must be sent away without delay—every second is jeopardy for him. Do you wish to go with him?'

Unspeaking, Bianca turned and hurried out into the scented garden, where a dark figure beckoned her on, and in silence the three sped through the shadows of the garden to where the fires in the stableyard leapt and sparked. Once in the yard, they followed the deeper shadow round the wall, and before Bianca was ready she saw a tall figure, and behind him, Shaibani was holding two saddled horses. Sher Khan, strange to her in the plain dark clothing of a hill man, his face hidden from her by the darkness, stepped forward, and the moment of their confrontation was caught and held by time, so that in silence and darkness they seemed to stand for an eternity—and then the spell was broken as the musicians began to play in the garden in front of the palace, and Sher Khan took her into his arms, and into a warm turmoil that shook her whole being, so that she barely heard his murmured words above her head. 'Thank Allah the merciful, you got here safely—'

His arms held her so tightly that she could not breathe, then he released her, and turned, and Shaibani brought up the horses. She was lifted in Sher Khan's arms, and into the saddle. Goki's hand lay briefly on her leg, she heard the creak of Sher Khan's saddle as he mounted, and then he struck heels to his horse to take the lead. Once through the stable gates, they rode in the dust on the soft side of the road, the dust muffling to silence the sound of the horses' hooves. A hundred yards from the Madoremahal, Sher Khan kicked his mount into a smart canter, and Bianca, settling into her saddle and following his lead, forgot everything in the pleasure of fast movement through the soft night air, and in the feeling that she had control over the splendid animal she rode. It was as if memory could bear no more pain, and therefore sank away. She knew both horses, Sher Khan's mount was one of his uncle's best animals, and Bedami, the horse she rode, was Sher Khan's own. She wondered fleetingly what had become of the wonderful new horses that he had been bringing up from the Rann—they would miss Sher Khan at the polo matches after the Durbar! Her thoughts flinched away when something whispered that there would not—could not possibly be a polo match on the strange tomorrow that would be dawning over the Madoremahal when she was far away. The sound of music from the Mahal garden still sounded faintly in the quiet night, and somewhere a bird screeched harshly. Her eyes fixed on Sher Khan's dimly seen figure, Bianca gave herself up to the ride.

The music, so quiet and delicate, borne on the night wind to the the riders, was loud in Khanzada's quiet room, loud and out of place, so that the Rani's tear-wet face clenched in protest as she moved about the tasks of putting Khanzada's little body in readiness for the final ceremonies. The women and the Moulvi had done their duties, and Hardyal had been in, had wept and torn his hair, and rushed out, overcome—and all the Rani could see were his cold eyes, cold as black stones, eyes that never changed however much his mouth writhed in grief's grimaces. Khanzada and her daughter—the child so dreaded, that had never breathed—they were undisturbed by all the turmoil of mourning. Zada had smiled at the last, and had put a trembling hand protectively over the little head. 'So, my daughter—you were in too much of a hurry to wait for your mother. Oh discourteous! Never mind—I come.' On the whispered words, she had died, and now the baby lay in the curve of her mother's arms, and the Rani drew a soft white veil over them both. The smell of jasmine and marigolds and roses from the garlands that had been hurriedly brought, filled the air, and a lamp burned in the open window, to light the two spirits to freedom.

'Go in peace, children,' said the old Rani, looking at the quiet figures on the bed. 'Go in peace. But my beloved children, go slowly, for I follow very soon.' She lifted the curtain, and left the room.

The night wind rose higher, and the lamplight leapt and wavered over the walls of the quiet room, as if the shadows were dancing to the music from the garden.

5

The musicians, seated on carpets among the flowers on a side lawn, obeyed orders, and played louder, as the guests began to gather. The women were all in a small pavilion, screened with fretted marble, so that they could see out without their precious purdah being violated. They sat eating sweets, and chattering like birds in an aviary. The air in the pavilion was heavy with the scents of musk and rosewater and sandalwood, and there was a constant ringing, as of little bells, every time the women moved a hand or arm, for they were all wearing all their jewellery. The eye dazzled on gold and on the flash of diamonds, rubies and emeralds, their colours repeated in the heavy silks, lavish with gold embroidery, that rustled and crackled like fire in straw. Khanzada's death had been kept from the guests, so there was no mourning.

Lady Willer and Mrs Morton, their full skirts spread round them, sat together trying to catch up on a year's news and gossip. Margaret Willer came from Rajsarda, where her husband, Sir Hubert was commanding the Maharaja's Forces, and Sophia Morton was from the small State of Joaldar, where Richard Morton was the Nawab's military adviser. They spoke of Blanche O'Neil's absence, and Margaret Willer said that she would go and see what had happened to their friend, but the Rani of Lambagh arrived at that moment and told them that Blanche was exhausted by her journey and was sleeping, and that Bianca was staying with her mother. Margaret and Sophia returned to their chatting and the Rani sat quietly beside them, letting the talk go by her as she watched the scene outside.

Servants were moving through the crowd with trays of fresh drinks already. Voices were loud, and faces flushed, there was a wildness in the air, almost as visible, it seemed, as the unbuttoned tunics, the turbans set awry on hot heads. The Ruler of Lambagh stood among his guests, Colonel O'Neil at his side, talking and laughing, but his eyes were grave and watchful, and constantly turned to where Hardyal stood, surrounded by a sort of court of splendidly dressed young men. The Subedar Major, Shaibani Khan, was close behind the Ruler; both looked with pity at O'Neil, but neither said anything as he murmured to the Ruler how glad he was that his daughter had decided to stay with her mother. 'I was surprised when Goki brought me the message—but very pleased. I am glad too that Blanche still sleeps. Though how she can, with this noise, God knows.'

Blanche O'Neil had wakened to find Goki at her side with a bowl of iced soup, had drunk it obediently, and had sunk back into fathomless sleep. Goki had left then, going quietly down passages and corridors, to the oldest parts of the palace, where, in an empty, long unused courtyard, she had spoken briefly with the Rani, who had given her a small package. Then the two women had parted, and Goki had slipped through the garden to a place near a small side gate, where she had waited, sitting inconspicuous among the shadows, watching and listening to the noise from the main gardens.

The musicians played louder, and the music grew shriller, like the voices of the guests as the wine jugs went round. Beneath the sound of the horns and the flutes, and the drunken laughter, the insistent note of the drums sounded like the beating of a frightened heart. Beyond the lights, in the darkness under the trees and in the darkened corridors, men stirred, moving uneasily, shadows blown by the evil wind that had risen throughout India, disturbing the habits and loyalties of years, a wind that was going to blow some things away for ever. These men, here in the old Madoremahal, were searching, quietly, unobtrusively, they quartered the palace, and the gardens. Goki saw two of them, and moved without noise to the wall, and crouched, and they passed her, unseeing. Then she went back to her vantage point, to wait.

The night was more than half over, the moon moving down the sky, when Hardyal came over to the Ruler, the lights sparkling on his jewelled coat, and salaamed low, so that the Ruler looked for a moment at the top of his turban where a great ruby glowed—part of Khanzada's rich dowry. As Hardyal straightened, he said, 'The evening goes well, my uncle—your guests are filled with gaiety.' The Ruler nodded, his eyes hard.

'Yes. All is very well with my guests. But I am surprised to see you make such a happy showing!'

Hardyal lowered his eyes. 'By your orders, Lord. You said there was to be no mourning until the guests left. If I sat apart, with ashes in my hair, it would avail Khanzada nothing, but your guests would surely wonder.' Unanswered, he turned, like a striking snake, to confront Terence O'Neil.

'Well, Colonel Sahib! Did you have a good journey down from the hills, and visit with all your old friends?'

There was a subtle undercurrent in his voice, which Terence did not like, but he answered civilly. 'Yes—but the journey was long for my wife, who is not very well—and also—' Something made him pause, a sudden tenseness in the Ruler, a movement from Hardyal, as if he leaned forward trying to hear better. Terence was not a man for atmospheres. He had been bedevilled all the way down from the hills by an intangible feeling of evil. Suddenly, he was tired of shadows. Better to bring everything out into the open. 'There were rumours of trouble, Prince,' he said, speaking firmly, 'stupid stories, babblings, but the men were listening, and were worried, I could tell.'

Hardyal gave a small sigh, and Shaibani Khan lifted his head, and began to look about him, counting friends.

'Ah,' said Hardyal, 'stupid stories, Colonel Sahib? As for instance, the tale of unclean cartridges?'

His voice was raised loud enough for others to hear, and heads began to turn, as O'Neil, flushing, said, 'Aye—I have heard that story too. It is a lie.'

Shaibani Khan moved quietly up behind the Ruler, and in the women's pavilion, the Rani rose to her feet, and went out. Gradually, the noise of talk and laughter in the women's pavilion stopped, and the women huddled close together, their eyes wide with fright. Margaret and Sophia moved forward to stare out into the garden with frowning attention.

Hardyal was laughing, and conversation was dying all round him. 'A lie, is it, Colonel Sahib? I ask myself, who is lying?'

Terence O'Neil straightened, his eyes hot. 'What do you mean to say, Prince?' On his lips, in his tone, the title became an insult, and Hardyal moved closer, showing his teeth in an ugly smile.

'You tell me who is lying, who is telling the truth, between us, Sahib. For I have proof. The story is true, and the Company is trying now, too late, to withdraw the cartridges. But this is only half the story, Sahib. There are so many things, that the account is long overdue—long overdue. So long, that the very air of our country cries out for a reckoning. Have you not heard the sound in the wind, Sahib, the cry for justice?'

A small circle was forming round the Ruler, and his companions, and with a sudden feeling of sickness, a horrified incredulity, O'Neil recognised that this was more than just drunken belligerence, this was trouble. He saw one of the English colonels, a man commanding the Forces of another Native State, similarly surrounded, and heard his angry voice. All over the garden little groups, it seemed, were forming, like whirlpools on a river, where rocks break the flow. At the centre of each group, was an Englishman, and sometimes one of the northern princes would be standing with him. Behind the Ruler Shaibani Khan felt someone come up beside him, and turned to see the Rani, her hands hidden in the folds of her sari, her head erect, her face calm.

'Greetings, oh my brother—we go in good company,' she said, as one who sets out on a journey in the hills, and he smiled as he replied, 'Yea, good company, indeed, and the joys of Paradise wait for us.'

O'Neil was speaking quietly, his eyes on Hardyal, his soft Irish voice persuasive. 'Come, Prince! This is no time for us to quarrel! Come to me tomorrow, speaking as a friend to a friend, and I will answer your questions. There is an old friendship between myself, and your country. You know that. Let not foolish mischief making come into our dealings together. Come tomorrow—'

Hardyal looked up at the tall fair man in his splendid uniform, and then looked down again, and laughed unpleasantly, and said, 'Tomorrow is already today—Sahib—and today there is news. Great news. The reckoning time is upon us, and today I, and all loyal sons of this wronged land, leave for justice, and the gathering of the brave in Delhi!' His voice rose on the last word, and shrilled out, louder even than the music, so that the word Delhi! rang like a tocsin over the garden.

'That is the signal, Lord,' said Shaibani Khan, loosening his sword.

'Look there—' The whirlpools swirled together, and there was the bright flash of drawn swords. Hardyal stood in front of the Ruler, and began to laugh, high and baying like a mad jackal, a curved sword glittering in his hand, and Shaibani Khan drew, as did the Ruler and O'Neil, and three of the northern princes who were in the group.

It was then, in that moment of stillness before the first clash of sword play, that the Rani moved, like a running partridge stooped low, she moved, and brought a small knife up, stabbing at Hardyal's belly.

'Delhi will do without you, murderer of children,' she said, and rammed the knife home.

But there was a metallic clink, and the knife turned sideways in her grip. Shaibani, defending the Ruler's back, saw her fall, a sword a hand's breadth in her side, then the fight absorbed him, and he settled to the deadly cut and thrust of sword fighting, determined to sell his life as dearly as he could. The three northern princes fought silently beside him, and the everlasting music was a dreadful background to the sound of men in battle, and in death.

'Oh God have mercy on us—look there, Margaret—they've gone mad—and little Charles is asleep in the palace. I must get to him, I must—' Sophia was on her feet and running out as she spoke. Margaret Willer had no children, and all she wanted to do was to be with her husband. She ran out, towards the spot where she had last seen him, and was cut down before she had taken more than a few steps, her head almost severed from her body, her beaded bodice and full crimson skirt hiding the blood that poured from her wound. Dying, her blue eyes were still fixed on her husband, where he stood, fighting like a demon, until he too fell, cut down by a dozen jabbing swords.

Sophia, after one horrified look at the carnage behind her, did not stop running for a moment and had almost reached the palace when she was caught. Her scream as she felt the hands that held her, and the knife that spilled her blood, cut through the other terrible sounds of men in combat like a shrill silver trumpet will rise above an orchestra. Terence O'Neil, fighting at the Ruler's right hand, heard her scream, and was badly wounded almost at once, for his mind became full of thoughts about Blanche, and he could no longer find the single-minded concentration a fighting man needs. A few minutes later, he was mortally wounded, and fell at the Ruler's feet.

Hardyal, watching, saw that with Terence gone, and the three northern princes who had been guarding the Ruler all dead, there only remained Shaibani Khan, fighting alone at the Ruler's side—and fighting blind, blood streaming from a gash on his forehead, one arm hanging useless.

'Now,' said Hardyal, and working his way round, while two of his creatures engaged the Ruler and the dying Shaibani, he took out his dagger, and drove it home in the Ruler's unprotected back.

There was a rush, as of jackals when the kill is made, and the Ruler and Shaibani Khan fell together, their fighting done for ever. They were fortunate, those two brave men, for they died quickly.

Terence O'Neil died bravely, but his last few minutes were a torment, as he lay, hacked and helpless, but still conscious, thinking of his wife. His fears for her at the last, took from his mind all thoughts of Bianca; it was as if his beloved child had never lived. His physical pain he could discount, but for the five long minutes that it took him to die, he agonised for his wife. Death was a kind friend to him, cutting off thought.

But he could have spared himself those fears. Goki's drug was strong, and held Blanche in a deep and peaceful sleep. She did not wake when they broke into her room, and did not see the hand that wielded the knife. She died smiling, her hand under her cheek, a child again, among the green hills of Ireland.

Dawn came slowly, reluctantly, to the gardens. It was still dark, but the sky had a faint haze of light about it, when the musicians stopped playing and hurried away, their faces all set in one mould, a grimace of fear and horror. The torches guttered out, the lamps were burning low, no one had replenished the oil. The women's pavilion was in darkness, only a sound of muffled weeping betrayed that it was still occupied.

The killers had done their work—some for the joy of killing, some to settle old scores, some for payment. Now they had gone into the Madoremahal, swiftly, talking with deep purpose, as men who needed a reason suddenly for what they had done. Blood cools swiftly in the early hours of the day.

Hardyal, a surgeon working swiftly on the superficial wound inflicted by the Rani's knife, was hearing the unwelcome news that there was no sign of Sher Khan, and that the girl Bianca had vanished too—and that the Emerald Peacock, that precious symbolic chain, had not been on the Ruler's person when he was finally cut down. It was during the eruption of rage that was caused by this news, that Goki rose to her feet and disobeyed orders.

The Ruler had told her, through the Rani, that when she saw him killed, she was to go, making for the hills with all speed, and give the news to Sher Khan. But now she hid the small package she carried, forcing it down among the roots of the tree near where she had been crouching, and went quietly over the grass, keeping as much as possible in the shadows of the trees, until she came to where the bodies were heaped about the Ruler, the coloured silks and the blood all uniformly grey in that dead light.

Between them, the Ruler and his supporters in that tight circle of death, had killed twenty men. Goki dragged the bodies aside, calling on a strength that no one of her years could have been thought to possess—and at last she had the body of the Ruler free, and could straighten his limbs, and try to wipe the blood from his face. It was while she was doing this that a sound, a sigh, barely loud enough to hear, made her turn, and she was looking into the Rani's eyes, live and tormented, a few feet away. Once again, Goki tore and pulled, until the Rani was free of the bodies that had been lying over her, but there was no moving her then. Death was close, but not close enough for the Rani.

'Goki—in the name of all mercy—speed my spirit. I pain—I pain greatly—and my Lord waits!' Goki, without hesitation, fumbled her knife free, and raised it. 'Go, sister, in peace—' The knife swept down, and the desperate eyes closed, peace growing on the still face. Goki hid her own eyes and wept for a second, but purpose woke in her again, and she bent to her task.

The pale light was sifting through the trees and the parrots were waking to scream the sun up into the sky as she finished laying the bodies of the Ruler, his wife, and his friends in a neat and orderly manner, their limbs composed, where possible, their terrible faces covered. She took the bloodstained turban from the Ruler's head, and cut the bloodiest piece from it, then wrapped it over his head again.

She stood above the bodies for a short while, as the light grew, murmuring prayers to send them safely on their way. Then she turned, retrieved her package, and left the dreadful garden, to set off on her long trek to the hills.

6

The growing light caught up with the riders, and out-raced them, and suddenly the mountains, haloed by the rising sun, stood like a high black wall on the skyline. Sher Khan did not slow his pace until they reached the outskirts of a village in the foothills. Then he slowed to a trot, and clattered up to a house, and a man ran out at the first sound of his voice. It was as if they were expected—no one else appeared, the village was silent, none of the usual early morning activity disturbed the narrow streets, and the houses were shuttered. Not even a pariah dog appeared to sniff around the travellers.

Sher Khan talked to the man for a minute, and then the villager ran back to his house, and Sher Khan dismounted and came over to Bianca. She was stiff, and stumbled when he put her on her feet—the horses were lathered and blowing, although Bianca's mount was in fairly good shape because of her light weight. Bianca unsaddled and opening the blanket that was under the saddle, threw it over her horse when she saw Sher Khan doing this for his animal. Sher Khan came over and gave her a drink from his silver flask, unspeaking, holding the flask out to her with raised eyebrows. Bianca, never having tasted anything stronger than watered wine, choked over her mouthful of fiery native spirit, but she did not speak—somehow she knew that Sher Khan did not want her to say anything in this place of listening silence. The villager was back, leading two horses. Then Sher Khan spoke to her.

'Up—we have been here long enough. Take the food from your saddlebags, Lady, and put it in the new bags. Keep a chapatti to eat as you go.'

'Lady'! Bianca raised her eyebrows at the formal title, but she obediently did as she was told, and allowed herself to be lifted to her saddle, and Sher Khan said something to the waiting man and mounted and, turning away from the village, they started to ride.

Her new mount was a sturdy hill pony, saddled and bridled in country fashion. Bianca thanked God that she had learned to ride astride, as the pony settled into a fast choppy canter, following Sher Khan. The wind began to whip her long hair against her cheeks. She had not even been given time to re-tie her hair! Sher Khan's desire for haste seemed a trifle unnecessary to her now. The events of the previous day were blurred in her mind by the exciting present. She was eloping with Sher Khan, just as they had planned—the only pursuit she feared was a loving one, the only danger was that her parents might catch her up, and delay with argument, her marriage. Khanzada's fears, the threat of Hardyal's hatred, the stories of terrible trouble to come—like phantoms of the night, they had faded, in this exciting daylight. Her only worry was that her elopement would have distressed her mother—but this would all be put right. Her mother and father loved Sher Khan, and had a great opinion of him. They would certainly be angry, but it would not be a lasting anger. The Ruler and the Rani would be delighted. She knew that. Faced with the Ruler's pleasure, and the marriage accomplished, her parents would give in gracefully, and would be happy with her in her happiness. They would probably come up and stay in Lambagh for the summer months—it would be a great pleasure to welcome her mother to her own home, on the delicious equal footing of being a married woman too.

Her horse changed the rhythm of his movement, and Bianca was jolted out of her happy daydream. She saw that they were following no set path now, but were picking their way up goat tracks and dry gullies. The going was very rough, but the pony was sure footed, he climbed almost without slackening speed. She caught at the high leather pommel of the hill man's saddle, and tried to help the beast by keeping her weight balanced and steady. Looking ahead, she saw Sher Khan riding easily, his horse picking its way like a cat over the rough ground, and suddenly no speed was too great, nothing mattered but that they should soon reach somewhere where they could be together, could talk together, and be in each other's arms. She longed for the night because they would have to rest then—and then, at last completely alone, she would be able to show Sher Khan something of the love she had been holding all this long year.

Sher Khan rode through the day with no pleasure, and saw the beginning of evening, and knew that now, when he entered Lambagh, he would be entering the State as Ruler. By this time, his uncle must be dead, and Bianca's father with him. He wondered how far the troubles, of which the tragedy of Madore was only a small part, would spread. He felt sure that the whole of Central India, Delhi, and the areas round Meerut, Lucknow, and Cawnpore were already contaminated, but would the north hold steady? Delhi, Cawnpore, Meerut, Jhansi, Lucknow. He told the names over to himself, names that seemed to have a terrible ring about them, a feeling of horror which, in fact, would never really leave those places. But the north? It was his duty to hold the three hill States steady—and also to keep the northern borders of Lambagh safe. He had a great deal on his mind. His love for Bianca was not lessened by his anxieties—it merely receded to the back of his mind for the time being. He rode, planning the next few days, thinking of men, and arms, and undefended mountain passes, and grain stores, and at the same time, managed to know that she was riding well, keeping up with him, and showing no signs of fatigue. Somewhere in his thoughts, he found room to be proud of her and to be thankful that she was not weeping for her parents. There was no sign of pursuit, but he would feel no ease until they were over the passes, and on the further side of the mountains, going down into the valley of Lambagh. There, at last, he would be among his own people. Until then, there must be no delaying, however tired they were.

Bianca watched the flaming sunset burn itself out, and night sweep suddenly down the slopes of the mountains, and her body felt as light as air—her head felt a little dizzy, as if she had been drinking too much wine. Perhaps I have, she thought, for each time they stopped, Sher Khan held out his flask to her, and she had never refused—to refuse his offer would be like refusing his love—for surely the offered flask was at present the only way he could offer her love. But soon—her heart quickened, and she caught her breath, yearning for—yearning for what? Bianca rode through the darkness, longing for love, and her lover's arms and his kisses, without altogether knowing what it was that she was so burningly eager to experience. Half child still, her dreams were all of burning love, of perfection and adoration, of passion that never ended, of eternal happiness.

They rode into a small village, a poor little place, with only two or three mud-walled houses, and no cultivation to speak of as far as she could see. It was getting very dark, and there were no lights. Then she saw a flaring torch ahead, and looked eagerly to see the place where they would spend the night. But the torch revealed yet another man standing with a pair of hill ponies, ready saddled—her heart dropped.

'Are we not to stay here for the night?' she asked, when Sher Khan came up to help her to dismount.

'No. Not here. Not yet. We must go further into the mountains before we stop. Are you too weary?' His eyes, looking up at her as he reached to lift her down, caught the light from the burning torch, and seemed to burn in the same way. Bianca, with that burning glance turned on her face, could only shake her head—indeed, as she felt his arms close round her, she felt anything but tired, and was embarrassed by the beating of her heart, which she was sure he must feel. If he did, he gave no sign, though he did not set her on her feet for a moment, but held her high in his arms, pressed against his body, and she could, for a breath-stopping moment feel his heart beat—steady, even, like a drum—then she was up on her new pony, and he left her and mounted his own horse, and the man waving the torch was behind them, while they climbed, it seemed, up to the very stars themselves.

When they finally stopped, in the lee of a huge rock, on a high wind-swept pass, Bianca was too tired to speak. The air was thin and cold, and it hurt to breathe. She was barely conscious of Sher Khan's hands, rolling her into a blanket that smelled of woodsmoke and horse dung, but she gulped gratefully the cup of hot gruel given to her by a man who had appeared out of the scattered rocks. As she drank, the stars in the cold sky seemed to whirl in a crazy dance. Sher Khan took the cup from her, and laid her down, and she fell, stunned by fatigue, into a deep sleep. Sher Khan spent the night sitting beside her, his back to a rock, facing the way they had come, a long rifle across his knees. He slept very little, and woke her before dawn, a steaming bowl of the same gruel in his hands. Over his shoulder, she saw by the light of a smouldering torch, that there was no change of horses this time. The hill man waited with the same two ponies, who looked as tired as she felt. She was stiff and aching, and when she put her hands to her hair, it felt like tangled straw—and probably looked like it too, she thought ruefully, trying to keep her back to the torchlight. But Sher Khan gave her little time to think about her appearance. Under his firm command she drank her gruel, and struggled to her feet, to be lifted into her saddle, too tired now to question anything. The torch made a flickering circle of light, a little bit of civilisation among the dark rocks. They rode out of this circle, into the pre-dawn darkness, and away, and the friendly island of light dwindled and died behind them.

It rained for the first part of the ride, and Bianca felt her thick woollen clothing for the first time with pleasure. At least her body would not get wet, though her hair and face were running with water. The way was rough and her horse stumbled badly several times, once flinging his head back and catching Bianca a hard blow as she leaned forward. She could hear a river, faintly, and began to lose all sense of direction as a choking curtain of mist came down, adding texture to the darkness. She could not see Sher Khan, but she could hear his horse stumbling ahead of hers, an eerie echo of her own progress—or was she the echo? Every story she had ever heard about the evil ones who come with the mist to trap souls, came back to her—also Goki's tales of the great bears, who live in the mountains round Lambagh. The path she was following was a mere track, winding round the side of the mountain. What if they met a bear on this narrow way? Her horse stumbled again, jerking her half out of the saddle, and she heard the voice of the river again. Tears and rain mingled on her cheeks as she clung grimly to the saddle, biting her lips in an effort not to cry out, not to show fear; fear in a woman was an inconvenience, and must be quelled before it took hold. She could hear her father's voice: 'Bianca—to be afraid—ah now, everyone is afraid at one time or another. We are but human, and the best and bravest of us have a fear of something or other hidden away in our hearts. But to show fear, to cringe and cower, that is a terrible weakness, and that we can conquer. We must conquer, because otherwise, fear becomes our master, and worse still, my girl, someone who is constantly in a state of fear is a terrible nuisance—and a terrible bore.'

Alone on the mountainside, in darkness and discomfort, his voice sounded in her memory. That had been the day she'd fallen from her horse, and had wept and refused to remount and had held the whole expedition up, while her father had gently and firmly persuaded her back into the saddle again. How many years ago was that now, wondered Bianca, stretching her fifteen years into lifetimes. But the memory helped. She stayed in her saddle now, and kept her tears under control, and tried to breathe evenly, without gasping. The air was keen, and a wind got up, blowing the rain into sleet, but at least the mist was clearing. The mountains, towering, overwhelming, slowly materialised out of the shredding mist, the path turned steeply downwards and the voice of the river grew loud.

It was a narrow, twisting stream, boiling along between the rocky mountainsides, deep and swift-flowing, and a mist of white spray hung about it where the black rocks thrust up. The path led straight down to it, and Bianca had a clear view of the bridge that spanned it—a single pine trunk, flung over where the river narrowed between two enormous overhanging rocks. On the opposite bank were two men, and two ponies.

Sher Khan dismounted, and then lifted her down, and tied both horses to a birch tree, and came back to her, where she sat, trying to rub some feeling back into her numbed feet and legs. He sat down before her, and took her feet between his hands, rubbing hard, and looking up at her with a smile that soon turned into a laugh. 'Ah, my poor Bianca—what a way to bring you to Lambagh! You should have come slowly, in a palanquin, wrapped in silks and covered warm in furs, with only twenty miles covered each day, and the roads lined with cheering people—that is how princesses enter their kingdoms. But never mind. See—we cross the river, and a day's ride ahead is Lambagh, and you will be able to rest and recover. And, Lady—' His voice caught, and deepened, and the smile was gone. 'Lady of delights—no princess has ever shown so much bravery.' He bent suddenly, laid his lips to her insteps, kissing first one and then the other, and got up and turned away, saying, 'No more time—I will go over first, to make sure the tree is firm, and then you follow as soon as you see me on the other side.'

During this time, Bianca had not spoken. She felt numb, and

as if the stiff coldness of her feet and legs had travelled all over her body. In fact, she had hardly registered what Sher Khan was saying.

Overshadowing everything, the boiling, foam-embroidered river, and the crooked pine bridge loomed in her mind, nightmares given tangibility, horror come close. The only fear that Bianca had never been able to conquer, that in fact even her father had been tender with, was her fear of heights. Sick and giddy, she had turned away from the slender towers of the Madoremahal, where the other children played, racing up and down the curving narrow stairs and peering over the low marble balustrades. The other children—but never Bianca. Her father had taken her to Delhi, where the high tower of the Kutb Minar had been one of the sights to see, but she had stayed at the foot, dizzy even looking at the outside of the tower.

Now she confronted a slender pine tree, lying over a rushing torrent, and she was paralysed with fear. Sher Khan was halfway over, treading one foot after another, slowly but surely, the tree swaying to his every step. She saw him reach the other side, and the two men run forward to prostrate themselves at his feet—then he turned to call to her, his voice drowned by the roar of the water, but his gesture plain enough: 'All is well— Come over.'

Bianca got up slowly, and walked to the end of the bridge, where the thick stump of the pine was dug into the earth, and steadied with boulders heaped about it. She stood there, looking across at Sher Khan, and wondering what he would do when he found that she could not cross. She could see that it was impossible for anyone to help her. No man could guide another over that narrow trunk, rough with bark, and knotted where the branches had been chopped off. She looked despairingly over—such a short distance, a mere twenty or thirty steps—and as she looked, her teeth bit into her lip, and she screamed to Sher Khan, and knew, with terror, that he could not hear a sound. He was standing, both feet on the far end of the bridge, and with him stood the two hill men, all three looking towards her—and behind Sher Khan, towering, it seemed, over him, was a great black bear. Bianca could see the white V that spread over its broad chest, and the enormous paws, almost human looking. She gestured frantically, and Sher Khan waved back, and the bear lumbered nearer. Bianca did not wave again, lest Sher Khan's answering movement should annoy the bear into hostile action. Without another thought, with, in fact, only one thought in her mind, to get to Sher Khan before the bear did, Bianca launched herself on to the bridge. The river, loud beneath her feet, the mists of spray that made the wood wet and slippery, the spring and sway of the slender trunk as she moved—she noticed none of this. Almost running, she skimmed over the tree trunk, and Sher Khan, amazed, stepped up and caught her in his arms.

'Indeed, Bianca, you are a brave girl—and a sure-footed one! I would never dare take that bridge at such speed—' The two hill men muttered astonishment, and salaamed deeply before her.

Bianca got her breath back, and half said, half gasped, 'Sher Khan—the bear—there, look, up on the rock—' Exhausted, nerves in shreds, frightened into hysteria, Bianca burst into tears. It maddened her that he should waste time trying to comfort her, that the two men with him merely stared, and looked sympathetic, until at last, his flask was rattling against her teeth, and she could make a little sense out of what he was saying.

'Bianca—that bear is not going to hurt us as long as we leave him alone. He is out looking for berries and grubs, and honey—or even young tree shoots. Tell me, Bianca, was that why you ran over? To warn us?' He turned to the men, and said something to them—and their faces broke into delighted smiles, their eyes almost hidden by their smiling, and both spoke to her in their hill patois, and salaamed again.

'They thank you for your thought, Bianca. You will be a heroine to the people hereabouts because you ran to save them, believing that you were running into danger—' He paused, and looked down at her, a memory stirring. Of course! She hated heights, and avoided all high places. He had forgotten this fear of hers, and looked at her with love and respect, and led her to her pony as if he were leading her to a throne. But Bianca did not notice this. She felt exhausted and miserable, and very stupid, as if she should have known that the bear was harmless. The journey to Lambagh was not as she had expected it to be—she longed for it to be over.

Suddenly, they began to climb into better weather. They came round a corner, and there below them, in a cup of mountains, lay the valley of Lambagh. Green and gold, the meadows of Lambagh glittered in the distance. She could see, scaled down to miniatures, the clustered villages, a blue lake, and a white-walled building set in trees. There were mountain ridges and valleys to cross, but at least there lay Lambagh, in sight at last. Sher Khan drew rein to give her an encouraging smile, and gestured downwards, and then they went on, the journey beginning to seem endless.

Indeed, they had to travel on for the rest of the day. The cold sunlight flickered out over the black range of mountains as they came up the final long slope towards the crest of the last pass. The day was dying fast, shadows sweeping in like great bird's wings, darkening the sky. Bianca was suddenly uneasy, her depression deepened; there was no welcome feeling of coming home. The shadows seemed to threaten, the rocks leaned close, the stream rushed and murmured like a thousand of Goki's evil mist spirits. A fear too great to control fell on Bianca's soul. She cried out to Sher Khan, her need overcoming her and he heard her, and turned back. She could only look at him, tears rolling down her face, past speech. With an exclamation, he leaned towards her, and dragged her from her horse's back into his arms, and so, held warmly against him, she entered Lambagh.

They were seen, a man called to them, Sher Khan answered, and suddenly the darkness was blossoming with lights, as the villagers, holding burning pine knots were all round them, their cries of welcome ringing up to the stars, and back to the dark mountain passes—cries of joy, that filled the narrow twisting streets of Lambagh, the largest village in the valley, cries of joy that, like the torches, helped to push back the dark.

Sher Khan and Bianca rode between lines of men holding torches, up the winding streets, where the balconies leaned over their heads, laden with women from the houses, all crying and calling their welcome—up through the village they rode, and out through the last of the houses, and then up again, the steep path twisting, to the little white-walled, domed, and arched palace she had seen from the first mountain pass. The gate in the high white wall was open, and people were waiting for them.

There was a roar of welcome that sounded like the waves of the sea breaking in Bianca's head. She felt herself being lifted down, staggered when she was put on her feet, and pitched forward into someone's arms, and into darkness and the peace of unconsciousness.

7

When she awoke, the air tasted fresh and cool. It was early morning, and the light coming into her room, filtered through silken hangings, showed her the luxury in which she lay. Piles of cushions were heaped round her on the big bed, the marble floor glowed with Persian carpets, and heavy silks covered the high arched windows. Someone had undressed her the night before, and she now wore a thin robe, white, and of so fine a silk that it rippled away from her when she moved like water. She stood up, and found that she was terribly stiff, in fact it hurt her to move, but her curiosity helped her, and she stumbled over to the deep window embrasure, where there was a day bed, and kneeling there, dragged the curtains aside to look out.

What she saw she never forgot, for the rest of her long life.

The lake lapped gently at marble steps just below, and behind it, the mountains reared, crested with white, insubstantial in the pale light, dream mountains guarding a dream country. She knelt there in the window, enchanted, her breath caught, unconscious of the cold striking through her thin robe, watching a fish eagle hanging in the still air of the early morning. Then, as he made his first splendid swoop, a sound behind her brought her back to the room.

A woman servant stood in the door, salaaming deeply, a woman dressed as Goki used to dress, and of almost Goki's age.

'The Lady wakes—' she called through the door, and then shutting it behind her, came into the room, and wrapped Bianca in a warm robe, and shut the window firmly, and brought a bowl of warm water, and Bianca found herself having her face sponged, and her hair combed as if she were a child of six. A voice called outside, and the door was opened and a younger woman came in, with a laden tray, and a long stare for Bianca.

'This is Kusma,' said the older woman, 'and I, thy servant, Lady, am called Ragni.' She arranged a small carved table in the window and heaped cushions behind Bianca. There was coffee in a fine porcelain pot, a bowl of raspberries, and a dish of little flat cakes, thickly flaked with almonds. Bianca could eat little, but she enjoyed the coffee; she drank two cups, and found herself dropping with sleep over the second. Ragni and Kusma lifted her back to the bed, and then sleep, solid and deep, took everything away from her.

This was the pattern of her life for the next three days, and on the fourth day, she woke, and stretched, and lay back again, and then stretched tentatively—and sprang out of bed. All the stiffness had gone, she felt light and rested, and full of energy. The woollen robe lay over the foot of the bed. She put it on, and opened the arched french window, and stepped onto the balcony outside, to watch the mountains turn from airy battlements to purple splendour, and the lake catch the blue from the sky. It was a sight she was never to tire of, and the fish eagle became a part of the morning that she loved.

Ragni called her in to breakfast, and then when she had bathed and dressed in the soft woollen robes of a Lambaghi woman, Bianca returned to the balcony, to sit in the sun, and wonder where Sher Khan was.

It was then that she first met Kassim. He rode up the path beside the lake, and stopped under her balcony, looking up, and smiling so infectiously that she smiled back before she could stop herself.

'Good day, Lady,' he called to her in English. 'May I come up?' It might have been an English boy speaking—his accent was faultless. While Bianca was wondering who he was, and what to say, he dismounted, threw his reins to a syce who ran up, and walked into the palace and was out on the balcony beside her, while she was still trying to make up her mind what to do about him. He was very handsome, a big youth, with untidy black hair tumbling over the grey eyes of the hill people—Sher Khan's eyes.

'So my uncle chose well! But you do not know who I am, do you, and you are wondering whether to call Ragni and have me thrown out. But do not worry. You have heard of me—I am Kassim, the son of Mumtaz—I only came back from England last year, and have been here ever since. So we have never met.'

This was the son of Sher Khan's eldest sister, the girl who had married an Englishman, and gone back with him to England, borne him a son, and had been happy, until her husband suddenly died, and she had returned to Lambagh Valley, with her son.

Bianca looked at him with curiosity, and pleasure. He was so near to her in age—perhaps three or four years older than she was—and he knew her mother's country better than he knew his own, for his father had gone over to Ireland with his regiment, and the boy had been brought up there. While she looked at him, he said laughing, 'What big eyes you have, Aunt-to-be. You look at me as if I might be perhaps the wolf, in the story of Red Riding Hood—but we are almost relatives. May I share your coffee? No one will mind, because I am almost your nephew—and I have been longing to meet you.'

They drank their coffee together companionably, and he soon had the story of her flight and professed himself fascinated.

'Romance of the highest order and it ends as it should. You will be married tomorrow—' As he saw her widened eyes, he frowned and said, 'Did you not know? But you are happy—you want to marry Sher Khan, surely, after all this frantic elopement?'

'Of course I want to marry Sher Khan, but I have not seen him since I got here, and no one has told me anything about the wedding—' She spoke forlornly, and then in honesty had to admit that she had been asleep most of the time.

He nodded, smiling. 'I know. We all know. Ragni was told to keep you sleeping, and to give you something to get rid of the aches, and the rattle in your chest. It seems that you sounded like stones being shaken in a saucepan when you breathed. But Ragni did her work well, and I would say that the results do her credit.' His eyes were very full of admiration—Bianca felt flattered, but also that she had found a friend, and decided that it would be all right if she asked after Sher Khan. Kassim laughed.

'Sher Khan? He is eating his heart out, in the intervals between seeing the elders of the State, paying the priests, speaking with the Moulvi, and interviewing the Commanders of the State Forces of the three States. He has been very busy, and of course, he is not allowed to see you until he lifts your veil on your wedding day—tomorrow.' He stopped speaking, and sat looking at her for a moment before he said quietly, 'You know all our marriage customs, don't you?'

'Of course I do—I was at Khanzada's wedding, you know.' She remembered Khanzada's wedding—days of noise and celebration, and Zada sitting, veiled and motionless in the midst of all the gaiety—and the last rowdy journey, with the tipsily swaying palanquin, and the shouting young men firing their rifles at the stars, while Khanzada was escorted to the door of her new home—which in her case, at that time, had been just another part of the Madoremahal. How she wished that Zada could be with her now, to help her laugh her way through the next few days! No memory of Khanzada as she had last seen her came to disturb her. In her mind's eye she saw her charming companion, the happy girl of the time before Khanzada's marriage; she would have made all this wedding business amusing. As it was, Bianca was beginning to feel very nervous. Kassim saw the shadow on her face, and wondered. Then she said, 'No wonder they wanted me to rest, with all this in front of me—' and while he still stared at her in dismay, she added, 'How many days will it take?'

Kassim was astonished. 'How many days—my dear girl, what are you talking about? By tomorrow, by nightfall tomorrow, you will be Sher Khan's wife, the Begumsahiba of Lambagh. Did you think it took weeks to marry?' He was half laughing, half anxious, when Bianca answered, 'But Khanzada's wedding took days—' Oh God, thought Kassim, anything to keep her mind from Khanzada! Indeed, this poor girl needed a woman to advise and help her.

'Khanzada was married under southern customs, with southern rites. Listen, Bianca, please do not distress yourself about anything, just take things as they come. Tomorrow the Begum of Sadaa arrives, and she will help you through all the ceremony. It is hard for you to be alone at this time, but you are marrying Sher Khan, and that is worth all the trouble—no?' He saw, to his relief, that he had struck the right note. She smiled, and answered happily, and they spoke of other things. Bianca had a good many questions to ask about surroundings, and he could answer most of them. At length, he got up, and smiling said, 'Well, little Aunt—I must go. I shall not see you again until after the ceremonies, but do not be worried about anything. As I said, you are marrying the man you love—and furthermore, Sher Khan has loved you for at least a year—is that not a triumph to think of with pride?' She laughed, and blushed, and waved him away cheerfully, which was exactly what he had intended her to do—her face had cleared of worry, and she looked gay and relaxed, and very beautiful.

But as he rode away, Kassim was full of anxious thought. His years in Europe had taught him a great deal about the way in which a young girl of good family was brought up in England, and he hoped that Bianca was telling the truth when she said that she knew all about the marriage customs of the hill people of the three States. After all, he reasoned, she had spent all her life in the country, and Khanzada had been her greatest friend. She must know all that she needed to know. But the nagging worry remained, and he wished that his own mother was closer to Sher Khan. He shut his mind to the breach between his mother and her younger brother—he already had more than enough to trouble him. He paid very little attention to all the bustle that was going on around him, as the people prepared for the coming festivities.

Splendid wooden arches were being erected over the road that ran from the old palace in the town to the smaller Mahal where Bianca was living. Green branches, spicy and fresh with the smell of spruce and pine were being laid in piles, ready to spread before the feet of the bridal cortège, and several times Kassim had to rein back his horse as the Temple gods, carried in their decorated palanquins by sweating bearers, reeled past on their way to the painters, to be refreshed and refurbished in new and brilliant colours. The Mosque was quiet, but there was already a crown of little oil lamps round the parapet of the minaret, and along the wall surrounding the garden, where jasmine bushes sprayed white blooms, and the grass was green and deep under the trees. Kassim saw the white, starry blossoms, and was immediately reminded of a wedding he had attended in a village in England, with the quiet voice of the priest intoning prayers in the old grey church, and the bride, beautiful and veiled in shining white, and the sprays of white flowers everywhere. White—the colour of mourning in his country. Tomorrow would be a riot of scarlet and gold, with beating drums, and the high shrilling of horns, and the deep roar of the conch shell, blown by the Temple priests, and the chanting of the Moulvi from the Mosque—his thoughts were as confused, he thought, as the religious ceremonies attached to the wedding of a Ruler who ruled over a people of divided religions, who had yet managed to live at peace with each other for many years.

He rode on, and tried to think of other things, for there was enough to worry him without these thoughts of his uncle's wedding. The news that had come with Sher Khan from Madore had appalled him and he could discuss it with no one. All he could do to help his uncle was to go round alerting the frontier posts, checking armaments and men and food stores, and doing it all without causing alarm. His brow creasing beneath the untidy black hair that he had inherited from his father, Kassim hurried on, swerving his horse to avoid yet another tipsily-carried god, going to the painters to be made glorious for the wedding.

8

That night, Bianca slept well, against all her expectations. But she was wakened very early, before it was light, by Ragni's hand on her shoulder.

'Wake, Sahiba—it is time for the dressing—'

Bianca was broad awake on the instant, and looked towards the alcove, expecting to see her coffee, but Ragni shook her head. 'Nay, my child. You go fasting today. Come—' Again, Bianca heard Goki's tones in this other voice, and obediently followed the old woman to the bathroom, and stood while Ragni bathed her. Then, wrapped in towels, she went back to the room she had learned to think of as home for the last few days, and found two strangers there, big muscular hill women, salaaming and smiling. They took hold of her, and laid her on her bed, and rolling back the sleeves of the loose robes they wore, they began to work. Bianca was rubbed with scented oil, and pummelled and massaged and kneaded, until her skin glowed like satin, and she felt as supple and as free of bones as a snake. Then Ragni took a small sharp knife, and every hair on her body was removed, first by the knife, and then by paste rubbed all over her, so that she looked like a small grey statue. She was bathed again, and oiled again, and once more the women stroked and massaged until the oil was completely absorbed by her skin. Her hair was combed, and combed, and coiled in a great mound on top of her head. Ragni came with a small silver bottle of antimony, and drew a thin black line round Bianca's eyes so that already large, they looked enormous. Kusma, the younger servant, then came up with a bowl of henna, and taking Bianca's foot, began to draw with a thin stick, the fine lace patterns that Bianca had seen drawn on the palms and on the feet of other Indian women. The work was very fine, and the patterns so intricate, that she forgot all her nervous apprehensions as she watched.

Kusma was very young, her hair was long and black, and lay on her shoulders thick and shining, and as she traced the whorls and zigzags following a pattern that was in her mind, her tongue was nipped between her teeth, pink and pointed, like a little snake's head. Bianca thought she looked charming, and was enchanted by her clever drawing; then Kusma looked up, and her eyes, wide and very dark, stared for a second into Bianca's eyes. Bianca felt, on that instant, an antipathy for her, a revulsion so strong that she would have drawn her foot back from the girl's touch but she was so confused by all the strangeness of the morning that she put her repulsion down to a kind of hysteria; part of her general excitement. The painting of her hands and feet seemed to take hours, but at last Kusma stepped back, and Ragni, after a close examination, nodded, satisfied, and to Bianca's relief, Kusma left the room.

Ragni opened a great chest in the corner, and drew out a flame of red and scarlet and gold silks. Bianca was dressed in these splendid veilings, fold upon fold of gold-spattered scarlet, Ragni arranging each pleat and gather with an expert hand. There was no *choli*, but there was no need for one, there were so many folds of silk. For an hysterical second, Bianca felt that she was a very expensively wrapped parcel. But Ragni's intent eyes and busy hands left her no time to think very much. Her head was still bare, and Ragni arranged in the coils of her hair sweet-smelling white flowers, jasmine, and little white roses, and a fine gold chain, with pendants which hung over her forehead. The central pendant was a ruby, burning a deep crimson fire with every movement Bianca made. A gold veil was thrown over her head, completely veiling her face, and the dressing was finished.

All through the dressing process, Bianca was conscious of the intense interest of the women. Their hands, when they touched her, were trembling slightly, their eyes were large with excitement. Her own feelings, already in a turmoil, took fire from theirs. When she was dressed, and the veil was in place, she could feel the silks and muslins that draped her, moving like leaves on a tree in a high wind, because of the beating of her heart. She felt that she was swaying as she stood, but the women appeared to notice nothing, and after salaaming to her with joined hands, the hill women went out, leaving Ragni collecting up the debris of the dressing.

Bianca turned to the windowed alcove, and tried to calm herself by looking up at the high peaks, just flushing in the dawn light, but her hands were shaking, and she could concentrate on nothing. Neither the view nor the hovering fish eagle could hold her attention; her ears were straining to hear each sound, she found that she was holding her breath, as if the act of breathing would unleash something terrible. She was not waiting for her lover, her dear friend and companion, Sher Khan. She was waiting for a stranger it seemed, and she was afraid. She would have given all the world to feel as she had felt on the journey but now she was cold and frightened, facing something unknown that she had thought to find familiar.

Somewhere in the palace, a silver gong was struck, and she heard the sound of many voices, as if a door had opened on a crowd. She turned towards the door of her room, just as it was opened, and a tall old man entered, and bowing before her, his hand on his breast, said in a deep cracked old voice, 'Sahiba—we are here to take you to your Lord. Will you come?'

It sounded like a ritual question—Bianca was on strange ground. She drew on courage and resolution from somewhere, and bowed to the old man, and as he turned, she followed him out, and down a passage lined with staring, murmuring people, all thought having left her except amazement that she could walk so steadily, on legs that were made of nothing but water.

There was a small scarlet-curtained palanquin waiting at the foot of the marble steps, and the old man drew back the curtains, and Bianca, gathering her silk about her, climbed in, and sank back into the cushions. She raised her head, and saw opposite a kind face and a wide toothless smile—the old Begum of Sadaa. Bianca, who had known the old lady all her life, fell forward into her outstretched arms, and was embraced, and laughed at and scolded all at once. 'Nay, child—do not weep—the eye black will run. See, look through the curtains, through this crack, and watch the crowd, and enjoy your day—indeed, you have no cause for tears—foolish one!'

Bianca laughed, and gulped, and was herself again, everything was wonderful, she was a girl going to her wedding, and was among friends. The old Begum, her mind turning to what must be happening down on the plains, the horrors from which Bianca had just escaped, marvelled to herself, and was very relieved.

She had been prepared for a weeping distraught girl, and was pleased that the child had her feelings so well under control. Then, watching the expressions on the beautiful young face, she realised the truth of what Sher Khan had tried to explain to her. Bianca had no inkling of what she had left behind her, and it was better so.

The rest of the day passed in a blur of noise and strange faces.

The sunset came and found Bianca jogging back to the Chota-mahal in the palanquin with the old Begum. So many strange ceremonies had taken place—Bianca realised that all the religions of the State had been represented in her wedding rituals. But when had she actually become Sher Khan's wife? There had been no ring—the moment she remembered most clearly was when Sher Khan had come into the room where she was sitting, veiled, with dozens of women laughing and talking beside her. At Sher Khan's entrance the women had all stood up. There had been a sudden outburst, an extra flowering of excitement, the women pushing forward to watch as Sher Khan bent down, smiling, and raised the gauze veil from her face. He had not spoken. He had given her a long look, so that before all the women she had blushed and lowered her eyes. Then he had gone out, and she had been bustled off into the waiting palanquin.

Now, with bands of young men all round the palanquin, firing off muskets and making the air reel with their shouts and wild cries, she still did not know when the actual moment of her marriage had been. Sher Khan, she knew, was somewhere behind her, riding with his men. But Bianca was so tired, and so hungry that she could think of nothing but food and sleep. The old Begum looked at her anxiously, then laid a jewelled little claw on her arm.

'My child—are you tired?' Bianca nodded, her eyes heavy.

'I am so tired I thought I was going to fall down when we had to walk round that fire in the Temple, and exchange garlands with each other—Sher Khan was tired too, he did not speak to me.'

The old lady drew in her breath. '*Speak* to you! My child, he could not speak to you then, in the Temple—it is not the Hindu custom. It does not matter that you marry a Muslim, child, in our States, we have always kept the customs of all three religions

—think of my wedding! I was married on the plains, where the ceremonies last for close on thirty days. This is nothing, this one day.' She paused, and then spoke again, striving to catch the girl's attention.

'Bianca—listen to me. You know this is a wedding—a marriage? That you are now his wife, in truth, and his Begum—and he did not need to do this?'

Bianca stared at her foggily, and said, 'Of course it is my wedding—he told me that we would be married, and be together always—but this kind of wedding I have never imagined, or seen before, and I am tired—so tired that I can hardly sit up.'

'Did you never go to one of the State weddings in Madore?'

'Only to the last three days of Khanzada's wedding. My mother said that I was too young, the parties were too late for me—' As she mentioned her mother, Bianca felt a clutch of homesickness and longing.

The old Begum sighed gustily. 'Truly the Western people bring their girls up very strangely. Now, I knew what to expect when I was married. I was trained for marriage, from the time I could walk—'

A rose, heavily drenched with rose water, fell into the palanquin, and the old lady returned from her memories, to the exhausted girl at her side. She saw the tears in Bianca's eyes with misgiving. 'Bianca, the Yuvraj did not need to marry you. He could have put you in the *bibikhana* of his house, and kept you there, and no one would have thought anything of it.'

Bianca was outraged, and no longer too tired to reply. 'I do not understand what you are saying, Begum Sahiba! The women in the *bibikhana* of a young unmarried man's house are not his wives—they are girls from the town! My father and mother would never have allowed this to happen to me—of course Sher Khan married me—'

The Begum shook her head, interrupting, 'You forget, child. Your father and mother knew nothing of this in any case.' The old face contracted into a mask of sadness for a second, and was smooth again too quickly for Bianca to have seen her expression. Then the Begum went on, speaking firmly, and quietly.

'Bianca, this is Lambagh. You are now beyond the frontiers of any jurisdiction save the Ruler's. Believe me, the Yuvraj could have taken you without marriage, and no one could have said him nay, and you would have been considered a fortunate girl. Instead, he has chosen to make you his wife, and his Begum, and to do so, for three days he has argued and fought with the priests and the ministers, and the Mullah.'

Bianca looked out at the laughing, cheering, singing crowd, and said unbelieving, 'You mean they did not want me?'

'Nay, child—for yourself, they wanted you—to see you is to love you. But you will be the mother of a future Ruler—did you forget that?'

Before Bianca could answer, they had arrived at the white palace, and the palanquin had stopped. The old Begum pulled a fold of the veiling over Bianca's face and then helped her out. Dimly through the smoke of torches, and the doubled veiling, Bianca could see a crowd of men, resplendent in jewelled uniforms, their turbans and silks seeming to burn in the flaring torchlight. Then she was surrounded by women, and was taken into the palace in their midst, almost lifted from her feet, there were so many pressing round her.

The two hill women were there, in her room, waiting for her, and Ragni, and Kusma. The room was quiet, a haven after the noisy crowded day. Ragni took her silks off, and soon Bianca's eyes were closing under the skilful hands of the women, and the old Begum, watching her for a minute, made a sign to them to stop. 'My child,' she said, 'listen to me—this is not the time for you to sleep.' Bianca groaned, and turned her head. 'Then, Sahiba, I hope it is time for me to eat, and *then* sleep, for I am dying of hunger, and I cannot keep my eyes open.'

The Begum's lips tightened, and she turned to Ragni, standing at her elbow with a silver cup. The Begum took it, and made Bianca drink it. It was cold, and bitter, and burned on Bianca's tongue, but in a minute or two she was wide awake, her eyes clear.

'Ah ha, that is better. Now Bianca, we speak together. You know our marriage customs?'

'Truly Sahiba, I begin to think that you are overtired too. Have I not been through all the ceremonies today? You yourself said I was the fortunate bride of Sher Khan, and lucky to have been married and not kept in the *bibikhana* of his bachelor establishment.' There was genuine anger in the girl's voice, Bianca was tired and hungry, and felt insult and ignominy where she had not expected it—from one who was now her relative.

The old Begum nodded at her. 'Yes, my child, you are angry. But my beloved child, I told you why you should feel so honoured.'

Bianca did not answer. Where was Sher Khan? The wedding seemed now like a barrier between them, or a long absence, during which they had lost touch, and knowledge of each other.

'Then am I to believe that he married me only because he hoped to father a suitable heir to his throne?' she said eventually, her eyes full of angry tears, and she turned away, feeling a stranger, and homesick for her own mother, and the smell of the scented room, and the noises from outside were so alien to her that she wished that she could close her eyes, and wake, as from a strange dream, and find herself home with her mother and father again.

Ragni said quietly to the Begum, 'Heaven born, leave it now. All will follow in order, without words, and what is unpleasing will be forgotten by morning.'

As the Begum hesitated, Ragni touched her arm. 'The lights show on the road from the town. They are coming. Best to leave it now, Lady. Truly, I have seen this before. All pain will be forgotten.'

The Begum looked for a moment longer into Bianca's lifted eyes, and saw there, as well as rage, an innocence and an ignorance that, to the old lady was frightening. This was no girl of the hill people, trained and taught and brought knowledgeable to her marriage. But it was too late now. She bowed her head, and stepped back, and instantly the two hill women, and Ragni and Kusma were back at their work, rubbing and sleeking Bianca's body, their hands firm and soothing, until she relaxed and stretched like a little cat, her anger almost forgotten, sighing with pleasure. Then the women stopped, and Ragni took her into the marble bathing place, where an oil lamp burned scented oil, and threw Bianca's shadow leaping ahead of her on the shining marble walls. Ragni raised a dipper of water, and said some words that sounded like an invocation to a god, and then poured the scented water over Bianca's shoulders. Dipper after dipper was poured, at first warm and comforting, it gradually got colder and colder, until Bianca stood gasping under streams of water that were so cold that her skin burned, and she lost her breath. Then it was over and she was wrapped in towels and taken back to her room—but the room was now full of women, the walls blazing with oil lamps, the sound of the women's whispering, and the rustle of their silks was like wind in dry grass—or like the hissing of snakes, thought Bianca, furious at the invasion. All faces were turned towards her, and when Ragni began to take away her towels, Bianca gave a small angry cry, and tried to prevent her, but the Begum was at her side in an instant.

'Bianca—let them disclose you. This is an important part of the ceremonies. Hold up your head, girl, and do as we bid you—'

Bianca heard the note of love under the authority in the old voice, and did as she was told. She had come too far now for any withdrawal, she thought sadly, and stood naked, her skin gleaming under the flaring lights, her head up and her eyes unflinching, as the women pressed close around her, discussing her body and her beauty, as if, thought Bianca, I was one of the horses Sher Khan values so much. Again she was stung by the thought that she had only been married to bear a child, and her eyes burned, but she stood quietly, as several women took sandalwood oil in their hands and smoothed it over her arms and shoulders. The laughing faces looking into hers were kind, the compliments, some of them very uninhibited, were spoken with admiration, and love. Bianca tried to smile back, for after all, these were friendly people, and none of them meant her anything but good. Then a hand touched her more roughly, she looked up into an unsmiling face, and thought, somewhere at the back of her mind—'That was Kusma. I do not care for her—she must go.'

The smell of sandalwood oil, and the heat in the close crowded room began to oppress her, her eyes dazzled, and she swayed on her feet, and then it was over, and the room was blessedly empty of all but the Begum, and Ragni.

'My child—my good child. Are you still angry with me?' Bianca turned to the old lady, unable to hold her anger. In any case, it was not directed against the Begum. Held in that kind embrace, she heard the old lady's praise. 'You did so well—a queen indeed. It is almost over now—endure for a small while longer, and then be at peace with your heart's desire—'

Bianca's body was as hot and sticky with oil and sweat as if she had not been bathed. Ragni took her back into the bathing place, bathed her again, and brought her back, her long hair streaming over her naked shoulders, her face beginning to look all bones and eyes, she was so tired. The Begum stood before her, holding a silver flask, and spoke softly. 'Bianca—child, do not be afraid, or ashamed of anything.'

Ragni gently forced Bianca to lie down, and the Begum, with intimate, swift moving hands, anointed her body with scented oil, smoothing and rubbing until there was no oil left, and Bianca's body was as smooth and hairless as the figures of the little dancing goddesses in the frieze that was carved round the walls. The Begum stood back, and said quietly, 'I am an old woman, Bianca, and have prepared many brides for their husbands, but never one so beautiful as you. You have endured custom and necessity well. Now will come the time of the pleasures of love, the flowers and the fruit of passion that take you to paradise. Stand, my girl—we have to robe you now.'

Ragni was waiting, with a light gauzy robe, so transparent that it was like a mist, rather than a covering. She put it over Bianca's shoulders, and the Begum spoke quietly, but with a firm authority in her voice. 'Bianca! Turn to me—'

Bianca turned in surprise, and as she turned, the Begum called in a loud voice, 'The woman of my Lord is ready—'

The door, flung open by Ragni, disclosed a row of men, holding gleaming swords, and Sher Khan strode in, unfamiliar in heavy robes and glittering turban, a great emerald glowing above his forehead. The door was pulled shut behind him.

He stopped in front of Bianca, and before she could do anything to prevent it, Ragni and the Begum had snatched the robe from her shoulders, and she was once again left naked, but this time Sher Khan looked down at her, and his face was a stranger's under the high folds of his turban. There was a silence that seemed to Bianca to last forever. She stood, lost in an icy agony of rage and embarrassment. 'I am a brood mare,' she thought furiously. 'I am. And there he stands, trying to decide if I will throw a good colt.' She tried to stare back into his eyes, tried and failed, and closed her eyes and scarlet, bent her head as well, and missed the smile that Sher Khan gave her, a smile that was meant to convey a good many things, including friendship and admiration, and delight.

There was a stir of movement, the Begum said, 'It is well, my Lord?' and was halfway out of the door before he had answered, his deep voice ringing in the room, 'It is well, indeed, very well.' Ragni then came up, and salaamed deeply, and suddenly, Bianca could hardly stand. She was burning one moment, and as cold as ice the next, and the room seemed to be closing in around her, the walls moving, the floor flowing like a river. Sher Khan said sharply to Ragni, 'Take all these cursed lamps out—this room is hotter than hell.' Ragni began to unhook the lamps from the walls, and soon there was only one left, the tall silver lamp standing beside the bed. Bianca had snatched up her thin robe—it was better, she felt, than nothing. Sher Khan, seeing the convulsive grip of her hands on the silk, frowned, but did not say anything to her. He removed his turban and his heavy robes, and then dragged back the curtains over the window alcove. A gush of cool mountain air came in, blowing the flame of the lamp sideways, so that the shadows leapt wildly over the room, and the carvings around the walls moved and stretched their arms, until the flame stood steady again, as Ragni trimmed it. Bianca had not moved all this time, clutching her robe, her eyes wide, and fixed on nothing. Sher Khan said something in an undertone to Ragni, who left the room, and came in again with wine and silver cups, and covered dishes of food. She put her laden tray down on the table in the alcove, and with a quick smiling glance at Bianca, put her hands together, bowed low over them, and went out.

Sher Khan did not speak to Bianca. He busied himself pouring wine into the silver cups, which were full of ice. In spite of herself, Bianca found she was relaxing a little. Everything began to seem more normal. The room was quiet and peaceful now, full of the stillness of centuries, a tranquillity that could not be disturbed permanently by the brief noisy events that had, like stones flung into a deep pool, only rippled the surface of peace. Now time, and memories of time past had closed over the colours and echoes, and there was nothing to disturb the mind or the spirit. The dancing statues were still, only the curtains moved a little in the fresh air from the window. The bed had been spread with clean white sheets, and heaped with pillows, and Sher Khan, bare headed, without his jewelled robes, looked himself again, at least a likeness of the dear companion of her dreams and of the journey through the mountains. Invisibly, deep within herself, tensions began to loosen, and as if at a signal, Sher Khan turned and beckoned to her, holding out a cup of wine.

'Bianca—drink this, and come and rest. This has been a terrible day for us both. I feel like a beaten dog, and I fear you feel worse.'

Bianca did not move, but the kindness of his voice broke through her anger and fear, and tears at last began to pour down her face. Sher Khan groaned within himself, but outwardly paid no attention. He continued to urge her to come and sit, piling up the cushions invitingly in a corner of the window alcove. He went to the chest, and pulled out a warm robe, and coming to her, wrapped her in the warmth of the wool. Bianca wept on, unchecked, and with the tears came relief, and she could move and speak again. She choked on a swallow of the wine he had brought her, and allowed herself to be led to the cushioned alcove, and seated there, drinking the wine, and at last eating a little of the chicken and rice. Sher Khan did not sit with her, but stood in the window, leaning against the arch, his silver cup in his hand, looking out at the moonlit snows that covered the high peaks, and were doubled in ghostly reflection in the lake. Presently he turned back, and looked down at her. 'The wine and food have made you feel better?'

His voice was very formal. Bianca was restored enough to be angry all over again, and, indeed, so angry that she could not control her voice to reply, so she turned her head away from him, her mouth trembling. Sher Khan came and knelt beside her, and gently turned her face back to him. 'My dear love—do you turn away from me, after all this? Are you sorry that you came?'

'How could I be sorry, when you have honoured me so greatly?' Her voice was like cold steel, thought Sher Khan, what in the name of heaven could have caused this anger against him? She looked at him as if she looked at a snake. Sher Khan, in his time, had gazed into the eyes of many enemies—but they had never been the eyes of a woman he loved. He sighed, and let go of Bianca, but did not move away from her.

'Bianca, you appear to hate me. Tell me what I have done to bring this grief to us both? Because when we left Madore, you came willingly, I thought.'

Bianca kept her head up, and her eyes steady on his, but her heart was very sore. The days of their journey, and the evening when they had left Madore together, seemed centuries away, and this man in front of her was a man of different customs and habits from her dear and gentle lover, the Sher Khan she had built so many dreams about. This was an Indian Prince, a man who needed an heir, just as Hardyal had needed an heir.

'I left Madore willingly, that is true, but I left it not knowing—not knowing all sorts of things. I had no idea that you wanted—' She stopped, fighting the lump that was growing out of all proportion in her throat. Sher Khan was now really worried. This was not the poutings of a child who did not care for the tiresome ceremonies of her wedding. This was something else, and he was afraid that Bianca had suddenly realised that she had left her parents to their death, without even saying goodbye to them. Out of this fear, he spoke sharply.

'What did I want, Lady?'

'All you wanted,' said Bianca, breaking into loud and childish sobs, 'all you wanted was a brood mare.'

'A brood mare?' Sher Khan stood up, and looked at her in blank astonishment. 'A *brood mare*?' His voice expressed so much amazement, that Bianca's sobs died away, and she was able to command herself enough to tell him everything that was boiling in her mind.

'And furthermore,' she ended furiously, 'I do not intend to do nothing but bear children, and sit in here. So.'

Sher Khan was very tired, and desperately worried about his family, and his friends in Madore. He had also spent three long weary days fighting over his marriage to this small mutinous girl who sat glaring at him like a cornered cat from among her cushions.

'Well,' said Sher Khan quietly, 'if that is what you think I brought you here to do, if that is the reason for your coming, then let us begin.'

'Begin what?' asked Bianca, sitting with dignity in her corner.

'This,' said Sher Khan.

He snatched the woollen robe from her, and holding her close in his arms, began to kiss her, taking his time about each kiss, paying no attention to her struggles, and muffling her furious cries with his mouth.

The lamp in the corner by the bed guttered and went out, the moonlight moved over the floor, and touched the dancers into shivering light—but there was no one to watch or care. Bianca was climbing the mountains of paradise, and tasting the fruits of delight, as the old Begum had promised she would, and her companion was as lost as she was.

Once in the night, sitting in the crook of his arm, and drinking from his cup, she said, 'I did not know that love could be like this.'

'Like what?'

'Oh, warm and sweet and burning and desperate and—oh, everything, in and out of life—'

'So much?' Somewhere in the deep tired voice there was laughter.

'Did you know that love was thus?'

Sher Khan was definitely laughing now. He took her wine away from her, drinking thirstily himself, and then picked up her hand and held it against his mouth as he said, 'Yes, I knew.'

'How? How did you know?'

'Oh, I knew. Men do know these things.' Just as well for you, my love, he thought, watching her happy relaxed face, and thinking of the raging, fear-crazed girl of a few hours before. Two virgins together would have made a pretty mess of this bridal night.

'What is this scar, and that, and this mark like a little red claw, and that scar—where did you get those?'

'So many questions! You are a talkative child! This scar I got from the lance of a friend with a bad aim, when we were pig sticking. That one is a knife wound from an old quarrel. The claw—that is my birthmark—all my family bear that mark somewhere on their bodies. That scar there is new, and you gave it me, and it still hurts—very sharp teeth you have, little tiger cat.'

Again the voices died away, and presently she slept, and he lay watching her, and thinking of what she was like, but also with half his mind free now to wander, he thought of Madore, and how many men he could spare from guarding the higher passes against the old enemy, Russia, how many could be spared from that duty, to go down and guard the lower passes on the road that led to the plains, and the new enemy of mutiny and revolt. The moonlight crept as close to the bed as it could, a dog howled somewhere, and Bianca stirred, and he turned back to her, and forgot, at last, in sleep, all the thoughts that disturbed him.

9

As morning edged the window, and the lake lay cold and grey in the first light, before the sun rose, Bianca woke, and turned her head, stretching out her arms, but she was alone.

A laugh from the alcove brought her head round. 'Oh my queen, what do you search for?' Sher Khan, fully dressed, came to her and looked down at her as she lay, her hair all about her on the tumbled bed.

'Not tired?' he asked, his voice full of admiration. 'Not at all tired? Well! Do you think we made a suitable attempt to get me an heir?'

Bianca reached up to his arms, as they closed round her, and he said, 'Because if you think I failed you in any way, we can try again—' He watched with pleasure the flush that rose from her neck to her forehead. Her voice was very small when she answered.

'If you feel that we have failed, lord—'

His pleasure at her reply spoken in his own language was great. 'Dear love, I shall always speak to you in my own tongue. Love, told in another language, never finds full expression. Listen now, Bianca while I tell you—'

In his deep voice he built for her an unforgettable house of words of love and passion that had not before passed between them. All her life afterwards, Bianca remembered what he said, recalling every phrase and every tone, and how the room had looked, and the growing light coming from the windows. She was held close in his arms, while he spoke, and afterwards they sat together in the window, silent and still, in contentment.

But he could not be still for long. His sigh, and the feel of his coat under her fingers, brought Bianca back from her happy dreaming.

'But you are dressed. Sher Khan, you do not leave me again now, surely—not for days am I to be alone again? Not now that we are married?'

'Bianca, I have to go. I have to arrange so many things, and see so many men, that I should have seen when I first returned, that the only way to deal with it all, is to go early, and at least get some of the ordinary work over, before the beginning of the talk. The courts start within ten days, and heaven knows how many petitions I shall have to hear, with my head stuffed with other thoughts—'

Bianca pushed her hair back from her face, and put her arms firmly round his neck. 'Stay with me Sher Khan, my dear love. Within ten days who cares if the courts will be open! The Ruler will be here by then, and probably my parents as well, and then we will have to spend all our time talking with them. Let us have this time alone together. The Ruler has not asked you to do this, has he? Anyway, I know from Jindbagh custom, that nothing can start until the Ruler returns—we never had the courts until he came, never—is it different here?'

Sher Khan held her close, looking over her shoulder to where the high snows were slowly flushing red in the dawn. He was full of a complete astonishment at her words. Her apparent ignorance of all that must have happened since they left Madore, appalled him. Had she forgotten her talk with Khanzada, and the reason for the flight from Madore, the threat that had caused their haste? Then he remembered something Shaibani Khan had said, that Bianca would not come if she knew that her parents were in danger, but that she would not know, all she would be told was that he, Sher Khan was in danger, and must be got away and that all else was in order, that the Ruler's army had everything in control. Her love for him, her faith in her father, and in the power of the Ruler, passion—all this had combined to wipe her mind clear of shadows. His little love. Did she really think that if he had been in danger, and could have stayed, he would have run away?

She was now speaking of her father and mother. When they first came, they would be angry, very angry with her, but after that they would be happy in her happiness, and it would be all right. He sent a thought to those two brave spirits. Perhaps they would in any case be happy in their daughter's happiness, perhaps spiritual knowledge spanned the barriers of time and death. He took Bianca's face in his hands, and turned it up to him, as he had the night before. But what a different face. He looked down into her loving eyes, shadowed by the night's passion, and could no more have disturbed that happy serenity by telling her the truth, than he could have taken a knife and stabbed her. He kissed her deeply, and lifting her, carried her back to the bed, and tumbled her in.

'Lie, lazy one, sleep again. I will come back and share your coffee and fruit that they tell me you ask for every day, and then we will go out for a ride.' As he left her, he reflected that the sight of his bride riding out beside him on the first day after his marriage would probably startle most of the villagers into verbal hysteria, but they would have to get used to new habits.

Bianca lay in a lovely languor, bruises, strange aches and sore lips all forgotten, or merely happy reminders of Sher Khan and the wonders of the past night. She watched the lake leap into flame, and turn blue as the sun rose, and was asleep again when Ragni and Kusma came in. She had forgotten any animosity she had felt towards Kusma. She smiled at both the women impartially, and went in to be bathed, and sleeked with scented oil, to have her hair combed and perfumed, her eyes outlined with khol—a wonderful thing, to have her beauty enhanced, knowing that it was to please Sher Khan.

But when they brought out shimmering silk robes, and jewels, she shook her head firmly, and demanded other clothes. 'I ride with my lord, this morning. Bring me *salwar* and *khamise*.'

She dressed in the wide trousers and loose shirt of heavy raw silk, and had her hair braided down her back, and looked a beautiful version of any one of the hill women. In fact, Kusma was more richly dressed than she was. Ragni was obviously put out by this.

'Will you not wear even the garland of the moon, Sahiba?'

'The garland of the moon?'

'Yes—this, the head dress that you wore yesterday. It is the custom for the second day.' Ragni held out the glittering chains and the big ruby pendant that had hung between Bianca's eyebrows all the day before.

'I cannot wear that while I ride, Ragni. Perhaps I will wear it tonight instead.'

Muttering, Ragni put the beautiful thing away in a sandalwood box, which she then placed in the large chest that held all the rich silks and jewels that now belonged to Bianca. Bianca was utterly without interest in the new clothes and the adornments of countless Ranis, the gold chains and the heavily jewelled earrings and pendants and rings that had come to her through her marriage. She watched for Sher Khan's return, and cared for nothing else until she heard the sounds of his arrival. He found her seated among the cushions in the window alcove, a slender figure in her peasant dress, the fruit and coffee spread out in front of her. He admired her appearance, and wondered how she had persuaded the women to dress her so simply; there were set robes for the first days after a marriage. When he remembered how he came by his knowledge of what was customary for brides, he frowned. This was yet another problem which he had to deal with shortly—but not just yet. His frown went, he sank down beside the girl who waited so eagerly for him, and they ate breakfast together, their voices and laughter filling the room with pleasant echoes, and making people passing by outside look at each other and smile.

The room, empty of everything but themselves, seemed to shut round them protectively, keeping out the world. Every moment that passed brought them closer in understanding, both, the mature man and the young girl were inwardly astonished at their discovery of each other.

The sound of horses stamping and jingling outside was an added pleasure to Bianca. She longed to be off with Sher Khan on a sort of celebration ride. She had a sudden desire, sharp as a knife, hot as fire, to go with him into the mountains, and there, in some lonely place, lie in his arms and take his love again. She looked at him sideways, under her lashes, and put a seeking hand on his thigh, but as he felt the demanding hand, Ragni came in to say that Sheik Nur-el-ahi wanted to speak to him. Sheik Nur-el-ahi was the commander of the Lambagh Garrison, and Sher Khan got up at once, excused himself to Bianca with a rueful smile and hurried out, leaving her feeling flat and impatient. She finished her coffee, and Ragni brought water for her to rinse her fingers, and then, at her order, a mirror for her to look at her face, while her mouth was coloured again. She tried a pair of gold earrings, and a light gold chain round her neck, and still

Sher Khan did not come, but there was the sound of another arrival, a horse's hooves tapping on the wooden causeway below.

A voice called in English, 'Oh, little Aunt—may I come to wish you good fortune?'

Kassim! Bianca had not seen him at her wedding ceremonies, or at any rate had not recognised him if she had seen him. Now she exclaimed with pleasure, and he came in laughing and sat with her, eating left over raspberries and teasing her, his handsome face so like Sher Khan's that he could have been his younger brother instead of his nephew.

Presently Sher Khan himself came in, and Bianca sprang up, anxious at once that Kassim should go, so that she could start her ride. But Sher Khan greeted his nephew with relief.

'Kassim! No, do not go. I am delighted to see you, I need you. Bianca—Lady, I regret I have to go at once. There are matters that do not go well. These accursed courts! Kassim will ride with you instead, and I will be back this evening. Forgive me—'

He saw her sadly downcast face, and paused to say low, 'I wished to be with you, as much as you wanted me, dear love, or more! But at least we have the night—'

He took both her hands, kissed the henna-decorated palms, and went. Bianca was so disappointed that she could not hide it, and Kassim saw the tears in her eyes.

'Oh come, little Aunt! No tears! He does not want to go, which is all that should matter. You will ride up to the head of the lake, and I will show you the lotus flowers, and the shrine of the Greek general who once came to Lambagh, hundreds of years ago. Do not be unhappy, Aunt, on your first day as a married woman!'

Bianca no longer wanted to ride, but she went out with Kassim because she did not, even in her disappointment, wish to hurt anyone so kind.

She came out with him on to the little verandah, with its carved wooden balustrade, and saw the horses waiting. Two riderless horses, held by two syces, and two mounted men.

'Do they come too?' she asked, and Kassim nodded.

'Yes. Wherever you go, now—' He looked at her, and stopped abruptly. Although the Ruler was almost certainly dead, the news would not be brought for many days yet, and this was no time to bring grief to a bride by letting her guess that as her husband was now Ruler of the three States, she would have an escort as a matter of course.

Bianca frowned at the bodyguard; her dream of riding alone with Sher Khan was doomed to disappointment anyway. She turned to look at the blue lake and saw a sort of banner, stretched between two poles, just beneath her window. Kassim was saying something to her, but she did not hear him, transfixed by what she saw. That stained and crumpled banner was a sheet. The sheet from her bed.

Nothing she had ever heard discussed among the women of the palace in Madore had she applied to her own life with Sher Khan. That her bedsheet would be displayed to prove that she had gone virgin to her marriage bed was something she had not thought of, and now, confronted with it, she turned crimson, and her eyes filled with angry tears. The men of the bodyguard, Kassim beside her, people passing on the road beneath—she turned her head away, unable to move, shaking with anger and embarrassment. Kassim bit his lip, and cursed his uncle, the customs of his country, and himself for being present at such a time. Indeed, it was better if the bride stayed indoors for at least a week after her marriage! But this was not a hill girl, this furious child beside him. He took a deep breath, and said quietly, 'Aunt—no, I do not call you Aunt any longer, I am much older than you. Bianca. Please do not be distressed by old customs. If a thing is customary, it must be performed according to that custom. If one part of the marriage of a Ruler was left undone, later perhaps it would be remembered, and there could be great trouble, and danger for any son of yours, if it could be whispered that you did not come a virgin to your husband. Forgive me for speaking to you like this. It is not fitting; I should have brought my mother to you. But think this—that I stand here instead of your family. I am as your brother now, and I cannot see you unhappy.'

His low voice, so fluent in English, and yet so like Sher Khan's voice, reached Bianca through the waves of hot misery that were overwhelming her, and she was able, after a few seconds, to lift her head, smile at him, and walk past the fluttering sheet, and down to the horses.

As they rode to the lakeside, the bodyguard fell in behind them, and in the familiar rhythm of movement, and the sound of jingling harness, the fresh air blowing around her, Bianca began to feel better. It was a morning of crystal and sapphire, lake and sky reflecting identical blue, and the mountains so close that they could, it seemed, be touched by just stretching out a hand. Bianca kicked her horse from a canter to a gallop, and was away, and Kassim with a shout of pleasure urged his horse on to try and pass her.

When, breathless, they pulled their horses to a walk, Kassim gestured with his whip. 'That is the road we would take to see the shrine, and the lotus flowers. But I think that Sher Khan might wish to take you there himself. Instead, we will go back this way, and I will show you where I live. My mother will be so happy to welcome you.'

They rode away from the lake, and came to a large tree-shaded house, with wooden balconies, and a *chibutra*—an open verandah—outside. There were several women sitting on the *chibutra*, and one of them got up, and came forward, calling out with pleasure.

'Khanum! Come, come in—my house is yours—I saw you during the ceremonies, but there were so many strange faces around you, that you will not remember mine. Kassim, my son, how good that you have brought the Khanum to me!'

She was tall, and beautiful, with the hill people's clear grey eyes set in a calm, unlined face, now smiling with warm welcome. It was strange to Bianca to think that this woman had lived for many years in her own mother's country, and had seen the places that her mother had spoken of with so much longing and homesickness. She found herself taken into a warm scented embrace, before she was led forward to the other women. Kassim did not come with her—the women on the *chibutra* were not all related to him, and therefore they would have had to veil themselves in his presence. He went into the house, and Bianca was presently sitting among the women, feeling very much at home. The women were all older than she was, but were all so friendly and she had the heady knowledge that she was deferred to, even in this circle of her elders. She was the Begum, Sher Khan's wife, and for the first time began to realise all that this could mean. Coffee in a silver pot, and fruit and sticky sweets, and laughter in the shade of the trees—Bianca enjoyed herself.

Her hostess, the Begum Mumtaz, suddenly clicked her tongue

and lost the thread of a story she was telling, there was a murmur and a sudden silence, and Bianca looked round to see a girl coming towards them, leading a child. Mumtaz got up, and went forward, almost, it appeared to Bianca, as if she would stop the newcomer, and Bianca had the strong feeling that this woman was not popular, in fact, judging by the faces around her, she was disliked. But their faces were smoothed of all expression when the woman joined them, and coffee was poured for her, and the conversation started again, though nobody spoke directly to the woman. Bianca, frankly staring, could see why this girl, Kurmilla, who could not have been more than twenty, might be unpopular in a circle of older women. She was very beautiful, with long almond eyes, and a full, curved mouth—and a full curved figure too, thought Bianca, envying the rich bosom and opulent hips. The girl radiated an animal vitality, and a sort of contempt that seemed to embrace all the women. Her eyes flicked past Bianca as if she had barely looked at her, but Bianca felt that the woman knew every detail of her appearance and thought little of it. Secure in a new-found certainty, born of her night with Sher Khan, Bianca merely smiled serenely, and the woman suddenly caught her underlip in her teeth, and turned away.

The child, a girl, was charming. Small, slender, as delicately formed as the blossoms of the white roses behind her, she stood among the women, her grey eyes as clear as water, looking at each face with smiling pleasure. Bianca was enchanted by her. She was the most beautiful child she had ever seen.

'Come to me—see, here is a sweet—come here to me—' The child smiled, and came to her at once, settling herself into the curve of Bianca's arm, to eat the sweet she offered. Bianca felt as if the child belonged in her arms. She held her close, and while she was talking to her, did not see the women's clashing glances, nor see the flat angry stare that enveloped her, as the child's mother watched them together.

'What is your name?'

The child parted sticky lips to reply, 'Sara.'

'That is a beautiful name—'

'Well, it means bitter—' said the child matter of factly.

Bianca stared at her, with nothing to say. Why should this beautiful little creature be called by a name meaning bitter?

Sara placed a confiding and sticky hand in hers.

'You see,' she said, 'when I was born, I should have been a boy, and my father was very angry because I was not a boy, and he was not kind to my mother, and so she named me "Bitter". My father, you know, is a monster. He is—' Kurmilla said something sharply, and Sara stopped speaking.

The story of a necessary heir again! Bianca looked at Sara's beautiful mother with sudden sympathy. So she had failed her husband, and he had been angry, and the beautiful little failure was called Sara—Bitter. She felt again, for a moment, the anger she had felt the day before, anger against Sher Khan, and found that anger against a beloved person brings great pain. Her pain made her deaf and blind to everything else around her—but then she heard in memory Sher Khan's words of the morning, and her sight cleared, and the day was sunny again. There had been a commotion among the women, she noticed—two of them were standing, asking for leave to go, and Mumtaz Begum was beside her, gently detaching the child from her arms, and saying, 'Khanum—Kassim says it is better for you to go back now, the horses are hot, and should be walked.'

Of course! Bianca, feeling a fool, and yet proud at the same time, got up quickly. These women could not go until she left, and Kassim was right, the horses had been ridden hard. She bent over Sara, and said, 'Sara, next week you must come and see me—will you?'

The child nodded, her hand going out to take Bianca's hand and hold it closely, as if she could not bear to let it go. Her mother broke the sudden silence that had fallen, saying silkily, 'The Lady is kind, and honours my child. My house is not far from here, anyone you ask will direct you to the Lalkoti. Will you please visit me at your convenience, my child and I would welcome you—'

The queer silence still held, and into that silence Bianca spoke her thanks and her farewells. She turned to her horse, suddenly glad of her slim body, as she swung herself up into her saddle before Kassim could get round to assist her. She turned to wave, and saw that all the women were standing, staring after her, all but the child, who waved furiously, calling, 'Goodbye, Khanum—I see you again very soon—'

'That is the most beautiful little girl,' Bianca said to Kassim as they rode off. 'Such eyes—the grey eyes that so many people here have. You, and Sher Khan, and your mother, and I have seen many others. But that child—she has taken my heart. Imagine a man being so foolish as to call that lovely child by a name that means bitter.' Kassim's answer was lost in the pounding of hooves. He rode past her, calling, 'My turn now, Bianca—' and Bianca forgot everything again in the sheer joy of movement. She forgot almost everything—but the child's eyes, and the clutch of the thin sticky hand remained with her.

The rest of the day was as Bianca had dreamed it might be. Sher Khan was there, to lift her from her horse when they got back to the little white palace, and when he heard that they had not been to the head of the lake, arranged that he would take Bianca there that evening. Kassim stayed with them for a little while, servants bringing wine and little savoury cakes to them, as they lounged, talking, in the windowed alcove. The sheet had gone, Bianca saw with relief. She took little part in the conversation, indeed she did not understand much of what they said as they spoke in the quick hill patois that she had never properly mastered, though she spoke Urdu as she spoke English. She was content to sip her wine, watching the two men, so alike, and both so splendid to look at.

At one stage in the conversation, Kassim said something that made Sher Khan angry; she saw the muscles in his cheek tighten, and was lost in the sweet surprise of finding how well she knew his looks after so short a time. He snapped a question at Kassim, who answered with equal fury, and some of the words she understood. 'It will not be a secret long, you fool!' but she was not really listening. That Sher Khan could look thus, like a snarling tiger, his lips drawn back in a rage that transformed his whole face! A shudder shook her at the thought of arousing that rage—this man was a stranger again. Sher Khan and Kassim sat glaring at each other, mirror images of fury, until Kassim said, 'Nay, Lord of the Hills, I do not mean to meddle—I speak for the good of all.'

'Yes. Very well. It is understood. But I will deal with this in my own time—'

Kassim shrugged, and answered, 'Lord of the Hills—it is as you say. I am your servant.' He bowed his head over joined hands like a suppliant, and Sher Khan's face slowly cleared and he laughed, and they began to speak together again, and Bianca did not even wonder what the sudden storm had been about, or why Kassim had called Sher Khan 'Lord of the Hills', one of the Ruler's titles. She sat, happily relaxed, half dreaming, her eyes on every move that Sher Khan made, until he became conscious of the beautiful eyes so faithfully watching, and turned, smiling at her, to take her hand. Kassim got up then, stretching and laughing, and said goodbye, and laughed again when he got no answer.

That evening, an hour before sunset, wearing woollen robes against the sudden chill of the mountain evening, Bianca rode beside Sher Khan along the lakeshore. The bodyguard were a discreet distance behind, and she was able to feel that she was alone with her husband. The evening light was all about them, the lake burnished, the mountains deep purple tipped with flame coloured snow.

They rode slowly, talking, relaxed, able to look about them, and see the extra beauty that the world wore, and always has worn for lovers. The villagers in the small village that straddled the road were lighting their fires—they stood, salaaming and smiling as their Yuvraj rode by with his bride. Riding through the wreaths of sweet smelling woodsmoke, Bianca knew that she would never forget the smell. She was so happy, she was held in a golden web of joy, and no unhappy memories or thoughts touched her on that gentle evening ride. Sher Khan watched her with pleasure, but marvelled to himself that she had forgotten everything so easily and so soon. The girl he was beginning to know better with every hour he spent with her, was not a shallow person, and not so lost in self-importance that pain or sorrow could not touch her. Therefore, he could not understand her complete withdrawal from any memory of Madore, and that fraught and desperate departure. He had not been prepared for the effect of a returned love, and successful love-making, on a passionate girl—she could think of nothing but him, and his touch and her body's response—all else was gone. Serene, smiling and beautiful, she rode beside him, her eyes constantly turning to meet his, and he, watching her graceful movements and her lovely face, found it easy to live in the present, and think of nothing but the coming night.

The lake narrowed, steep slopes, pine trees climbing them, led up to the first rises of the mountains, and the lake rounded into a small wood, where the night seemed to have already gathered. The last light still burned on the water, and at first Bianca thought she was looking at a reflection of the sun, but it was the lotus flowers, raising their beautiful cups in hundreds, not yet closed against the night. They flung a great stain of coral pink over the edge of the lake, completely covering the water, their flat leaves lying below them, and Bianca could smell their scent, heavy and sweet, and she stopped to stare, enchanted.

There was a small marble building glimmering white in the shadows on the shore, deserted and silent, but someone had been there, for in the darkness within the shrine, Bianca saw the flicker of fire. A little lamp was burning steadily on the altar stone.

'This was built by the Greek Alexander's soldiers, when he camped hereabouts on his way to India. He stayed here some months, I think, and one of his generals was left here, ill. He recovered, and took as his lover one of the women of my family. He loved her, and she loved him enough to bear him children—one of them was a son, who was my ancestor. I think the general took too long to rejoin Alexander—in any case, he was left behind here forever, and some say he is buried here. I do not know, it was a very long time ago.'

The escort had come up, and dismounted. Sher Khan took Bianca's horse's bridle, and pulled her a little distance away, before he dismounted, and reached up for her to slide down into his arms. When they wandered back to the shrine, dazed by even the few minutes they had stolen to kiss and be close, they found rugs spread, a fire blazing, and food and wine laid out before them—and the escort riding away round the curve of the hill. 'I will call them back when we are ready—this is our land, sweetheart, we are safe enough here.'

He poured wine into a silver goblet, and stretched out, leaning back against her raised knees as she sat, supported by a fallen tree.

The night came down, the lake was a sheet of dark glass, and the only light was from the fire, leaping red and yellow flames against the dark. Sher Khan was hungry, and made a good meal, but Bianca could eat little. Her body was loosened, and burning with desire. The turn of his head, his hand holding their shared goblet, the flash of his smile in the firelight; Bianca sipped wine that ran in her veins like another fire, and sat, learning over again, everything that she liked in his looks, as if she had never seen him before.

Presently, he put his plate down, and they sat silent together, his arm over her knees, staring into the fire. Then, as he turned his head to look at her, she moved, and slid down into his arms.

Bianca, who thought that she had learned everything about love the night before, forgot it all. Something in the night, and the place took hold of them both. His passion matched her demands, grew greater, and mastered her, carrying her to heights of ecstasy that she had not known existed. She cried out, and was answered by the lonely call of a bird, disturbed in the forest behind the shrine. The fire died down to embers, and the moon rose, and the silver lake gave back the trees and the mountains in faithful reflection, but no one remarked this black and silver beauty.

It was very late when they went home, riding together on one horse, Sher Khan holding Bianca before him, her head on his shoulder, too heavy for her to hold erect. He carried her into their room, and she was asleep before the women had finished undressing her. He sat for a little in the alcove, before he joined her, but she did not move, and soon there was nothing for them both but quiet and deep sleep.

10

Bianca slept late the next day, and woke alone. Sunlight was moving in the water shadows on the walls, and glittering on the silver on the table in the window. Her breakfast of fruit and coffee was waiting for her. Ragni came in, smiling, at her first movement, ready to help her rise and bathe. Bianca was suddenly completely at home in her new life, and knew, with no impatience, that Sher Khan had many duties, and would return to her when he could. Her soothed body calmed her mind, and she could wait. A single white rose, perfect among its green leaves, lay on the table—some one had picked it from the bush outside the alcove window, and Bianca, raising it to her mouth, knew whose hand had picked it for her. Shadowless, beautiful, her life stretched ahead of her, and she was at home and content.

It was two or three days later that she found herself with no one to ride with. Kassim had gone out on a day long journey with Sher Khan. It was a beautiful day, too good to spend sitting in the alcove looking at the lake. Bianca ordered her horse, and set off with her bodyguard, taking the road she had taken with Kassim on her first ride. She passed the big house where the Begum Mumtaz lived, and thought of calling there, but she could see no one about, and the shutters were closed. It was when she had ridden on some miles that she saw a large house with wooden balconies, a house as red as the red plastered walls of the Madoremahal. Of course—the Lalkoti, where that beautiful child lived. Then she heard a voice calling, and the child Sara ran out, delighted, followed by an ayah, who pulled the big gate open so that the little girl could run through.

'Oh Miss— You have come! Come in, and we will have coffee and cakes if you come, and my mother will be glad—'

'Sara! You must not call the Khanum "Miss"—she is the Begum Sahiba.'

Sara's beautiful mother was standing on the steps of her house, her hands joined in greeting, her face, to Bianca's astonishment, unveiled, in spite of the bodyguard. Bianca herself, at Sher Khan's request, had started wearing a white veil over her head, and covering her face when she rode out—muslin, so fine that it did not prevent her seeing clearly, nor indeed did it hide her face, but it was a veil, and pleased Sher Khan, and so she wore it. But Sara's mother was not only unveiled, she was bare headed, and Bianca looking at the thickly-coiled black hair, and the folds of the sari she wore, knew suddenly that this woman was not a hill woman. She was from the south of India.

'Sahiba, will you enter, and take coffee with me?'

Bianca felt it would be rude to refuse, besides, the day lay ahead of her, and this interlude would help it to pass more quickly. She would not admit to herself that the real reason was the child, standing there, looking up at her in anticipation.

The senior man of the bodyguard was saying something, and surprised, she turned to him as she slid down from her horse. 'If it pleases the Begum Sahiba—the horses are hot—should we not return, instead, to the Chotamahal?'

Bianca stared at him. The horses had been ridden at an easy canter, and were as cool as she was—what did he want, standing there looking into her face, and talking nonsense? It came to her then, that this man was set to guard her, and was responsible for her to Sher Khan. Any departure from normal would worry him of course.

'I shall not be long, Nasir Dost. Walk the horses if you are worried about them.' She smiled at him, and followed the excited child into the house, not seeing how the bodyguard exchanged glances with tight worried faces.

The entrance hall of the Lalkoti was dark and gloomy after Bianca's white room with its wide windows and clean marble floors. There were many silk hangings, and the floor was covered with thick Bokhara carpets, dark in colour, and everything seemed to smell of dust and disuse.

As they drank their coffee, poured from a beautiful but very tarnished silver pot into little porcelain cups, Bianca asked Kurmilla where she had lived before she came to Lambagh.

'Before my marriage, I lived in Calcutta, and in Darjeeling. Where do you come from?' The heavy lidded eyes were not turned on Bianca—the question was asked as if the reply would be of no interest.

'I am Irish—but I was born in Madore, and have lived all my life here—either in Jindbagh, or in Madore. My father serves the Ruler—he commands the State Forces of Thinpahari.'

'Oh yes. The famous Irish soldier, so beloved of the Ruler. He is known.' Still the indifferent voice, the downcast eyes. Bianca suddenly thought of her father, saw him as clearly as if he were standing before her, smiling his kind loving smile. She felt a longing for his presence, and it was the memory of his pride in her that stiffened her spine and made her sit where she was. She wished very much that she had not paid this visit. It would have been better if she had listened to Nasir Dost and ridden home. Only the child seated on a stool at her feet was friendly. As she smiled down into the grey eyes raised to hers, she was conscious that the other woman was now staring at her, a hard searching look that compassed her whole person, and seemed to probe for her very soul. She looked up quickly, and spoke at random, to break the strange tension that was beginning to grow in the room.

'I love these mountains, like a great white-topped wall, protecting Lambagh—'

Kurmilla shrugged. 'Mountains? To me, these are not mountains. I have looked from the windows of my father's summer house on to the snows of the Great Mountains. These are but hills, the foothills of the giants.' Bianca thought of the towering ranges she had seen from the passes on her journey from Madore, but she said nothing. Kurmilla clattered her coffee cup down, and without looking to see if Bianca had finished, clapped her hands for her woman to come and take the tray away. Bianca thought she detected homesickness in her voice, and felt a kindliness that made the atmosphere easier.

'Did you like Darjeeling?' she said, 'I thought you must be from the south, because of the way you fold your sari, and you are unveiled—I saw some of the southern Ladies when they came to the Madoremahal for the Nawab of Sagpur's wedding—' Khanzada! Her mind flew back to the last time she saw Khanzada, flinched away, and then remembered Goki's words. 'It is well with the Lady Khanzada—the Rani is with her—'

Yes, of course Zada was all right, and safe, before she had left Madore with Sher Khan that night. Once the Rani knew of her troubles, it would not matter even if she had a daughter—

Hardyal could not harm her in her own home. 'The Pool of the Women—' a sorrowful frightened voice sounded for a moment in her ears, and Bianca felt cold, and quickly turned her thoughts back to the present. She saw Kurmilla put a hand up to her shining black coils of hair.

'I go unveiled here, yes, custom or not, there is no one here to see that matters to me. But in Calcutta we do not wear the veil in any case—sometimes, when we go to parties, we would be veiled, if the parties were, as you would say "Fancee Deress"—' She preened at Bianca's surprised stare. 'Oah yess—I speak Eenglish veree vell. I had manee reech Eenglish friends in Calcutta. The great jute merchants, you know, there were plentee parties in their houses. It was a most entertaining life.' Her sigh was heavy, her accent abominable. Bianca, used to the splendid unaccented English spoken by the native princes of the Ruler's household, and of his friends, had never heard the kind of English spoken by the half-caste. Bianca's father had called it 'Calcutta Welsh' and now Bianca knew what he meant. But she complimented Kurmilla on her fluency, and little Sara smiled, and said softly, 'I would like to learn to speak as you do Miss—' but no one heard her, for her mother was saying, 'Yes—that was a good life. I was a fool to leave it for this hole. You said you saw the wedding of the Nawab of Sagpur? You know him well? He is my cousin brother. I was born in Sagpur, a very beautiful place, and also the climate there is good, warm and gentle, not like this bitter prison of mountains. But Hardyal married a woman of these hills—so he also was a fool. I did not go to the wedding because Sara was too small for the journey, and in any case I had no interest. A native State wedding is all drums and shouting, very dull.'

'It was a beautiful wedding,' said Bianca, the heat rising in her face. 'And the bride is a dear friend of mine—I have known her all my life. She is the Ruler's niece, Sher Khan's sister.'

There was a silence again, a listening silence, and then Kurmilla shrugged her arrogant, indolent shrug. 'Yes. Hill people.'

Bianca found her anger was beginning to get out of control.

'And did you think my wedding was all drums, and shouting—but I do not remember seeing you there, there were so many people. Perhaps you thought my wedding was not interesting enough for you to attend.' She was interrupted by the other woman's furious stare. For a second she looked into eyes that held mortal hatred, and was astonished. Then Kurmilla began to laugh, harsh grating laughter that rose to a shrill peal, and brought the ayah out from an inner room, to stare in fear. Bianca felt Sara leaning against her knees, like a little animal seeking shelter, and put her hand down to press the thin little body to her, before she rose to her feet. Kurmilla caught her breath, gulped, and was in control of herself again. Bianca could not give her the conventional smile, and when she made her farewells, she was shocked within herself at the coldness of her own voice.

'Thank you for my coffee, Kurmilla. May I send one of my women with a palanquin for Sara one day? I would like her to come and spend a day with me, perhaps we could go on a picnic.' And I have no intention of asking you to come too, my good woman, so do not expect it. The other murmured her thanks for the Begum's kindness, her eyes once more cast down, her manner perfect, but Bianca felt that she was close to something evil, as if a snake had come near her, and now lay hidden, a threat out of sight. Strange that this beautiful woman should make her feel exactly as Hardyal had made her feel; it must be something in the blood line. Khanzada's terror-filled face came into her mind's eye again, to choke the words she was speaking, and she was only able to bow and turn away to where the bodyguard had brought up the horses. Sara had followed her out, and watched her settle herself in the saddle, and then said, 'Miss—but my mother says I must not call you Miss. Are you a Rani?'

'Of course not Sara—I am the wife of the Yuvraj, Sher Khan, who is the nephew of the Ruler. The Rani will be coming back very soon, and then we will have big parties at the Chotamahal, and you must come. Would you like that?'

'Will there be music, and garlands, and little sweet cakes? We had no cakes today. And another thing—can I see the peacocks?'

'My little rose—you can see and do anything you like. I will send for you.'

She took with her, as she rode off, the memory of the child's thin little face, lit by those beautiful grey eyes, now smiling happily as she waved goodbye.

11

The days in the Chotamahal, the little palace, passed pleasantly. Bianca was often alone, and rode a great deal. The villagers became used to seeing the small cavalcade clattering by, Bianca always well in the lead, with the bodyguard keeping a good distance behind, at her orders.

She explored the lakeshore thoroughly, and the surrounding country, but she did not go towards Kurmilla's house again, nor did she fulfil her promise to send for Sara. The unease and anger she had felt in Kurmilla's presence had grown into a strong reluctance to see her again, and she had not decided how to arrange a day with the child without at least some contact with the mother. She was happy, but a little lonely. Sher Khan was away nearly every day, and now Kassim went with him.

Bianca had never been alone before in her life. Inevitably, her thoughts turned back to her mother. Her father had often gone off on long trips. Her own loneliness told her something of what her mother must have suffered, and she felt miserable when she recalled how she had left the Madoremahal that night, without even a farewell. She knew that Goki would not have insisted that she should go like that if it had not been necessary—but how unhappy it must have made her mother! A small thought, as frightening as a ghostly whisper in an empty room came to her—had there been danger for her mother too? Surely not. She remembered all that Shaibani Khan had said, and comforted herself with the thought that her father and the Ruler between them were more than capable of dealing with anything that Hardyal could do. She set her mind on how she would welcome her mother when she came. Blanche would be very angry with her of course, that was to be expected. But when she saw how happy Bianca was, and how she loved Sher Khan, it would be different—for had not she herself said that nothing else mattered once you had found the man you truly loved? Bianca comforted herself with this memory of her mother's words.

When Sher Khan returned, Bianca's happiness was almost too much to bear, his glance, smiling and warm, his voice, his touch, and the knowledge that they belonged together, that no one could intrude into their lives once they were alone and behind closed doors, transported her, and she could think of nothing but his presence and his love. He appeared to be as completely enthralled as she was, but she felt sometimes that his thoughts were on many other things, and remembered Goki saying that men lived lives apart from women, that women were as nothing without their husbands, but that men could have many interests. This brought her no unease—so long as he loved her, and she was sure now that he did, she was happy. Once or twice she woke in the night to find that his place beside her was empty, that he was sitting in the alcove, looking out at the lake and the mountains, so deep in thought that he did not hear her when she called to him. Her arms about him, her kisses on his throat, brought him back—'What are you thinking of, so far from me, beloved?

'A thousand things, but none of them as interesting or as beautiful as you—come to bed, my bird, you are getting as cold as a fish—'

'Fish, bird—what kind of animal am I, Sher Khan?'

He looked down at the glowing eyes, the waiting passionate mouth, and laughed. 'A tigress, my heart—that is what you are—a hunting insatiable tigress—' and bent to kiss her. The answer was enough. Held in his arms, Bianca would sleep again, and Sher Khan would stare over her head, into the darkness, wondering desperately when the message would come from Madore, and what disasters would come with it. The passes would be closed very soon, the first snows were already on the lower slopes above the lake, and there were charcoal burners selling their coal in the villages. The wind had a bite in it now, that spoke clearly of the approach of winter, though the leaves on the great Chenar trees had barely begun to change from summer's green to autumn's flame. Bianca wore thick woollen robes on her lonely rides, and from her windows saw the roofs of the village below begin to glow scarlet and orange and gold, as the villagers dried their harvest of maize and peppers and tomatoes on the most convenient flat spaces they had.

The fields had been gleaned and ploughed, and the little platforms that stood on high poles at the edge of each field no longer held vociferous small boys with little hand drums, who had spent many of the summer nights in their rickety eyries, calling and drumming to frighten off the birds and the goats. The first stories of villagers meeting wolves below the snow line began to filter down to Lambagh. 'And that is another thing to waste ammunition on,' said Sher Khan bitterly to Kassim, 'They fire off their guns as if there was never going to be a shortage of gun powder or cartridges. At this rate we shall be defending the passes with sling shots and swords.'

'If it comes to that,' said Kassim, 'and I do not see how it can. The British are not children or fools. The mutineers will have few victories, and will not get as far as the passes, I swear.'

Sher Khan sighed deeply. 'Please God, and Allah in particular—but in any case, the whole plains country is going to be upset, and there will be many men anxious to find sanctuary up in the hill States, bringing every sort of evil and mischief with them. Against these, we must hold the passes, and keep these States free of unrest. In the name of Allah the compassionate, when will that messenger come?'

Goki was making less speed on her journey than she had hoped. She walked along the tree-shaded road to the north, travelling mostly by day, keeping well to the side of the road, and moving through scrub and undergrowth, where the edges of the road were merging with the fields. She did not travel by night because that was when everyone else seemed to be on the road, the great road that ran right through Hindustan, from the south to the north—the Grand Trunk Road. To Goki, struggling along the overgrown verges, it seemed a very frequented road. At night she lay hidden, while parties of furtive men, who themselves kept to the verges, went by, hurrying from one patch of dark shadow to another, as if they feared the light. Goki knew them for enemies, the hyenas and vultures hastening to the killing grounds of the big cantonment cities in search of plunder.

She also avoided, with a sad heart, the terrified, straggling little companies of white people fleeing down the road, sometimes with a faithful servant to guide them, sometimes alone, running from terrible scenes, wounded and distracted, going they knew not where. She could do nothing to help them, and they might hinder her, and so she hid from them too. During the day, she was able to travel, because the noisy parties of Indian troops gave plenty of warning of their coming. When she heard the drunken voices, and wild laughter of men unaccustomed to power, Goki would move even deeper into the *rukh*, the wilderness, and lie quiet until they had passed. She could not go very far in a day, because she was old and very tired, and in a state of great sorrow. One thing kept her moving, slow though she might be—the knowledge that she carried with her the Ruler's last commands and messages, and the Emerald Peacock, and Sher Khan waited for her in Lambagh.

She kept her eyes and ears well open, and gathered every item of news that she thought might be of use to Sher Khan. Village shops, early open in the mornings and willing to sell for a few coins not only milk, but information, sometimes inaccurate, were her sources of both food and news. She did not beg, but went along the road, a traveller towards the safety of the hills, and the passing people had no interest in one so old and decrepit. She was certain that Hardyal would search for her untiringly. Now, with both the Ruler and Shaibani Khan dead, she was the only person who knew where the Emerald Peacock was and the only one who knew the short route to Lambagh. For this reason, she did not follow the short route, but went by known ways. She was unafraid for herself. More than her life lay dead behind her in the garden of the Madoremahal—now only Lambagh and the two who were there waiting for her mattered.

Strangely, Hardyal did not search for her. He saw the neatly arranged bodies of the Ruler and his wife and his friends, and superstitious fear turned him cold—had the spirits of the slain returned to compose their own bodies? For a moment he shivered, but only for a moment. Then he turned on his hirelings, and raged at them, telling them to search the gardens and the palace again, 'For he is still here—who else could ready the Ruler's body, and arrange the corpses of his followers? Find Sher Khan, and that girl—and for every day that passes with him at liberty, one of you will lose his head.' He did not tell them that the Emerald Peacock was not on the Ruler's body—they were paid assassins, and he did not trust them. His threats did not help him. In twos and threes they slipped away, and joined the looting, murdering gangs of men who found good pickings and little danger in many of the cities in that terrible time.

Bitterly, Hardyal admitted to himself that he had bungled his attempt to get the throne of Lambagh, and the Emerald Peacock. He had not been prepared for the speed with which the Ruler had moved to protect his heir and the three States.

Hardyal sat thinking in the empty silence of his room in the Madoremahal, and it seemed to him that someone was watching him. He glanced uneasily over his shoulder to the piles of silk cushions in the corner of the room. A wind moved the silk curtain. Hardyal shuddered, and went out of the room and into the garden, and then, as the trees rustled and doves settled for the evening, crooned with a soft sound of sorrow, Hardyal found the garden no less populated with ghosts than the palace, and shouting for lights, and a drink, he came to a decision.

He would start now, with men he could trust—there were a few—for Lambagh State. Lambagh was the capital of the three States, and the most important. There was a great deal of damage he could do up there, and there were those already there who would be able to help him.

It was still dark and empty in the garden, with blowing leaves that rustled like voices. Hardyal shouted again, and clapped his hands, and when a servant finally came running, he said, 'Send Haridass, and Shankar Lall—and bring lights, thou fool, and cognac—and hurry.'

There in the darkness, with the cool evening breeze putting words to the doves' crooning, Hardyal sat, and began to plan.

Goki had come, late one evening, after many days' travel, to the outskirts of Sandalla, and was carefully avoiding the inhabited areas, pushing her way with difficulty through the thick bushes and thorn trees that grew in the barren land surrounding the town. This was the last large town she would have to pass. After this, twenty miles further on, she would turn on to the smaller roads, to the dirt tracks that wound up into the foothills, and would be within a few weeks' journey from safety and the end of her mission.

The mutineers were ahead of her. As night fell, and she looked about her for a suitable place to sleep, she saw flames flowering from the cantonment area, and faintly on the light evening breeze she heard shouting, and smelled the acrid smell of burning. An uneven rattle of rifle fire sounded above the shouts, and she thought she could hear screams and the crackle of burning wood. Otherwise the night was deathly quiet, as if the earth and sky were both keeping silence in horror at what was being done. Goki turned her mind from what she could not bear to think of, and found a thicket of trees and a low stone wall, that ended in a broken culvert. This would provide safe shelter. She lay down, her white cloth pulled over her head and face, and in spite of the distant noises of disaster and terror, slept until the false dawn woke her, and with her old bones creaking in protest, she struggled up, twitched her robes into place, and set off to find somewhere to buy her milk and bread.

The people in the small wayside shop that she finally found, were not inclined to speak. They hurriedly filled her brass pot with milk, and gave her two flat rounds of bread. To her careful questions, the shopkeeper replied, 'Nay, old one—we be poor folk, and know nothing. But blood will pay for blood, and last night's work in the cantonment will bring us nothing but trouble.'

'Yes,' said his wife, her face sallow in the grey light, and her eyes haunted, 'old one, it is better that we do not speak of such things. Go, old one, go in haste. The killings last night must have been terrible, and there will be a curse on our heads here for ever—'

Goki went quickly, wanting to hear no more. She made a wide detour and was some distance from the last houses of the town, when she saw a good stand of thorn trees, and went over to sit and drink her milk and rest a little.

She had just settled herself down, when from within the thicket, clear and chilling as a fall of ice on her spine, she heard a long shuddering moan, that ended in a gasping cry of pain. Trembling, Goki sprang up to run away, but could not make herself move. She had to stay and see who it was, humanity demanded it, for the sound had been one of mortal agony. Goki made her way carefully through the trees into the heart of the thicket, and then stopped, her breath catching in her throat. It was a woman lying there before her, or what was left of a woman

—an Indian. How anyone so brutally hacked and slashed could have dragged her body here, Goki could not imagine. Looking beyond the torn body, Goki saw a waist-thick trail of blood, where flies already buzzed, and then, a little to one side, she saw the child, lying quiet and still, face down, dark hair tumbling in dust-covered curls.

The poor thing on the ground at her feet moaned again, and opened her eyes. There was no sight in those eyes, they were long past earthly seeing, but slowly Goki sensed that the woman knew there was someone near her. Tormented by the agonies she could see, Goki felt for her little knife, and the woman spoke.

'Oh may the gods have mercy—my child, my little girl—Oh save my child, and whoever you are, the gods will bless you. I can do no more.' The words ended in a choking cry, and Goki grew terrified lest someone should hear. 'Hush! Be silent—I am a friend.'

Somehow the pain-clouded mind heard and understood, and forced itself to coherence. 'Oh friend, whoever you be—take my child—'

'Tell me her name—she will be safe, I promise, but tell me her name so that she will be at ease with me—'

'Her name is Charlotte—' The poor creature fought for breath, and conquered. 'Her father they killed last night—he was an Englishman, a soldier. He named her for his mother, and would have married me when he took his discharge from the army. But they took him and killed him in the night, and took me to kill as well, because I lived with him—but they did not find my child, and when they had left me for dead, the gods were good to me, and I found strength to bring her here. Now I go—and leave her to you. I go—'

There was no need for Goki's merciful knife. The effort of speaking had been the final stroke. The head that had once been beautiful fell back, the crying voice stilled, and Goki turned to the child, unharmed, alive, and just beginning to move. Swiftly the old woman picked the child up, lest she should see her mother's body, and went as quickly from the thicket as she could. The child was quiet, lifting great dark eyes to the old woman's face. She showed no fear, and when Goki sat down, the child drank some milk, turned her head to Goki's shoulder, and fell peacefully asleep, held against Goki's heart—while the old woman, watching her quiet sleeping, was greatly troubled, knowing she could not now desert the child, and also foreseeing the extra burden she would be.

But the child was a good child. She made no sound, showed no fear when she woke from her sudden sleep. She rested confidently in Goki's arms, as the old woman crept very slowly with her burden back to the edge of the road again. She stopped when she thought it was safe, and gave the little girl another drink, and took off the tattered, blood-stained little clothes, so carefully embroidered and be-ribboned, and wrapped them into a bundle, which she hid far back under the roots of a thorn tree. Then she tore her *chadder*—her head cloth—in half, and wound the child into it, thanking her stars that Charlotte was dark-haired and in spite of her fair skin could pass for the child of a Pahari—a hill-man. 'But your name—your name is Muna now, my pretty one. Pray the gods you are too young to have remembered anything. Muna—?' She spoke questioningly, and the child turned her head, and eyed her gravely. Goki wondered how old she could be—light of body, very small boned, she could be any age between three and five.

'Your mother has sent you with me, while she rests, my little flower. You must be a good quiet child, so that we do not have any trouble.' How much of the terrible doings of the night before had the child seen? The dark eyes looked back at her, unsmiling, expressionless. 'How old are you, *pyari*?' asked Goki.

'I have five years. They made a party for me last week. But then, last night, bad men came, and took my father, and cut off his head—and they beat my mother with their swords, and made her bleed very much. Are you sure she is resting? Will she follow us?'

Goki's eyes filmed with tears, but she spoke firmly. 'She is resting now—Muna, remember your name is Muna, and I will keep you safe until—' The child's straight look stopped the lie on Goki's lips. After a short silence, the little girl said quietly, 'My name is now Muna.' Then she closed her eyes, her head dropped to Goki's shoulder, and she slept, with the sudden sleep of exhaustion.

Throughout the long days that followed, the slow miles that

fell behind, the child barely spoke. She trudged along beside Goki, she ate and drank whatever Goki gave her, but she only spoke when she was too tired to go on walking. Then she would say very quietly, 'Can we rest here, Grandmother? Is it safe?' They rested often, and Goki looked at the child in an agony of pity and fear. Each day that passed seemed to peel more flesh from her little bones, and her face was all eyes. Goki tried to carry her sometimes, but could not—her old arms would no longer bear the child's weight, light as it was. Their progress was very slow.

Now the roads were empty at last. They saw no one, and except for some scattered villages, where Goki went to buy her milk and bread, there were long stretches of empty countryside; even the goatherds were not out with their flocks in this terrible year.

The days were growing cooler as they joined the smaller roads that began to wind upwards into the foothills—indeed, the nights were cold, and Goki knew that she must find warmer clothes for Muna, and some other form of transport. The mountain passes lay ahead, and the snows would already be there. Ten days after she had found Muna they came to the largest village they had seen for some time. Goki knew it well, as a staging post for the Ruler on his way down to Madore. This was a village where they had stopped to rest the night in those days, and the head man was from Jindbagh, and knew Goki well. But that did not mean he was honest. These villagers were still villagers of the plains, the people were a shifting population here, going down to the cities to find work in the winters, and only coming back during the long hot summers, when the plains lay in a coma under the onslaught of the heat. Goki knew that whatever the risk, she had to ask for help here; Muna could not walk far at a time, and the last nights had been cold enough to make them both lie shuddering in each other's arms.

Goki reconnoitred carefully, and choosing the hour just after sunset, when everyone was within doors, she left Muna hidden under a tree and went into the village, and up to the head man's house. Her knock was not answered by an immediately opened door and her heart sank. News from Madore had obviously preceded her, and this could be nothing but dangerous. Almost, she did not answer when she heard the man calling, 'Who is there?' but necessity forced her on.

'It is a traveller,' she answered. 'I ask for shelter.'

There was a whispered consultation behind the closed door, and the man called again. 'If you are a traveller, what do you on the roads so late—a woman—and how many are you?'

'I am but one—and I would speak with Chundu—' The head man's wife had been a crony of Goki's in the old days. She heard the bolts being drawn, and pushed back her head cloth, as the door opened a crack, and she found herself looking into the muzzle of a musket, and the head man's frightened eyes behind.

'In the name of Allah—it is the old one, Goki—' The door opened wide and eager hands pulled her in. Looking at the two old faces before her, Goki could see no guile, only fear, and astonished welcome—and a questioning look that told her what rumour had preceded her. In silence she looked back at them, and then the old man turned away, his face twisting. 'Ai, sorrow—it is true then. We heard of the killing, but we trusted that it was a story blown up by many tongues. Goki, what do you here alone? Do you go to Lambagh?'

Goki, grim faced, nodded. If the tale of the Ruler's killing was ahead of her, she feared for Sher Khan. Were the passes already broached, and the killers on their way? She resolutely put the thought from her, and sitting down, told as much of her story as she thought needful, feeling her way as she talked.

The head man's wife, Chundu, was heating food and putting more wood on the open fire. The man, hearing of Muna, stood up at once. 'Where is the child? I will go and bring her here.'

Goki stood too, her bones protesting at every movement. 'I will come with you, Yunus. The child may be frightened if she does not see me.'

The man made a wry face. 'Indeed—such days, when a child is fearful of an old man.'

Warmed and fed, Muna fell asleep, rolled in quilts, while her elders talked. Then Goki too slept, as she had not slept for days, a deep black sleep, from which she woke with a start, to find it full day, and Chundu bathing Muna in a bowl of hot water, exclaiming at the beauty of the child. Indeed, it was a perfect little body and face, with richly curling hair. Goki thought fleetingly and with pain of how much this child must have been loved.

They left the village that night, on horseback, with Yunus Khan's son to go with them to the next safe village, a week's journey ahead. Goki had asked to go alone, for she feared the spreading of the news, but Yunus Khan had shaken his head. 'My son is the Ruler's man. He will not speak—but I fear the news will already be known in the hill villages. There have been many who ran from the terror—in the foothills, certainly, all know the story. But it is late in the year Goki—the passes may be closed. Let him go with you. Alone, you will die in the snows, and the little one with you.' Goki did not argue any more.

They evolved a plan that seemed good to Goki. When they came to the villages where they were to get food, the young man went in, and came back with the provisions, and in each case shook his head in answer to Goki's questioning. 'They have heard,' he said briefly, each time, and Goki travelled on with a sinking heart. But after another week he came back and told her that he had been received as an ordinary traveller, returning to his country. No news appeared to have reached the higher villages. Goki raised her eyes to where the high snows reared before her, and pulling Muna closely against her body, rode on with more hope, in spite of the terrible road that still lay ahead.

12

In Lambagh, the snows had crept down and lay in the meadows on the far side of the lake, where the slopes were higher than they were on the village side.

Bianca rode less now. The days were grey, and she found it hard to rise in the mornings. A heaviness seemed to have fallen on her, and she was content to lie and doze after Sher Khan had left her, and she took a long time over her dressing. Her appetite had left her too, and she had lost weight.

'What is this—and this—I can count your ribs, Bianca! You must not grow so thin, or I shall think you pine, and are not happy. Besides, your bones are bruising me!' Sher Khan's voice was anxious, and he looked narrowly at the new hollows in Bianca's face.

'You are thin, yourself,' she countered. 'Look—here is a bone, and here. You speak of my bones bruising you—but we are both thin together.'

Sher Khan smothered a sigh. He had enough to make him thin, he was never out of the saddle, it seemed, these days—riding out to all the posts and mountain forts with Kassim, with the shadow of what was to come hanging over his days.

The Ruler, his uncle, had taken three small, struggling hill States, and welded them into one country—Thinpahari, the land of the three mountain valleys, with Lambagh as the principal state. The State was a place of contented people, each man able to live his own life, practise his own religion, without fear. Muslim, Hindu, Sikh—it made no difference. Safe behind its mountain passes, the valleys prospered and grew rich—a prize that many began to covet. Sher Khan held it as a sacred trust, from his uncle—soon, he knew, the message must come, that would make him Ruler indeed. It was the holding of the passes against the upheaval in the rest of India that troubled him. The news of the death of the Ruler, and the news of the mutiny would come together—what other evil would try to creep in? He wished that he could ease his mind by talking to Bianca. But he could not understand her attitude. When she mentioned Madore, it was to ask how much longer it would be before the Ruler came—and would her parents come with the Ruler and the Rani? Sher Khan did not know what to say. Had she completely forgotten the desperate haste in which they had left Madore? He could not believe that. Was she secretly worrying, and afraid to say so, was that why she was so thin, although she appeared to be perfectly happy. He listened to her talking about how easy it would be to turn her mother's anger into pleasure in their happiness, until he could stand it no longer, and stopped her words with his kisses. It was already weeks past the time that the Ruler habitually returned from Madore, and she had expressed no surprise. He tried to tell himself that this was all to the good, but all the same, felt that there was something unnatural in this complete disregard of all life that had happened before these days—it was as if a curtain had been drawn between Bianca's previous existence and this life with him, and he dreaded what would happen when the curtain was forcibly drawn aside by the messages that would come from Madore.

If any came, he thought, staring out at the mists that hung over the lake. Surely news should have come already. But it was as if Lambagh had moved out of the world. Even the usual gossip of the small tribal fights that always broke out on the northern borders once the harvest was in, even these rumours had not been heard this season.

'We float,' he said morosely to Kassim, 'just as the stars float—far above the world, so far that we hear nothing—'

Kassim nodded, and then, greatly daring, spoke of the gossip he *was* hearing. 'They say that the Lady Kurmilla holds many parties these days—and that they are not all purdah parties. Men are also invited.

Sher Khan shrugged. 'What men? Grooms and sweepers? This is indeed the only kind of rumour we do hear—women's gossip.'

'Nay then—it can be of importance. Have you told Bianca anything of the past?'

At once, Sher Khan's face darkened. 'Kassim Bahadur—I have spoken of this to you. Leave my own affairs to me—they have nothing to do with you. You have enough to do, I should have thought, with the arranging of important affairs here. If not, I can find you more work.'

But this time, Kassim would not be silenced. He spoke firmly, and Sher Khan, after a furious moment of protest, was forced to listen. 'The Lady Bianca is seeing Kurmilla next week—the child is the cause, it seems that Bianca promised to send for her to spend the day in the Chotamahal, and then did not—and the child has been ill, and Kurmilla has sent word that Sara longs to see the Begum Sahiba—so, of course, Bianca goes. Do you think it wise that she goes into that serpent's nest, unknowing? For the sake of your own happiness, and hers, I think you should speak, for be very sure—if you do not, one of these women will say something, and then there will be heartbreak, for these European women are different from ours—they do not accept things that our women take as matter of course.'

Sher Khan was silent for a long time, and then, when he spoke, he was no longer angry. He sounded despairing. 'It is too late now,' he said slowly. 'Too late. She should have been told this long ago. I should have made my peace with your mother, and she could have told her—or Khanzada could have told her, when she first found herself in love with me. Now, it will be terrible. Better that she is never told.'

'But Sher Khan Bahadur—this is impossible! Let my mother tell her, please—' Kassim was looking at Sher Khan in horror. 'You cannot leave her untold. She is bound to find out! The women will talk, you know that they will—half of them were hoping to marry you themselves, or marry you to their daughters—'

'It does not matter if they talk,' said Sher Khan. 'She will either not hear, or not believe. But if I tell her—well it will break her heart. Now, let us speak no more of this, my dear nephew, lest I lose my temper, and do or say things that I regret later. Come—there is the Patwar of Khankhote waiting for me. His tales of bears in the streets of the village, looting the granaries, will fill an hour easily—and perhaps take your mind from my affairs.' He was trying for a lightness that he did not feel. Kassim, filled with anxiety, nevertheless followed his lead. Allah knew they had enough to distress them, it was best that at least they remained close, and did not quarrel. But from that time on he had a feeling of distress at the back of his mind whenever he saw Bianca—an ill-omened thought of disaster, that shadowed his pleasure in the obvious happiness of Bianca and Sher Khan.

Bianca dressed carefully on the morning that she was to visit Kurmilla. She did not admit it to herself, but she needed the extra confidence that adornment gave her. Ragni, usually so eager for her to take trouble over her appearance, and her choice of robes and jewels, this morning did not appear to be anxious to make Bianca look her best. Kusma, on the other hand, was full of suggestions as to colours and jewels—she painted Bianca's eyes and brows with fine artistry, and then, while Ragni, with a face of stone, arranged Bianca's hair, Kusma came forward with ear-rings of heavy wrought gold, and a great red gold bracelet to match.

'Ah—fool! The Khanum does not want those for a morning visit—' Ragni sounded really angry. But Bianca was pleased with the frame that the gold made for her face—Sher Khan was right, her face looked very thin, and all eyes—the gold earrings seemed to broaden it a little. She caught sight of Ragni's furious glare at Kusma in the mirror, and thought it was jealousy. The older woman usually made all the suggestions as to what Bianca should wear. She paid no attention to what seemed to be a servants' quarrel, and went out to find that a palanquin, splendid in scarlet and gold hangings, waited for her, instead of her horse. At first she was about to order it away, but suddenly the thought of lying back on those soft pillows, and arriving in state, was very appealing. She seated herself, was tucked in by Kusma, who was very solicitous this morning, and smiling her thanks, was lifted by the four men on the carrying poles, and carried off at a smart trot, the mounted bodyguard falling in behind.

The palanquin was an old one, heavily carved with the same dancing goddesses and beast-headed men that decorated the walls of her bedroom in the Chotamahal, as she was learning to call the white palace. The hangings of the palanquin were heavy silk, embroidered with gold, and the cushions were as soft as they looked. All the hangings and cushions were scented with attar of roses and sandalwood.

'Like a bride's palanquin,' thought Bianca, and fell to dreaming about her own wedding day, wondering in passing why this magnificent contraption had not been used for her then.

In the bedroom of the Chotamahal, Ragni waited for Kusma with rage in her heart—but the girl did not return. Ragni looked for her everywhere, and when she could not find her, her rage turned to apprehension, and pulling her *chadder* over her face, Ragni went out to speak to one of the watchmen at the gate and sent a messenger to find Kassim, and tell him he should come to the Chotamahal.

The messenger was lucky. Kassim was in his own house, and came at once, and listened to old Ragni with a grave face, all his fears crystallising as she spoke. 'That girl—I did not want her here, but all was arranged in such haste when the Yuvraj came back—Kusma is a creature of Kurmilla's, and takes money from her to give news of what happens here. Oh Kassim Khan Bahadur, the Khanum went off wearing the gold earrings and bracelet that *she* wore often—*and* in the palanquin that was used at that accursed marriage, and I am afraid. They have been coming and going from the lower villages to that bitch woman's house, and no one will listen to me—'

'I would have listened, Ragni. You have done very ill not to have told me.'

'Nay, Lord, do not be angry with me. When I saw the Yuvraj was happy with the white Khanum, and that he married her in truth, with due ceremony, and all was well, I did not see any danger. Only in the last weeks have I seen trouble, and now I am very afraid, for I think the Khanum is with child, though she does not know it yet. That other one will be like a disturbed cobra—all along she has been waiting for Sher Khan Bahadur to tire.' Ragni pressed her hands together, and rambled on, and Kassim stopped listening. He had heard more than enough and of all that he had heard, the comings and goings from the lower villages was the most disturbing information. Bianca's pregnancy and possible distress would have to take second place to that news.

He told Ragni to send word to him as soon as Bianca came back, and hurried off to look for Sher Khan, only to be told that the Yuvraj had already left for Salkot, a village about twenty miles away, and cursing, sent a message after him, and then tried to get on with the ordinary work of his day.

Bianca arrived at the gate of the Lalkoti, and was helped out of the palanquin by her bodyguard. This time, there was a gate man—he opened the gate, and she saw Kurmilla, resplendent in purple silk, standing on the steps. Bianca went up to her, greeting her as she came forward, but saw that the woman was not looking at her. As one who has seen a snake, she was staring past Bianca at the red palanquin—Bianca thought perhaps she was surprised to see that she had not ridden over, and said, half laughing, 'I grow lazy with the winter, as you see—this morning, it seemed good to me to have myself brought here with no effort. Is that not a magnificent palanquin—really fit for a queen?'

The other woman did not speak—she turned her eyes on Bianca, and her expression was so dreadful that Bianca fell back a step, almost expecting a blow. Was this woman Kurmilla deranged? Bianca did not know what to do. When Kurmilla turned and walked into the house, she found herself reluctant to follow her; only the ignominy of turning back in front of her bodyguard and the carrying coolies made her mount the steps and follow Kurmilla into the house—that, and the fact that she wanted to see Sara. But in the hall of the house she found no one, and did not know where to go. She called out softly, 'Is anyone here?' feeling a fool—for of course Kurmilla was here, but where had she gone? A little faint voice came from beyond the half open door on one side of the hall—she went in and found Sara in bed, looking very frail and small under the covers. Bianca went over at once to the outstretched arms; the child was feverish, she felt the hot little body in her arms trembling like a trapped bird. 'Oh, I am so glad to see you, you said you would send for me, and you did not, you forgot me!'

Bianca felt guilty and ashamed as she assured Sara that she had not forgotten, 'I have been busy, Sara, settling my house—and also, these last few days, I too have not been well—'

'Did you have a bad pain in your stomach, like me, and did you throw up all your food?' asked Sara, with clinical interest.

'Well, no, not exactly—I just feel heavy and tired. I am lazy, I expect.'

Sara was lying back, holding Bianca's hand and talking of what she was going to do when she was better. Bianca did not like her looks; the child was very thin, and flushed, and her eyes glittered with fever. Presently the ayah came in to say that the Lady Kurmilla had coffee ready for the Begum Sahiba, when she was pleased to come and Bianca thought it best to go at once, Sara should not talk and have such an excited look. 'Sleep now, my little one—I will come and see you before I go, I promise.'

The child's eyes filled with tears. 'But you promised before,' she said on a caught breath, 'and you did not come!'

'No, truly—I *will* come. Now sleep. See, here is my bracelet—keep it for me, and then you will know that I will come back.'

She saw the ayah's staring look at the bracelet, and wondered for a second if she had been wise—the thing weighed a ton, and was obviously pure gold, and worth a fortune, but the ayah was already leading the way out of the room, and with a last smile for Sara, she had to follow.

Kurmilla was waiting for her, lounging on cushions in an inner room. She made no effort to get up, and Bianca felt herself stiffen with rage, remembering the courtesy due to her as Sher Khan's wife. However, she sank down herself, thinking, 'Well, anyway, you would have trouble getting up and down with all that precious stiff silk—and all those curves too,' and accepted her cup of coffee with a smile that had malice in it. Kurmilla reacted at once. Her insolent eye ran over the other's body, until Bianca felt she had been undressed completely, and blushed scarlet under the indolent arrogant eyes. Then Kurmilla smiled slowly. 'Well, well. You grow thinner every time I see you, Lady. But love burns all away, does it not? In any case, from all I hear, you will be heavier soon.'

'I do not understand you,' said Bianca, her heart beginning a slow angry thumping, and her breath short.

Kurmilla laughed. 'You do not know? Nay, what do they teach European girls? Now, my people, we know at once when the flowers of love fall, and the fruit begins to form.'

Bianca, her coffee forgotten, stared at her, and the other, looking at the wide astonishment on her face, laughed louder.

'But you really do not know! Oh, but this is wonderful. You are so obviously with child—the bones of your face, and the great hollows round your eyes, they are not just from the long nights of your husband's loving—he is a lusty lover, is he not? But it is not his passion that has burned your flesh away. The seed has fallen, the fruit is formed—let us hope that all goes well for you.' She waited, her eyes burning on Bianca. Then as the girl was still quiet, she lost her temper completely.

'Yes, little white Sahiba. Let us hope you bear your Lord a son, and do not find that the earrings you wear are given to another, when you bear your husband a girl—as I did. You have no right to those earrings you wear so proudly. They were part of my marriage portion, and should have come back to *me* when Sher Khan put me away—'

Away— Away— Away. The words echoed in Bianca's head, sounding first loud, then faint. The walls of the room moved in on her, and the last thing she saw, as she fell into blackness, was Kurmilla's open mouth, a scarlet cavern that echoed with a screech of laughter, and got mixed up in her head with the voice that was crying sadly, 'Away—away—' in an endless parrot cry.

Ragni's anxious old face was the next thing Bianca saw—and the first thing she thought was, 'Oh—and I broke my promise to say goodbye to Sara—I must go back. *Why* did I faint?' Something stopped her thinking any further. 'Ragni! Do not weep! See, I am perfectly all right, I think that palanquin was not a good thing, the swaying made my head spin—and then the coffee was so strong—' But I did not *drink* any of the coffee, she thought—and memory, cruel and sharp and clear, came back, and told her all that had happened, and as poor Ragni watched, she put her hands to her head, and tore off the earrings, and threw them on the floor, and turned her face into the pillows, and began to weep, sobbing until her breath left her, and she had to fight to get it back, and lay trembling and white faced, and silent at last, while Ragni knelt beside her, rubbing her cold hands and feet, and weeping herself. Then Bianca raised herself on her elbows, and said, 'Ragni, you must tell me something. Was Kurmilla married to Sher Khan?'

Ragni covered her eyes, but Bianca's hand on her shoulder forced her to look up and answer. 'Yes. She was his wife. It was an arranged marriage, not as your marriage. It was like a fever at first, and like a fever it burned out in two or three moons—and then the child—'

'The child was a girl, so he cast her away,' said Bianca in a dead voice, and fell back into her pillows, with such a look on her face, and such a shadow round her eyes and mouth that Ragni cried out and ran to the door, calling on the gate man to send at once for the hakim, the Khanum was ill. She went back to the bed, and looked at the girl lying there, her eyes open and set, looking as if she was dead already.

Sher Khan arrived at the same time as the hakim. He waited, desperate with several anxieties, while the old man saw Bianca, and then spoke to him outside the room. 'She is greatly distressed—her mind is disturbed, in fact. It is too early to be sure that she is with child, but Ragni thinks that she is, and these old women are knowledgeable about such things. I think if you do not speak with her now, it might be good—she is, as I say, hysterical with shock and, I think, rage. These European women behave like mad women. I remember once in Madore—' Sher Khan had no time for his reminiscences, nor for his advice. He walked away, and burst into Bianca's room, and went to her bed, to stand looking down at the rigid figure, with both shame and love making him as angry as he looked.

'Go away,' said Bianca coldly, and turned her head from him. Ragni, on the other side of the bed blenched before the tone used to the Yuvraj—at a gesture from Sher Khan she left the room, in spite of Bianca's cry, 'Ragni—stay here!'

'And now, my girl, before we have any words, listen to me. You will never speak to me in that fashion in front of one of my servants again—that is understood. As for Kurmilla—it was wrong that you were not told before. But I could think of no way to tell you, I could not bear to hurt you. I was a coward. Kassim's mother is estranged from me—I was very angry when she warned me about Kurmilla. If I had not quarrelled with her and been too proud to ask her pardon, I would have begged her to tell you—somehow—that I had been married already. Bianca, this you must accept as being part of my life.' He paused, but Bianca gave no sign of having heard a word he said.

'Bianca—your people do not behave thus, but my people do. By marrying me, you have become of my people. Therefore, you accept what you cannot help. The woman is less than nothing to me—this you must know. She has been put away. That is all that should concern you. You are now my wife.'

He spoke with a firmness that he did not feel. Bianca was

silently weeping, and he longed to fling himself down beside her, and dry her tears with his kisses. Instead, he turned away, and went over to the window to give her time to recover. He was beginning to understand her pride, and therefore the extent of her hurt. A sob, quickly stifled, brought him back to sit beside her.

'Bianca, please—you must not weep like this—listen, and try to understand. It was an arranged marriage—you know, as Khanzada's marriage was arranged. Kurmilla is related to Hardyal and her family are very wealthy, and it was good for the three States, my uncle thought, to bring more gold into our valleys. I did not refuse—I was very young—five years ago! And she—well, she is a woman that men cannot help but desire, and she knows how to make a man burn for her—'

Bianca had stopped crying. She was lying as still as a statue, and Sher Khan, feeling more and more uncertain of himself, hurried on. 'As I say, it seemed a good match in every way—she was very beautiful, and very rich—'

'And I am not rich, and not very beautiful, and I brought no gold to the three States—' Bianca's voice was so choked and husky that he would not have recognised it. The thought of Sher Khan burning with desire for Kurmilla, lying with her through the long nights of loving as he had lain with *her* made her suffocate with a rage that was agony. Sher Khan tried to take her hand. 'Oh child—Bianca, you do not need gold—I would not take gold with you—I love you with all my heart and mind and body—from our first meeting, I loved you, and I chose you myself. It would not have mattered if you had been a street beggar—' Indeed, he thought, it would have been a great deal easier if she had been a beggar girl. He would not have had all that palaver of a wedding—she would have been in the *bibikhana*, and happy to be there. Now, here she lay, bathed in tears, and sick with pride, and he did not know what to do with her.

'Bianca—listen to me—you know I love only you, you *know* it, you know it within your heart—'

Almost, he reached her, his voice held such warmth and sincerity that Bianca felt herself turning to him. But there, in plain sight, was an earring, a gold earring, lying on the floor where she had flung it. The image of Kurmilla interposed, the thought that his voice must have spoken just so to her also—rage and pain fought within her, armouring her against him.

'And you will love me if I bear you a girl, my lord? Or will you build me a house, and let me live alone there with my child—how many houses will you build, Sher Khan, if each wife you take has no son? You could have a village of houses, each one with a woman and a little girl—what could you call the village, Sher Khan Bahadur?'

Sher Khan interrupted her with an exasperated oath, then grasped for the rags of his temper. 'You speak like a fool, Bianca, and would do well to listen to me. If all had been right with my marriage to Kurmilla, she could have had ten daughters, and would have continued to be my wife. Who have you been talking to? Kassim is the heir to the Ruler's throne after me, in any case—did you not know that? Only if you have a son, and he is accepted by the people, will he come to the throne of the three States. The son of the reigning Prince is never automatically the heir in the Thinpahari, surely you knew that?'

Bianca had not known. She remembered Kassim's unfailing kindness, his apparent feeling of family pride in her, and all that had seemed good before, now seemed, in her rage and bitterness to be a sham. 'In that case, if that is true, why did you throw away the beautiful Kurmilla? Do you tire so easily, lord?' Her words were spoken between her teeth, spat out as a little cat spits. Sher Khan got up and walked away from her, trying to keep his temper.

'Kurmilla is of bad blood,' he said quietly. 'Her father was a good man—but her mother was an evil woman. She took as a lover an English man, a man of low breeding who was working on the railways. The family hid the story for shame. The old man, her father, took Kurmilla, and said she was his child, because he could not bear being mocked—and all his life he paid that Englishman money to keep the story quiet.'

Bianca ignored Sher Khan's lowered voice, and obvious distress. She was determined to make a grievance of this too. 'So—because she has white blood, she is put away—a fine future I have then.'

Sher Khan turned and looked at her. 'You are not a fool, Bianca. Try not to speak like one.'

Bianca felt a chill deep inside her body. His voice was an angry snarl, his eyes cold and hard. She had never heard this tone before, nor seen him look so angrily at her.

'Now listen, Bianca. Kurmilla is the child of an evil-living woman and a man of no breeding. Do you equate yourself with such people? I think you should have more pride in your brave and noble father, and the great lady who was your mother. Your blood is as pure as mine, our child will be of good breeding—'

'Our child will be a half caste too,' said Bianca flatly. She did not register that Sher Khan had spoken of her mother in the past tense. She was instantly terrified by the fury on Sher Khan's face.

'MY child,' he said, 'MY child will be of pure blood, born of good parentage on both sides—or so I thought. I trust you will not continue to give me reasons for doubt or regret. Good day, Khanum. I will send your woman to you.'

13

Sher Khan did not come back.

Three days passed, without Bianca seeing him. She bore the terrible solitude as well as she could, too proud to show grief. She was conscious of Ragni's concern and misery, which seemed almost as great as her own, though the old woman did not say anything. Kusma did not appear, and Bianca did not ask for her. The girl was connected in some way with Kurmilla, Bianca realised that, and she hoped never to see her again. She thought of Sara with great sorrow, as if she had lost something of her own flesh and blood, but knew that she could do nothing about the child, without coming in contact with Kurmilla—and that she could not bear.

The days were long—or at least, seemed long. The daylight was short, the long winter nights were coming, the short periods of sunshine, the cold wind that blew from the lake, the mists that hid the mountains—the season fitted Bianca's mood, and she was more unhappy than she had ever been in her life.

On the evening of the fourth day, as she sat sadly in the alcove, looking at the reflections of the lamplight in the black windows, she heard horses, and her heart began a swift tattoo that made her feel sick and giddy. In spite of herself, she watched the door, but when Ragni opened it, it was Kassim who came in, alone. He spoke, at once, with no preamble.

'Bianca, what is this idiocy that is making Sher Khan as easy to deal with as a wounded tiger? And it appears to be turning you into a fountain—what is it?'

Bianca, furious that she could not hide her tears, turned away from him, but his insistence demanded an answer. 'Sher Khan is cruel—he is a monster—'

Kassim nodded. 'This is probably true. All men are at one time or another cruel monsters, and selfish as well. It is understood. But is that a reason for a broken marriage? Oh yes, little aunt. That is what you are playing with now, like a kitten with a snake—the means to finish a marriage.'

Bianca's tears dried on her hot cheeks. She felt a sick dismay, but said, 'Well—it will not be the first marriage he has broken.'

Kassim, who had been standing by the door, came swiftly over to her, and sat down. 'Bianca. You have married an Indian prince. He can take as many women, in or out of matrimony, as he wishes. *But*—this man, Sher Khan, is not like most of his kind. Kurmilla was a mistake, made first by my uncle, and truly, Sher Khan also. Five years ago, Sher Khan was taken by a pair of promising eyes and a figure that would make a stone man lustful. The marriage was an arranged marriage, but Sher Khan could have refused, but I do not know the man who, young and lusty, could have refused Kurmilla when she was trying to please. Sher Khan married a whore. Yes—a whore. She did not come a virgin to his bed. She used her arts to so bemuse him that he was totally deceived until, one day, he came back sooner than he was expected, and found Kurmilla with one of the grooms she had brought with her from the south. There they were, in her bed. This is why the old palace, down in the village is no longer Sher Khan's home. Kurmilla was pregnant, and Sara was born, and no one can say whose child she is. Kurmilla was divorced three years before Sher Khan fell in love with you. He loves you. You—do you love him?'

Bianca could not answer, but Kassim did not pause.

'I know that you love him. You love him so much that you have forgotten everything for his sake. Now, listen to me. If you want him, send for him. He will not come back of his own accord, Bianca. He is a very proud man. Send for him, and send soon—tonight. Do as I say, Bianca and take happiness for your companion again. Life is very short.'

Bianca had listened to him all this while, with her face in her hands. Now she lifted her head to look at him, and even blurred and smudged with grief, her face was beautiful, he thought, watching her. 'Very well. I will send for him. But how are you so wise, Kassim?'

'Bianca, I am wise with the wisdom of envy. I envy you two your joy, and I cannot bear to see it spoiled. You will truly send?'

Bianca nodded, and he took her hand. 'My brave good Bianca. Send quickly. He is driving us all mad, and is as dangerous to deal with as a caged tiger, and a mad elephant mixed together.'

After he had gone, Bianca called Ragni. The old woman came at a run, and between them, with weeping and laughter, they set about removing all traces of grief and tears and sleeplessness—bathed, dressed, and rested, Bianca leaned from her window and found a small bud, the last on the rose bush. 'It is small, and not properly open, but he will know where it comes from. Ragni, go quickly, take a horse—'

'A horse? I, at my age ride a horse? Nay Khanum, if I try to mount a horse, your message will never arrive. Do not worry. I will be swift—' Fluttering and giggling like a bride herself, old Ragni went, and Bianca sat down in the alcove, to wait.

The waiting was not long.

She heard the horse, being galloped hard, only one horse. The bodyguard must have been outstripped. Then hasty footsteps, and the door opened, closed—she turned, and was caught into an embrace that took the breath and bruised her ribs, and she was glad of the pain.

Presently he raised his head and said on a half groan, 'Bianca if anything comes between us again, take a knife, and cut out my heart from my body, but do not let there be anger or hatred between us, for I cannot live like that. These days have been death for me.'

Bianca, drying her eyes, vowed, with an unromantic sniffle, 'We will never quarrel again—never—'

Outside a wind had risen, and the bare branches of a tree shook roughly from precarious shelter a bird, that flew off, crying desolately in the darkness. Bianca's last word seemed to echo in the bird's cry, 'Never—never—' She shivered suddenly, and moved closer into Sher Khan's arms. It was wonderful to be safe, and warm, and together.

Ragni brought them food, and this time it was Bianca who ate, while Sher Khan sat and watched her, and drank copiously of warmed spiced wine, but ate nothing. When the dishes had been taken away, and Ragni had gone, Bianca waited, all her nerves and body clamouring for his lovemaking in a way that brought the blood into her face whenever he looked at her. She felt as if a fire was burning her up from inside her, and found it hard not to get up and fling herself into his arms. But their reunion was too new for this, she felt that he must make the first move. So she sat, and watched him pace about the room while he talked to her, and could make no sense of anything he said because of the way her body was clouding her mind with its demands. Then at last she heard him say, 'And now, my heart, you must sleep—come, let me put you to bed,' and raised her arms to his shoulders as he lifted her, clinging to him, until she found he was disengaging her arms, and none too gently, and then she sank back among her pillows, to hear him say, 'Sleep well, dear love, I am here, in the alcove.'

Bianca, her bare shoulders gleaming in the light from the single lamp that always burned at the head of her bed, stared at him in astonishment. 'Sleep *well*, while you lie in the alcove—Sher Khan, what is it? Have you not forgiven me?' Her voice broke, and she stretched out to catch at his hand, but he moved out of her reach, and answered her roughly, his head turned away.

'Let there be no talk of forgiveness or not—that has nothing to do with it, and you should know that. I cannot come to your bed, girl. In God's name, Bianca, don't start crying again. Do the Europeans teach their daughters nothing? You carry that within you now, that our love-making could harm, and in harming the unborn, I might kill you. Now—is that enough? Do not tempt me past my strength, or I will have to go away from you. Sleep, and let me be.'

He sounded enraged to a point that almost frightened Bianca, but she was past being afraid. She climbed out of bed, shedding her robe as she went to him and clasped her hands behind his neck, forcing him to look down at her. 'Sher Khan, I think my people have more sense than yours, they have certainly never taught me anything about love-making—but you have—and I do not believe that your love can do me any hurt. What old wives' tale have you been told? In any case, Ragni says that it is too soon to tell if I am really with child or not, although she thinks I am. Let us at least make sure that I carry this dangerous cargo before you leave me to sleep cold and alone in my bed—'

Bianca had not shown daring like this before—she had been an ardent responder to his love, but now, with flushed cheeks, she stood naked in his arms, begging for love, in a way that would have been impossible for her a few short weeks before. Scruples and the hakim's advice forgotten, Sher Khan gave a great cry of joy as he snatched her up into his arms, a shout that re-echoed in the room, and outside it, and woke the gate man, who was guiltily conscious of sleeping on duty, and shouted back in his turn, thinking that someone called him—but no one heard his shout.

For ten days, Sher Khan did not leave Bianca; it seemed as if he could not bear to go away from her. They rose late in the mornings to drink their coffee and sat long over it. They rode out, in spite of the cold, muffled to the ears in furs, chasing each other along the lakeside, the horses fresh and fidgety with the cold air, their breath blown like smoke, to hang in the air behind them as they rode. Ragni shook her head disapprovingly over the riding, but Bianca paid her no attention. She was in a dream of ecstasy, she moved in a golden haze of happiness, and it seemed that Sher Khan for once, had no worries. They sat late into the night, talking in the gentle intimacy of satisfied love, growing closer and closer in mind and spirit. He was the Sher Khan she had first met, glowing and vital, bearing no resemblance to the worried man who had left her so often to sit brooding in the night. Friends, lovers, happy companions, they were at ease, and it seemed there were no clouds in their sky.

They had spent one rainy morning sitting close together in the alcove, looking out at the grey lake scarred with the heavy rain. Bianca leaned against the window, her raised knees making a support for Sher Khan's head. His hair, thick and curling, seemed to spark under her fingers as she touched it, loving the lively feel and spring, until he laughed, and caught her hand to his mouth, saying she was lulling him to sleep, and he wanted to stay awake with her. They sat there, in their own climate of warmth and peace, the room glowing with lamplight and with the red flare of the wood fire. The weather outside was of no account to them, except as it served to accent their own warmth and comfort. Bianca saw some hill men going by, laden with logs of wood, their duffle robes dark with rain, but they were no reason for discomfort—they were laughing as they went, carrying their loads easily. There was no poverty in the State, as long as the Ruler was secure, his subjects were sure of food and warmth, even in time of bad harvests, and this year the harvest had been very good.

Ragni, tapping at the door, did not disturb Bianca and Sher Khan, she was part of their happy life, the messenger who had brought Sher Khan back, and held now a special place in their confidence. Sher Khan called 'Enter' without moving his head from Bianca's knees. But Ragni, when she came in, shut the door behind her with a snap, and frowning, began to speak firmly, so that Sher Khan who was not listening, was forced to pay attention. '*He* waits outside, Ragni? Who?'

'The white hakim, Lord.'

Sher Khan sat up suddenly, his tranquillity gone.

'He is here?'

'Yes, Lord. He had ridden down for the winter provisions, and heard some news, and now he asks to speak with you.'

Bianca had made great strides in her mastery of the hill tongue. Now she too sat forward. 'Sher Khan, what does she say? A white man? Who is he? A European?'

'Yes, he is, but not from England. He came here some years ago, and lives in Sardara, beyond Salkot, too far for him to come down here very often, which is good.' He was standing, tying his turban as he spoke, a frown on his face.

'Why do you say that; is he not a good man?'

'Oh, he is good enough, I think. My uncle did not care for him. He is not a priest, but he spoke to the people when he first came here, telling them to give up their worship in the temples and the Mosque, and that they should not have to bring a tithe of everything they harvest to the Panchayat—and various other things—' he remembered, as he spoke, his uncle's rage when he heard that the white man had been advising the young men to refrain from doing their service in the State Forces, and had heard the priests complain that he had advised the young women to refuse their husbands access to their beds when they took another wife.

'I seem to remember my father speaking of him—saying it was not his business to tell the people anything. I think he told the Ruler he was a nuisance and made trouble. Why did he come to the valley at all?'

'He is a healer, and came because of the lepers in the valley below—but they told him to let them be, and he came on up here because it seemed good to him, and he decided to stay here.'

'What did the Ruler do?'

Sher Khan had finished tying his turban, and was shrugging into his *achkhan*, the long embroidered coat with the high collar that Bianca loved to see him wear, it set off his splendid figure so well. 'Oh, he called him in and warned him that if he went on talking to the people and making trouble, he would be sent from Lambagh—and so the man was sensible, for he liked it in the valley, and now he does no more troublemaking. He treats those who go to him with illness, and he has trained some midwives. In fact, I think he is a good man, but he has strange thoughts, and beliefs, and could make trouble. There are always fools who are willing to listen to his kind of talk. Myself, I would have sent him out of Lambagh. I do not care for him. What are you doing?'

He watched Bianca, swiftly plaiting her hair, and putting on her overshirt and head cloth. 'Bianca, you do not wish to see this man.'

'Oh, but I must, Sher Khan. After all, he is European—it would be most rude of me not to see him, and my mother would be very displeased if she thought I had let a visitor go without speaking to him. Also, if he is, as you say, a doctor, well, I think I would like to talk with him, because perhaps it is time—if I am with child, he will know, will he not? And I could have two of his trained women here—'

All the anxiety that had been gathering in the back of Sher Khan's mind came to a head. He imagined, with dismay, the effect it would have on the palace hakim, and his midwives, if Bianca preferred the ministrations of the white hakim. He could understand that she wanted her own people, but why did Reiss wish to see him now, had news filtered through ahead of the messenger that was supposed to come to him? And still Bianca did not know, or did not care to know, what might, or rather, what most certainly had happened in Madore.

Sher Khan considered how he could see Reiss alone—and said eventually, 'Bianca, you can have two of his trained women here later. It is not seemly that Reiss comes here. You can, if you wish, see him before he goes back to his village; we will ask the Begum Mumtaz, Kassim's mother, to come and be with you when you see him. I will talk with him now. Goodbye, Bianca, be wise and quiet, and I will come back to you soon.'

Bianca watched as he went out, walking with the easy swagger that she loved. She turned back to the alcove, preparing to sit and wait for Sher Khan, wondering a little what it was that kept Kassim's mother from her—she had seen her several times, but she would never come to the Chotamahal, and Sher Khan's name was never mentioned. She decided that she would question Kassim the next time she saw him alone.

Suddenly, she heard raised voices outside. It was Sher Khan's voice that she heard, and he sounded furious. There was an answering voice, cold and firm, which was, she thought, speaking English.

She was sitting bolt upright, staring at the door, when it opened and a man came in, followed by Sher Khan, looking as angry as he had sounded. The stranger came forward, and stood a few paces from her, his eyes fixed on her in a most disconcerting stare. She pulled her filmy veil up over her mouth, and stared back at him.

He was tall and blond, with a full beard, and his eyes were very slanted in his high cheekboned face, like the eyes of the Chinese traders she had seen in Madore and in Jindbagh, except that his eyes were not dark—they were a clear and vivid green, and he stared so hard that Bianca blushed scarlet, and putting up her hand, pulled her veil right across her face. Then the man bowed, clicking his heels, and said, 'I am Doctor Johann Reiss, at your service, Lady. I could not believe that the stories I heard of you were true, and I had to see for myself. I have angered the Yuvraj, I fear.'

Sher Khan spoke through clenched teeth. 'Reiss—you have not angered me. You are finished here. You go too far. You will now leave my State.'

Reiss took not the smallest notice of Sher Khan. He said, still looking at Bianca. 'Well—you are very young. Let us hope you make the Yuvraj happier than his wife has done. You know of course, my child, that you have sinned in the eyes of God—and how your poor parents would feel if they could know—but never mind that now. I hear that you are with child. I am a doctor, and I cannot with honesty to my profession, leave you to the uncertain ministrations of one of these so-called hakims. Prince, I propose to examine the Lady—and I think you will allow me to do so. This is not a strong big-boned woman you have taken this time. This is a child—is she yet sixteen? She is very slight, and her bones are small. Could you forgive yourself, if by refusing my help you kill her?'

To Bianca's surprise, Sher Khan bowed his head. 'I will send Ragni,' he said, and with a long look at Bianca, he went out before she could stop him.

'Ah—so. Now this is better. May I sit until your woman comes?'

Bianca was so angry she could hardly speak, and Reiss gave her a sudden smile, and said, 'You are angry with me, child—because of what I said of the marriage? But you are happy?'

Bianca was startled into replying. 'Yes,' she said.

'Yes. I can see that you are. Perhaps it is all for the best. God has reasons for everything that happens, and we mortals cannot understand his reasons always. The Yuvraj—if he is still only the Yuvraj—is a good man, and deserves to be content in his home. But a white woman—this is not a good thing really, because of the succession. I do not like mixed blood.'

Bianca found it impossible to be detached and dignified, this man appeared so honest. 'The succession is already secure. You have lived here long enough, you must know that. Kassim Khan Bahadur is heir to the Ruler, after Sher Khan—and *he* is also of mixed blood—'

Reiss nodded. 'Yes, yes—this is for now. But in these States in the hills, things change so quickly that anything can happen. It is well known that Kassim would like to leave Lambagh and enter the army of the English—and if he is killed, then what? Your child would be the child put forward as successor—but it would be contested, of course. The child of Kurmilla has more right. Kurmilla is his wife—his lawful wife.'

Ragni, who had come in, looked at him with fear and fury.

Bianca determined to keep calm, and she replied quietly, 'You know—again, because you have lived in these hills a long time—you know that there is doubt about Sara's parentage, and Kurmilla has been put away.'

Reiss interrupted her. 'Oh, yes, there is a doubt. But I know that the child is legitimate—I examined her. She is Sher Khan's daughter. Tell me—what do you think?'

The question was abrupt, and Bianca was again surprised into giving an answer she had not meant to give. 'Yes, I think she is Sher Khan's child. It is the eyes—' she stopped, angry with herself, feeling she had been disloyal to Sher Khan, but Reiss, nodded, satisfied.

'Yes, the eyes, the carriage of the head, and other things. But in any case, it will not signify. Rulers, and States and thrones—all these things are of no importance in the final scheme of things. Time will sweep all these things away, and leave only humanity, and human beings.'

With a swift movement he bent forward, and placed his hand gently on Bianca's stomach. 'What you have here is important—new life. Are you sick in the mornings? No? That is good. How long is it since your menses stopped? Nearly three months. I see. Well, I think you carry a child. You are small, but you are a strong girl and should have no trouble, though you are very slender—here, and here—still, you look well. Now I must make an internal examination. Ragni—bring me hot water and soap. Now, Lady, here is nothing for shame or embarrassment. Lie back, please, raise your knees so—'

Binca endured his swift examination with closed eyes, and burning cheeks. He was quick and expert, and when it was over he smiled at her, a kind gentle smile that transformed his face. 'There. That is over. I will come again in three months, when I hope the worst of the snow will be finished, and the passes will open again. I go back tomorrow, and will not worry about you. You are a good strong girl. Eat well, sleep well, do not raise your arms over your head, and do not lift anything heavy.' Bianca, who was barely allowed by Ragni to blow her own nose, sat and listened to him in astonishment.

Ragni said, with a sidelong look at her mistress, 'And riding, Hakim Sahib? What about riding?'

'Riding will do no harm for another two or three months—but gentle riding. No jumping, and nothing done to exhaustion.' Bianca shot a look of triumph at Ragni. She was wild with impatience, and humiliation. Why did Sher Khan not come to take this extraordinary man away? His corncrake, heavily accented voice was beginning to make her head ache. It was a revelation to her that she could feel no kinship with this man, who, after all, though not of her own country, was a European—and seemed far more foreign than any of the hill people. Bianca wondered for a moment if her own father and mother would seem strange to her too, if she had become so much a part of Sher Khan's life that she would never fit into an English way of life again. Her own beloved parents! No, they would always be close to her, and yet, her mother had never seemed to have come to stay in India. She always spoke with longing of the day when her husband's service would be over, and they would be able to return 'home'. Home to Bianca had always been Jindbagh, or Madore—not her mother's dream place, Ireland, which sounded terrible to Bianca, a place of rain, mist and cold, full of people who wore grey clothes and talked of nothing but horses and servants and cooking, like the raw-boned ladies of the officers of British regiments that she had seen in Madore. For a minute or two Reiss and his admonitions were unheard as Bianca sat warm in her cushions, admiring her graceful woollen robes, thanking her fates that she would never have to leave the lovely land of India now. She was a part of it, forever.

Her wandering thoughts were recalled by a tap on the door, and Sher Khan came in. 'Reiss. You have leave to go. I have a litter for you, because of the rain. If you do not leave at once, I think the road over the hills to your village will be impassable—' His voice was cold, and he did not return Reiss's smile. The doctor did not seem at all upset by this. He made Bianca a heel-clicking bow, and told her he would see her in the morning, and left the room with Sher Khan. Then he spoke directly to Sher Khan.

'Your Lady is strong and well, and will, God willing, bear you a child in about six months. Do not, I beg of you, allow any of your hakims to give her anything. Highness—you will tell me if there is news out of the plains?'

Sher Khan nodded. 'Word will be sent. I will trust that the word stays with you, and goes no further.'

'Where else would I send news, Prince?' His tranquillity was in marked contrast to Sher Khan's obvious displeasure.

'It could be sent to many places—over the passes, and the great river, for instance. The reward, I feel sure, would be large.'

'Whereas you offer me no reward for my silence—at least

you pay me that honour, Highness—' Reiss bowed again, smiling, and left.

Ragni, when Sher Khan returned into Bianca's room, after a glance at his face, went away, closing the door after him.

There was silence in the beautiful room. Sher Khan broke it, looking over to where Bianca was sitting rigidly in the alcove. 'That man,' he said, 'that man is a thrice accursed fool.'

Bianca, smarting under various little wounds of the spirit, said tartly, 'Well—he may be accursed, but he did not seem to be a fool. What he said of Kurmilla and her child is to be expected, with two of your wives sitting in one small village. I wish Kurmilla could go *away*.'

'Well, it is impossible, I fear. She has nowhere to go. Her family will not take her back—and at least here, under my eye, she can bring no more shame on my name.'

He eyed Bianca apprehensively. She was now at her mirror, peering at herself, and did not seem to like what she saw. 'I am thin and small, and have a bony face, and no front—' She turned away from the mirror, and said, 'I do not know why you chose me out of all the big-chested, big-mouthed girls you could have taken. And I have no money either.'

'I told you why I chose you,' said Sher Khan. He had been told by Reiss that there was trouble brewing beyond the passes to the north, and that the garrison at Sadara was short of arms. It was hard for him to put the right emphasis into his voice when he spoke to Bianca, who was looking ruffled and petulant. She was silent for a few minutes, then said, 'You told me that Kassim is your heir. What happens if he is killed?'

'We hope that his chances of being killed are no greater than normal. But if he is, then our child, be it boy or girl, is the heir—if the people agree. And they will agree. It is the custom.'

'And if I have no child?'

Sher Khan sighed deeply. 'Bianca—what has this idiot of a man said to you, to start all this story again?'

'He is no idiot. He told me that Kassim wants to join the army in the plains, and that if he did, and I had no child, Sara is the heir. Her mother, of course, would have to come back here, would she not?'

'She cannot come *back* here, as you say—she has never lived in this place. She will never hold any authority in this State—or any other of the three States. She is merely the mother of a child that is possibly mine, as it was born while Kurmilla was my wife. Bianca—let us talk of other things—please.'

'No. I wish to talk of this. I think I shall bring Sara to the Chotamahal. If she is part of you, then she should be here, not thrown away like rubbish—'

'You will not bring her here.' Sher Khan's temper was gone. He glared at Bianca, and Bianca glared back at him, and he could not imagine how he had ever thought her either lovable, or beautiful. She looked now, like a little cat, ears back, spitting defiance.

'I shall bring her here, and I shall be glad of her company. I am lonely all the time—'

'Lonely—when I have been shut in here with you for the last ten days—how can you say you have been lonely?'

Shut in—was that how he looked on the wonderful days they had spent together? Bianca turned away with filling eyes, and Sher Khan, instead of taking her into his arms, said, 'Oh Bianca—*not* more tears. I cannot bear it. Could we not have one discussion without tears? I shall drown in the fountain of tears you have shed, you seem to have an inexhaustible supply. That child has been a trouble since she was born. It would have been better if she had never lived, for she has been used as a pawn in all Kurmilla's little plots, and now it seems that you are going to use her as a stick to beat me with every time I displease you—and God himself knows how much I have to think about at present without having to soothe the ruffled feelings of silly girls.'

Bianca flew at him like a little cat he had thought she resembled. He caught her hands as they clawed at him, and said through his teeth, 'So ho, my little dove has claws—listen you to me for a minute—'

'I will not listen!'

'Oh yes you will—' Sher Khan accompanied his words with a hard shake that jerked Bianca's head. 'You will not go to the Lalkoti again. Nor will you bring that child here—Bianca, can't you understand? She is a reminder of my most unhappy years, when I was, before the whole State, the husband of a woman who, chosen by the Ruler as my wife, and as the mother of my children, debased my bed and presented me with Sara—about whose parentage there is great doubt. Do you wish my shame to be forever before me?'

'Then send them away.'

'I cannot. For one thing, her family will not accept her. For another, she is a dangerous bitch, and set free could bring great trouble to me. As I told you before, she is better where I can watch her.' She would be better still got quietly and permanently out of the way, he thought morosely, remembering how various friends of his had suggested that she be given a quieting drink—one that would make her sleep for ever.

Bianca's jealousy rose suddenly as she had a mental picture of Kurmilla's perfect face and figure, and remembered that Sher Khan had admitted that he had found her pleasing at first. 'Yes, indeed—I can see that it is better for her to stay here—then you can visit her, no doubt, when I grow dull and boring.'

'You are dull and boring now, when you speak like that. Listen, Bianca, I am going now, but I have one thing to say. I will not have these stupid hysterics about a child that may or may not be mine, and a woman I have put away for ever. Behave as my wife should behave, or else—'

'Or else? I suppose you will put me away. But I would like you to know that I carry a child within me now, that be it girl or boy, or even, as seems likely to me, a monster, you will not be able to repudiate it—for all the three valleys and the hill villages know that *I* came virgin to your bed.'

She faced him, so hurt and angry that Sher Khan's anger died, and his hard grip on her shoulders relaxed. He pulled her into his arms. 'My dear love—'

Held against his heart, Bianca did not cry, she was too angry. But Sher Khan was a man of experience and he called on it all to bring her back, finally apologising so humbly that he made her laugh. 'I am a bad-tempered, evil-natured ape from the mountains, and I do not know why you have given me your love—but you do love me? For you have all my heart and soul and body in your keeping, for ever, Bianca.'

Bianca was not quite ready to forgive him, though she was

clinging to him as they stood in the alcove. 'You *shook* me,' she said accusingly.

'Yes. I shall probably do it again, because you are very enraging—but only little shakes, and never I promise you, when you are carrying my child. Bianca, believe me, I have so much to think of, and worry about, that my temper is not my own, but whatever I do or say, never forget that I love you—never.'

Bianca turned in his arms, and kissed him with all her heart.

'I will not forget. And you must not forget either. But what made you so cross? Did that man bring you bad news? Is there some news from Madore that has upset you?'

Sher Khan began to speak, looked at her, and changed his mind, and his words. He walked impatiently about the room. 'It is impossible to say if the news he brings is good, or bad, or even true—he confuses the story so much with his own interpretations. You see, he does not believe in Rulers and the ruled. All men must be equal, and none have authority. So when he says this or that is happening in the hills, he says it as if it was a great blow struck for the freedom of the peasants—as if the peasants could live without us! Oh God and the devil, I should have done with the man, and put him away. But I do not think he is an evil man, just an accursed nuisance. Enough. Let us forget everything for a little while, my soul and heart, and talk about ourselves.'

Late into the night the lamplight glowed from their room into the darkness outside, where snow fell, a thick white curtain that brought a heavy silence to settle over the village, and the Chotamahal, walling them in with their happiness. Bianca sat in the beautiful warm room, and listened to Sher Khan speaking of their future, and of the coming spring, and remembered nothing but the delight of being with him.

14

Morning brought Kassim, and the outside world, and trouble. Kassim had not been up to the Chotamahal for all the time of their happy reunion. Now he came in, stamping snow from his boots, and with him came, it seemed, a hostile wind, a dark and stormy sky. The climate of the warm, comfortable room changed with his coming, and was one with the snow-tossed grey weather outside.

Sher Khan looked up at him, and said nothing, and gave him no greeting. Bianca looked from one to the other, and her glad cry of welcome died on her lips. Kassim did not look at her. He answered Sher Khan's lifted eyes. 'Yes. The messenger has been seen. Before nightfall, I think, news should be here—it has been necessary to send a palanquin to Lungri Pass. The way has been very hard. Will you come, Sher Khan Bahadur?'

Sher Khan was already on his feet, and pulling on the boots that Ragni brought him. Almost, he forgot to say anything to Bianca, his whole mind was with the news that he would shortly have to hear. Kassim's hand on his arm stopped him, and he turned back. He had never embraced Bianca in front of Kassim before, but now he put his arms round her, and whispered close to her ear, 'Wait for me my dear love, I shall come to you as soon as I can—rest, and stay warm—'

He loosed her clinging arms gently, and went out quickly, followed by Kassim, who had not spoken to Bianca, but who tried to smile at her as he left.

The sound of their horses was muffled by the heavy snow on the road, but looking from her window, Bianca saw them already almost out of sight, riding fast, the snow kicking up into a long plume behind them. She turned back to drink her coffee, wondering what news the messenger could have brought that would send them off in such a hurry. She looked out at the flurrying snow, and decided to do just as Sher Khan said—rest and keep warm. Later, she would bathe, and get Ragni to dress her hair in some new way, and wear the brilliant scarlet robes that Ragni was always urging her to wear. Bianca preferred the soft natural cream of the undyed wool, but the scarlet was warm, and would give her colour, and please Sher Khan. Planning her day, she sat, half in a dream, forgetting, or making herself forget anything that might have troubled her. She felt lazy, and was glad that she did not have to do anything—that foolish man yesterday, with his warnings not to lift, or stretch! Bianca stretched like a little cat, and then curled into a more comfortable position, and watched Ragni put the room in order, and drank more coffee, and fell into a light sleep. Ragni took the coffee tray and went out without disturbing her.

A light tapping on the window woke Bianca. Was it a broken branch of the rose bush, or a bird, snow blinded? Bianca sat up, and pressed her face close to the glass to look out into the swirling whiteness, and looking back at her was a woman's face. With a start that made her blood leap, Bianca fell back from the window. Had she imagined that staring face, with snow lying thick on the head cloth? She could not force herself back to the window, but did not have to, for minutes later she heard a stealthy movement outside her door, and then the woman herself slid into the room, and stood before her.

Bianca kept the silence of shock, staring at the woman—a bedraggled figure, in snow-drenched clothes, with a constant shiver running over her body. It was Kusma—she flung herself down at Bianca's feet.

'Khanum—I would not come to you. I know what trouble I caused, but I was instructed and obeyed. But now I come of my own wish, to say to you that the little Sara is sick, sick to the point of death. She asks for you, and I know you would wish to have news of her. Oh Khanum, if you can, go to her—go. I must not stay. I hear Ragni coming, and she will kill me if she finds me here. But I had to come and tell you, I love the little one, and I could not see her as she is now, and not come and tell you.'

As swiftly as she had come, Kusma slipped through the door again. Bianca would have believed that she had dreamed the whole episode, if there had not been a pool of melting snow on the floor. Almost without thinking, she got up, and fetched a cloth and rubbed the patch dry, and put the cloth back in the bathroom.

Ragni came in, and Bianca said, as if the words were written somewhere for her to say, 'Ragni—I have a great desire for fresh parattas and vegetable curry—could you make me some?'

The old woman was delighted. 'Of course you have a great desire! I shall go now, and make you all you can eat.' Clucking with pleasure, she went out, and Bianca watched her go, and waited for a few minutes, and then got up, and robed herself in her warmest clothes, with her hooded fur cape over everything, and went quietly out, and down the steps to the gate. All the time, a voice in her head said, 'What are you doing? Sher Khan will not forgive this—' and another voice answered, and said, 'But you promised Sara you would see her again—you promised—' and she felt giddy and confused, but went steadily on, through the gate to where Sutla the bodyguard was sitting, his horse and himself sheltered in a rush matting shed. Sutla stood up as soon as he saw her, full of astonishment as seeing his mistress out in such weather, and dressed for riding. When he heard where she wanted to go, his face changed.

'Khanum—I regret, but my lord has ordered me on pain of dismissal, to prevent any visiting of the Lalkoti—I dare not let you go there. Nay, then, Khanum, do not be angry with me, I must obey my lord. In any case, this weather is not for visiting—' Where was that old fool of a serving woman, he thought wretchedly, his mistress looked strange, and ill—but she spoke quite calmly in the end, when she had looked at him in silence for a minute, an unnerving stare from wild blue eyes.

'Well then, Sutla, if you dare not, you dare not. But if you are going to sit out here, with Bedu, should you not at least loosen his girth, and cover him with a blanket?'

She wandered over to the horse, and Sutla followed her, thanking his gods that she was so easy to deal with. Some women in her position would not have cared to be told they could not go where they wished by a sowar, and he had been told that European women were very self-willed. But this girl was a beauty, and as gentle as a lamb. He stood admiring her, as she spoke to the horse—and then she suddenly swung herself up into the saddle, and kicking the startled horse into a fast canter, was gone in a spray of snow, before he could even cry out. Sutla ran for the gate, yelling for his lance naik and a second horse and telling himself that his job as bodyguard to the Begum Sahiba was gone forever.

Bianca rode as fast as she could down the untrodden snow of the road to the Lalkoti. She did not have time to wonder what her reception at the house would be, before she arrived at the gate.

There was no gate man to take the horse—she slid down from his back unaided, and tied his reins to a post beside the gate man's empty hut, so that he had some shelter from the snow. She went up the steps, and stopped at the high, closed door. No one answered her calls, so she pushed at the door, and it opened, and she went in.

The hall was empty, there was no one to greet her. The hall was also as before, very dirty. Dust lay in drifts on the window sills, the shutters were cobwebbed—the wall marked in one corner by the red stain of betel. Bianca thought—dust? Where do you get dust from, in such snowy weather?—and knew that nothing had been cleaned here, properly, for weeks. She opened the door of the room where she had sat drinking coffee with Kurmilla on her last disastrous visit, but it was dark, the shutters unopened. She closed the door again, and heard the silence of the house. It had an emptiness about it—where was Kurmilla, and where was the sick child—was Sara so ill that she had been taken away? She pushed open another door, and faced a dimly lit room, with an untidy, rumpled bed—and on it, seated staring at the door, was Sara. Her eyes, enormous with fright, slowly lit with pleasure.

'Oh Miss—you have come. How good this is, I am lonely, now we can talk—I am sorry there is no fire, it went out, and ayah did not come back to light it—'

Bianca looked closely at her, her hands on the thin little bird bones of the child's shoulders. Seen on the soiled, unmade bed, in the sordid room, Sara was like a blossom, clean and fresh, and as far as Bianca could see, not ill at all.

'Sara—are you well?'

'Yes—I am very well. But I am very hungry. My mother

was busy with some friends who came in the night, and no one brought me food. Listen—my stomach makes sounds—'

Bianca, remembering the unkempt look of the house, and the silence brooding in it, wondered where Kurmilla and her friends could be. All she could hear was Bedu, stamping and blowing outside, his bridle rattling and ringing to the tossing of his head.

'When did you see your mother, Sara?'

'Oh, she put me to bed last night. But then I heard some friends come, because I was still awake—and I have not seen my mother since—and the ayah did not come to dress me this morning—'

Bianca decided instantly what she must do. Sara would come back with her to the Chotamahal. There was no one in the house, she was sure. Where Kurmilla had gone, heaven knew—but Bianca had no intention of leaving Sara here alone and hungry any longer.

'Where are your clothes, Sara—in here?'

She opened a cupboard, and stared unbelievingly at a stained, tattered uniform jacket. For a moment her mind could register nothing but surprise. The jacket was, she thought, a Sepoy's, but torn and bloodstained, the insignia torn away.

Sara's voice from the bed roused her, and she shut the cupboard quickly. 'Is there nothing there? But I am not cold in bed. Perhaps the ayah took my clothes to wash.'

'But surely you have more than one set of clothes—oh never mind that now—I am going to take you back with me—perhaps there are some clothes you can wear, in here.'

She opened another cupboard, and the door creaked loudly in the silence. The cupboard had only sheets and blankets in it, but the door, although she was holding it, still seemed to creak—or did the noise come from elsewhere? Bianca whirled round in time to see Sara turn her head and stare at the bedroom door. 'What—what is it, Sara?'

The child looked back at her with wide puzzled eyes. 'It was one of the friends of my mother—but he did not come in—'

Bianca was suddenly terrified. Something in the silence, the emptiness of the house—and yet, it was *not* empty, and the silence seemed to have stealthy undertones. Was that a footfall, hesitating and then hurrying away? She ran to pick up Sara, and then carrying her, went to the door. It was urgent to go now—she had no doubt but that there was danger in the house. It spoke softly in the muffled noises outside, and whined of death in a sudden rush of feet in the hall—feet that were shod in squeaking shoes, not the soft slippers of the local people. Danger rose like an evil mist in the smell of smoke that came faintly into the room—the door, Bianca found, was locked.

Sara did not seem afraid. 'My mother often locks the door. She says that if she is going out, it is better that I am locked in—then no one can take me away.'

Yes, perhaps. Perhaps the man had looked in and had not seen Bianca in the shadow of the cupboard, and had locked the door as usual—but he must have seen Bedu, tied outside.

The smoke seemed thicker. A badly-lit fire in one of the rooms? But this smoke was too thick for woodsmoke, it was heavy smoke, that did not rise in blue coils like woodsmoke, it clung round the corners of the room, and made her cough.

Bianca put Sara back on the bed, and ran to the shuttered window. It was quite immovable. She could not hear if Bedu was still outside, for now all the creakings in the house seemed to have come together into one loud crackling roar, which grew louder as she listened.

'What—*what* is that, Miss?'

Sara was sitting, staring at the smoke, which was strangely lessening, but in its place Bianca saw an orange glow, a lance of brilliant light under the door. It was dark in the room, and Bianca knew that it must be dusk outside. Ragni would have missed her by now—the gate man would have been sent down to bring horses, Sutla would not have tried to follow on foot—but why had no one come yet? The Lalkoti stood in a fold between two hills—how long before someone saw the glow of the fire, and gave the alarm? Too long for us, she decided. The heat in the room had been building up. As she watched, she saw the floor-boards near the door blacken and add their own contribution to the smoke.

Bianca went back to the cupboard where the uniform was, and snatched up the cavalry sabre with its stained, dull blade. Two hands on the hilt, she beat with it on the shutters, but they were made of good stout wood, and were firm. After a few minutes frantic slashing, she had to stop, panting for air. Sara was beginning to cough.

'Miss—I think we should go from here. *Why* does someone not come and open the door?' She was fighting tears, and Bianca was despairing. How long before the smoke choked them, or would the fire get them first? If she took Sara into the cupboard, would that protect them?

The cupboard! Something else that she had seen in the cupboard nagged at her mind—she snatched at the door, and threw it wide—yes, there it was, a long-barrelled rifle. She had no idea if her sudden hope was justified. 'Wrap a blanket over your head, Sara,' she ordered, her voice terse with strain. '*Quickly*—'

The little girl obeyed her, and came to stand behind her, and Bianca put the muzzle of the gun against the lock of the shutters, shut her eyes and pulled the trigger.

The world filled with fire and smoke and pain. Dimly, she could hear Sara crying out to her, and she fought her way back to consciousness, to find the window open, and that the door of the bedroom had fallen in and a great wall of flame was leaping in its place. She tore at Sara, one of her arms seemed to be uesless, and she had to pull at the child one handed. Somehow they were up on the window sill, and the sweet evening air was in front of them, but there was a six-foot drop to the ground. She took Sara by one arm, and lowered her as far as she could, and then dropped her, and heard the breath thud out of her lungs as she landed. The flames were moving closer when she stood up, and jumped, and felt pain lash up all through her body when the ground was suddenly and solidly under her.

The sound of sobbing brought her back to bitter coldness and a darkness that was one sided—behind, terribly close behind, were the flames of the Lalkoti—now a complete torch, each window and cupola outlined in glorious scarlet.

Little desperate hands were pulling at her. 'Miss—wake up—the fire is too close to you—'

Sara!

Bianca's memory flooded back. With an effort that made her sweat with pain, she pulled herself to her knees, and then, very slowly, to her feet. Sara went ahead of her, still holding a fold of her robe. They staggered out of the smoke, and away from the flames, which seemed to be trying to pull them back, and came up hard against a barrier—the wall to which Bedu had been tied.

Bianca had no hope of finding him, but felt her way along the wall to the gate—and they were out of the compound, and on the road before she realised that it was no longer so dark, only twilight in fact, and that the moving shadow on the other side of the road was Bedu, his broken reins trailing, his eyes wild with fright, but his training still holding him near at hand.

'Oh *Bedu*—' Bianca's voice broke on a sob, and Sara's sobs became loud frightened crying at once. Bianca soothed her to silence, and called again to Bedu. She was deperately afraid of making too much noise. The house could not have caught fire by itself; where were the people who had started the fire, leaving herself and the child locked in a room? The house was now burning so strongly that the villagers should be here in crowds—but there was no one, and it was getting darker. She continued to call to Bedu, and he came slowly towards her until she could catch the trailing reins and hold him still under her soothing hand. But mounting him was another matter. A great throbbing pain had begun to beat in her body, and every move was agony.

'Sara—can you ride? Can you get up on Bedu's back?'

The child's tears had dried now that Bianca seemed so calm. 'Of course I can ride—see—'

She scrambled up as agile as a monkey, and sat looking down at Bianca. 'Now you, Miss—'

Bianca bit her lips and tried, but her legs would not raise her, and the pain was growing worse. 'I cannot,' she said eventually, leaning sick and faint against Bedu's side. 'I cannot mount.'

Sara looked as if she could very easily cry again, but she made a valiant effort, and looked about her in the fast gathering dusk, and as the flames of the house leapt higher, she saw what she was looking for. 'See—there is a big stone there—when I was very small, I used to mount from that—could you mount from it do you think?'

Bianca saw the rock she meant—it appeared to be miles away, but was in fact only a few steps. Once beside it, she dragged herself on to it, inch by agonising inch, and at last forced herself into the saddle. Disaster threatened again as soon as she was mounted, the first step Bedu took made her cry out in agony, and Sara, frightened, joined her cries with sobs of her own. Bianca clung for dear life to the pommel, and told Sara to guide the horse. 'Go to the Chotamahal, and I will hold on as well as I can. If I fall off, Sara, listen to me—try to remember where I fall, and go as fast as you can to the Chotamahal and send back for me—but do not stop on any account.'

The journey passed in a blur of pain and Bianca could not see the lights of the Chotamahal, her eyes were so blinded with agony. But when Bedu stopped, and she felt Sara sliding down, she looked up, and there was her home, the lights on, and all, it seemed, in order, with the gate keeper running to her, exclaiming in horror. Bianca whispered, 'Ragni—get Ragni—' before she finally fainted, falling heavily into the man's arms as he started to shout for Ragni.

15

The last few days of travelling had been terrible for Goki.

Ghila, the son of the headman of Patkote, had doubted that he would bring her and the child Muna alive through the high snow-swept passes of the last stage of their journey. But Goki, clinging to the horse, Muna wrapped warmly and tied to her back, had battled grimly on, her spirit holding her old body together, until at last they had clattered into Lambagh, and the journey was over.

The child called Muna was lifted down, and then willing hands were raised to help Goki. She could not stand, and they would have carried her indoors, but she refused, croaking out her demand to see Sher Khan Bahadur himself.

It was then that Kassim and Sher Khan had ridden down, and Sher Khan, flinging himself off his horse, had rushed to raise Goki. But she refused his aid, and struggled to her feet, and stood facing him. She took from her bosom the two precious packages she had carried for so long, and held them out to him.

'Sher Khan Bahadur, your uncle, the late Ruler, sent you this—and by the grace of all the gods I was able to bring you this. It is only a rag, but it was soaked in their blood. I could not bring his ashes, so I bring you the rag instead.'

Sher Khan, his face a mask, touched his hand to his breast and to his forehead, and bowed very low, before he took the small packages from her.

The priests, and the Moulvi, already warned, were there, and the carefully-wrapped piece of bloodstained rag, torn from the Ruler's turban by Goki in that grey dawn so many weary days before, was reverently received, and taken away to the sound of chanted prayers, and the roar of the conch shell and the beating of drums. There would be a ceremonial burning later. Now the news had to be broken to the people. There would not be a home in the valley that had not lost a member of their family, a son, or a brother or a husband. But above all, they had lost their leader, the man who had ruled them for so long, the one they trusted, and loved.

At first, as the message went round, it was received with blank disbelief. Then, as Sher Khan raised the green fire of the Emerald Peacock, never removed from the neck of the Ruler until his death, a great cry rang out, and the people of Lambagh began to mourn. No one noticed the red glow in the sky towards the lake—there was too much to think about and too much desperate grief.

Sher Khan, after telling Kassim to send messages throughout the three States rode off to tell the news to Bianca, and riding down, saw no flames, indeed saw nothing but the lights of the Chotamahal, and thought of nothing but how he could tell the girl the terrible news.

In the Chotomahal, Bianca had lain, still and cold, and it seemed to Ragni, without breathing, ever since she had been carried in and put to her bed. The hakim, hurriedly called for, did all that seemed right to him, and went away again, the messengers sent to Sher Khan did not return, just as Sutla had gone off that morning and had not been seen again. Ragni, after clearing up the stained cloths, and the sad, bloodclotted clothing, stooped again over the bed. A flutter of breath still moved between Bianca's pallid lips. At least she was still alive—but where was the Yuvraj? Ragni felt as if she were isolated, the only person alive in the mountains—or at least, still alive—it did not appear to her that her mistress would last for much longer.

She went to the door, intending to call the gate keeper, and ask if there was any sign of anyone, and as she put her hand to the latch, she heard a sound outside. She opened it, but at first, saw no one. Then she saw a movement, and stood fearful, looking out. There was a sound of muffled sobbing, and a very small figure stumbled towards her.

'Oh child—we forgot you—come with me, and be warmed and fed—no—wait—I cannot leave the Khanum—' Ragni stood, distracted, half in and half out of the room, but the child knew what she wanted, and was in through the door before Ragni could stop her, and had run over to the bed.

'Oh, Miss! Why is she so still? Is she dead?' Sara asked, her her eyes turned in horror on Ragni.

'The gods forbid, no—but she is very sick.'

Ragni had no control over the situation any more. Where was the Yuvraj—and the child, this child of all others—what of her mother? Sara's story was a strange mixture of a burning house, her mother's friends, the Lady—whom she called 'Miss' steadfastly, had obviously saved Sara from some peril, and had lost her own child as a result. Disaster upon disaster, thought Ragni, and wept, and Sara wept too, standing cold and hungry and frightened in the middle of the bright warm room.

Bianca returned to consciousness of a sort, to hear their combined weeping. It seemed terribly bright in the room—FIRE! Her scream was in reality only a faint whisper, but the child heard her, and ran to her. 'Miss—are you awake? Please wake—I am so cold and very hungry, and I have no proper clothes, and I am dirty—'

Ragni pushed her aside and bent over the bed. Bianca's eyes, sunk into her head, looked at her with nothing of recognition in them, no expression at all. Ragni looked, she heard something that made her turn to the alcove, and hurry across to throw it open. From the village below, there came the sound of a terrible wailing—Ragni pulled the window shut again and, back to Bianca's bedside, sank down beside it in complete despair. The end of the world had come—and she was alone with a dying girl. Something terrible must have happened to have caused that sound she had heard—and the absence of the Yuvraj was now explained. He must have been killed.

It was then, in the full dark of the winter evening that Sher Khan came. He came in so quietly that Ragni did not hear him. Sara, standing by the bed, stared at him from big frightened eyes, but Sher Khan did not see her, and bent over Bianca.

The child saw that as he looked at Bianca, Sher Khan wept—tears fell from his cheeks and down on to the pale face on the pillow. This, to Sara, was the most frightening thing that had ever happened. This man who wept, was a strong man, a man she had been taught to fear. What terrible thing could have happened to make him weep? All her life, Sara remembered seeing Sher Khan weep. The sight dried her own tears, and she stood there, ignored by everyone, in dark despair, fearing some unnameable horror.

Bianca opened her eyes, and this time she saw clearly. Sher Khan—she smiled, and tried to raise her arms, but they were too heavy. Sher Khan's face was very blurred and seemed to keep moving. If only she could pull his head down so that she could see him more clearly. Sher Khan saw the ghost of the smile he loved flutter about her grey mouth—he bent to lay his mouth on hers, listening to the voice that spoke in his mind.

'She is dying—your girl is going from you. Kiss her quickly, before her lips are too cold to kiss—'

The room, so bright and warmly beautiful, closed in around them, as so often before, engulfing their world in silence. But now it was a silence not of timeless ecstasy, but of timeless pain.

Down in the old Lambagh palace, Goki began to wake. She had not slept for long, but by the time she woke, the story of the burning of the Lalkoti, and of the young Begum's ride and its terrible result, had already reached the village, and added itself to the general distress that was filling the minds of the people. The Begum was said to be at death's gate.

When Goki stirred, the women around her brought her tea before they told her anything. Watching her drink it, they wondered if the news they would give her now would kill her, so old and frail, huddling there in her blankets, far too old to have survived such a journey—and now this news on top of it. Half filled with pity for her, half with expectations of drama, they waited for her to drink her tea, and then told their story.

Goki listened quietly, and then stood up slowly, reaching for her clean woollen robes. 'Is there a palanquin ready?' Her voice was strong, even though cracked. The women assured her that there was a palanquin.

'Good. I go now to the Chotamahal—'

She was hampered in her forward stride to the door by something that clung about her leg. One of the women swooped down and lifted the obstruction away. 'It is the little one,' she said, 'Muna—'

Goki looked briefly into Muna's appealing, frightened face—so many strangers round her, and now her only friend seemed to be leaving her. But Goki said firmly, 'Muna comes with me,' and went out to the palanquin like a queen, surrounded by the women, and Muna, warmly wrapped, was ensconced beside her. The carriers raised the palanquin, checked, broke into the quick lope of the carrying coolies, and the palanquin swayed off into the snowy darkness, a lantern held in the hand of the spare coolie who was running ahead to light their way.

Goki entered the warm silence of the bedroom of the Chota-mahal, like a person returning home. She knew this room well. Once it had been the *bibikhana* of the old Ruler, and Goki as a girl had shared many nights with her royal lover here. She cast a contemptuous glance at Ragni, weeping in a corner, and surged forward to the bed, Muna forgotten behind her. The child, bereft, looked round. There was only one other person in the room, if you did not see the figures on the bed. Sara, herself at a loss, moved forward and took Muna's hand. Together they went to the alcove, and sat, eyeing each other. At some time on that dreadful evening, Ragni had put milk there, on the table in the alcove, and fruit, and little almond cakes. The children ate, and drank, and presently, curled like puppies close together for warmth, they slept.

Goki, at the bedside, put her hand on Sher Khan's shoulder, and after a moment, reluctant, he raised his head. It seemed to him that the body he held in his arms was already growing cold and stiff.

'Goki—she is dead—'

There was a loud wail from Ragni. Goki, with a jangle of bracelets, pushed Sher Khan aside, and bending over Bianca, took one of the cold limp hands in hers.

'Child of love, Bianca—ah what fools you have about your house now, Maharaj! Tell that weeping idiot, who was always a fool, to bring hot bricks, and hot milk, and warmed blankets—move, woman, move!' Ragni stumbled, galvanised, through the door. Sher Khan himself became another pair of hands, another pair of feet to hurry to do Goki's bidding.

Presently, her body packed in warm blankets, her feet being roughly chafed by Sher Khan, Bianca began to move. Sugar-stiff milk was dribbled into her mouth. Sher Khan, staring from the end of the bed, saw the sunken eyes open, heard the faint

'Goki' from the colourless lips, saw the incredulous joy in the white face. He stood up, and went to look out of the alcove window, not seeing the children or anything, but at last beginning to hope that Bianca would live after all. His sight cleared—away to the west of the lake he saw a dull red glow in the darkness, that could only mean fire—where? He went and spoke softly to Goki, and went out to shout for the gate keeper and question him. So, for the first time, he heard the story of Bianca's ride.

When he went back into the room, he saw that Bianca was fully conscious, her hand firmly clasping one of Goki's old hands, her face wet with tears. Goki had told her the news from Madore. Sher Khan wondered that she had taken the risk of the shock that such news would give Bianca at such a time, but he was guiltily conscious also of a great relief that he had not had to tell her.

Bianca turned to him as soon as he came over to the bed, and as he took her in his arms, he felt the shudder of her suppressed weeping. 'They are dead, Sher Khan. They died before we had even reached Lambagh—'

There was nothing he could do but smooth back the roughened hair from her forehead. Her face was still smudged with dirt and streaks of black shadowed her temples and cheeks, Goki had been in too much of a hurry to get her warmed and nourished to clean her yet. The room smelled of blood and smoke. Sher Khan held Bianca closely, and said quietly, 'Do not weep for our people, Bianca. They died quickly, knowing nothing—when our time comes, may we have as easy a passage.' Over her head he met Goki's eyes—what was she seeing, her lined face so still, her eyes seeming suddenly blinded? Goki was seeing the Ruler's embattled figure, falling beneath Hardyal's treacherous sword—the Rani's agony—Terence O'Neil's tormented face. The gods protect this pair from such deaths, she thought, sight coming back to her eyes again. But she smiled at Sher Khan knowing why he had lied about death having come easily.

Bianca, weeping, knew that she would hear no more of her parents—but that they would be honoured and loved forever in the three States as the parents of the Ruler's wife, and the grandparents of his children. Sher Khan too had lost his beloved uncle and aunt, all the father and mother he had ever known.

'I weep for the Ruler and the Rani too,' she said, and took his head to her shoulder as she felt his body shake.

The children slept quietly in the alcove, the room was silent. Goki, tidying up, assisted by a cowed Ragni, threw a light blanket over the children, and they did not move.

Presently Sher Khan raised his head, and unashamedly wiped his eyes. He rubbed the tears from Bianca's face, and said, 'Enough—they would think less of us, if we mourn like children. Tell me, beloved—can you talk to me? Do you feel strong enough? I do not wish to tire you, but it is necessary for me to know—there is a large fire out beyond the lake—and the gate keeper says that you rode out this morning, and came back at dusk with the child Sara—what happened?'

'You will be angry—'

'No, love of my heart—I will not. Only tell me—'

'The fire is the Lalkoti—it was burning when I left.'

He did not ask her why she had gone. He went to the door and issued some sharp orders, and then came back, to get her story from her with quiet questions, while Goki fed her with spoonfuls of chicken soup between sentences. Stumblingly the whole story came out. When she told him about the creaking door, and the shutters bolted from outside, his anger glowed in his eyes, but he said nothing. She told him too, about the blood-stained uniform in the cupboard, and he groaned inwardly, catching Goki's eyes.

She frowned and nodded. 'Aye. Someone was ahead of me—but did not have time for much damage, I think. You have closed the passes?'

Sher Khan had closed the passes, and manned them as fully as he could long before Goki's arrival—only the one pass had been left open for her, and that was heavily guarded. He wondered how long, once the snows melted with the spring, he would be able to keep the passes. India was in a turmoil, and it spread to the north—and then there were those high, guarded passes that led to the dead lands between Russia and the valleys—he would have to go up there himself. He left Bianca, and went to the window, beckoning.

Goki came at once, and he said, 'How is she?'

'She has lost the child, Lord—saving your other child. Do

not forget, she saved the little one, who is of your blood.'

Through gritted teeth, Sher Khan spoke. 'That child is none of mine—'

Goki looked at him sharply. 'Think you so, Lord? Then let me show you something.'

She picked Sara up, while Muna still slept undisturbed, and undid the neck of the little torn nightshirt that Sara wore.

'Lord—look on this, and then repeat what you have just said—'

Sher Khan, his face stern, stared at the little thin body, and bending closer, stared again. Rosy against the pale skin was a mark he bore himself, a birthmark that had given him his name, Sher Khan, the Prince of Tigers. A little mark, shaped like a tiger's claw. He looked in silence, and Sara, frightened, looked back at him, her eyes slowly overflowing with tears. She made no sound and that slow fall of tears touched Sher Khan as nothing else could have done. He dropped to his knees and took the child into his arms. She stood, in the circle of his arms, rigid for a moment, then slowly relaxed and lay confidently against his shoulder.

'Is—is the Lady better now?'

Sher Khan nodded.

'That is good. I love the Lady. I used to call her Miss, but they say I must not. The Lady is very brave, you know. When the house was on fire she took me out, and was not frightened, although my mother and her friends must have been very frightened because they ran away. Listen—' She leaned close to his head. 'I want to tell you something secret.' Sher Khan held the little skinny body closer, and she breathed the words into his ear. 'Listen. I would like the Lady for my mother. What do you think? Can I choose? My mother will not mind. She smacks my face and tells me I am the devil's child. I would like to stay with the Lady if I could, and perhaps, even if I am the child of the devil, he will not come near here—will he?' There was an uncertain note in her voice.

Sher Khan turned her so that she was looking straight into his eyes. 'Listen small one. You are not the child of the devil. You are my child. And the Lady, as you call her, is now your mother, because she is my wife. How is that for you?'

'That is very good. But will I live here always?'

'Always. You have my solemn promise—'

Sara laughed, delighted, and the sound rang in the room like a silver bell. But although Bianca smiled, both Goki and Ragni stood staring at Sher Khan, their faces still and watchful.

The night had passed, and the clear white light of a snowy morning poured into the room. The children had slept well—fed, bathed, and rested. Goki took them out, saying firmly, 'You two at least had a night's sleep. Now you can go for a ride in the palanquin, while I see to the Khanum. She must sleep now. Ragni, send one of the women with these two. They can go as far as the lake and back, and then they can play in another room, where they will disturb no one.'

There was a stern look on Goki's face when she went back into the room, but Sher Khan was sitting beside Bianca on her bed, and Goki, looking at them both, knew that what she had to say could not be said then. She continued to straighten the room, apparently tireless, finally coming over to the bed and saying, 'Lord of the Hills—I must bathe the Khanum now, and make her sleep. I hear horses coming up from the village. I think it is the Lord Kassim. The time for your vigil must be near.' As she spoke, Sher Khan heard Kassim's voice outside, and kissing Bianca, went to join his nephew.

16

Sher Khan and Kassim rode down the hill to the village in silence.

It was the custom of the States for the new Ruler and his heir to keep vigil over the body of the dead Ruler. The body of the Ruler lay far away in Madore, but all the rest of that day they stood before the ashes of the bloodstained rag that Goki had carried for so long, while the priests of the three religions of the valleys said their prayers for the dead.

As night came, the chanting of the priests and their clashing cymbals disturbed the bats in the Temple precincts and sent them flying, little vocal shadows in the smoke of the flaring torches. Sher Khan, looking at the pile of ashes, heaped now on a silver tray, could not relate them to his brave sharp-tongued aunt, or to the splendid figure of the Ruler. But there they were, all that remained of a strong man and his wife.

'We all come to this,' whispered his mind. 'This is how I shall end, and my beautiful Bianca and all our loving—a heap of ashes, stirring a little in a night wind.' He bowed his head, and Kassim, looking at him through the smoke, thought he looked ten years older than he had the day before. 'And possibly a lot of hard fighting ahead of us still,' thought Kassim with sinking heart.

Bianca did not want to get up the next morning, in spite of having slept for twenty-four hours. She felt drained and empty, and terribly weak. But she was determined to be up and dressed when Sher Khan came—Goki shook her head, but helped her to get up, and Bianca sighed with pleasure as she felt the old familiar hands helping her. She bathed and was dressed in her usual cream woollen robes. Goki brushed her long hair, and coiled it smoothly on top of her head, and Bianca went over to sit in the alcove, and asked for the children.

'They are riding,' said Goki. 'No palanquins for Sara—she is teaching Muna to ride, and they are happy together. Children forget easily.' There was a shadow on Goki's face—Bianca, lost in sad memories of her mother, did not notice when Ragni called Goki over to the bed. The two old women stood, talking in undertones, and when Bianca put her coffee cup down, Goki came over to her.

'Bianca. You must come back to bed, and lie with your feet up. It is not good, so soon after losing a child to keep your feet down, or move about—you still bleed, you know.'

Bianca looked up at her sadly. 'I did lose the child then. I was not sure. Please Goki, let me stay here. I can put my feet up—see, thus—and I can watch my friend the eagle, and see the lake. I feel so sad in bed. I wanted that child very much, you know.'

'There will be others, my heart. Do not be sad. But stay if you want to—see, here come the children—'

With the smell of the fresh cold air all about them the children dashed in, bright eyed, red cheeked. Sara in two days seemed to have gained weight and energy. Muna was quieter, but appeared to be perfectly happy—she followed Sara over to the alcove, and settled herself confidingly into Bianca's arms.

'But there must be one arm for *me*,' said Sara, demandingly, and it was thus that Sher Khan, coming in after his long vigil, found Bianca—lying back in the alcove seat, pale but laughing, a child curled close to her in each arm. He stood for a moment in the door, unseen by Bianca, and looked at them, then she looked up and saw him, and gave a glad cry of welcome, and he went forward, lifting the little girls out of the way so that he could bend and kiss Bianca.

'How is the light of my life? You are too pale, Bianca. We have the dedication of the Ruler and his wife before us—do you think you will be well enough in a week's time?'

'Yes—of course I will—I am well now.'

Goki took the children out, and Bianca said, very low, 'Forgive me, Sher Khan. I lost your child.'

'You lost my child, saving Sara—and she is indeed my own child, whatever her mother was. She carries the mark you once asked me about—remember?'

'I remember—how well I remember that night. Yes, Goki told me she had the mark. It is so strange, I loved her at sight, as if she were my own child. I knew she was yours, Sher Khan. My heart told me.'

They sat close together, in silence, then presently Bianca shifted to a more comfortable position, her head on his shoulder, and said, 'What are the dedication ceremonies, Sher Khan? I have heard my—my father speak of them, but of course I have never seen them.' How strange and difficult it was to remember that she would never hear her father's voice again, and that the dedication ceremonies meant that the Ruler was dead—she hurried into speech again. 'Tell me—are they like a coronation?'

Sher Khan nodded. 'In a way. We, you and I, dedicate our lives to our people—and then the priests of the three religions bless us, and lead us up the steps of the Guddee, the marble throne in the old palace, and we seat ourselves there, before the people—all those who can get in. Then we hear three petitions, and that is the end. We are then the Ruler and the Rani of the Thinpahari States.'

They both became silent, thinking of the past and the future, Bianca with hope, Sher Khan with anxiety. The immediate future of the three States was secure enough, so far. But Bianca's story of the bloodstained uniform in the cupboard in the Lalkoti could only mean that at least one mutineer was in Lambagh—but where? So far, no trace had been found of either Kurmilla, or any strangers, nor indeed of the girl Kusma. They seemed to have vanished like the smoke from the burning house, now just a heap of blackened timbers.

Bianca moved uneasily in his arms, and put a hand to her stomach.

'What is it, Bianca?'

'I have a pain here, but it has gone now. It comes suddenly, and goes very quickly, so do not worry. Goki says I should go back to bed—perhaps I will—'

Sher Khan, all other anxieties swamped in this new worry, carried her to her bed, and shouted for Goki.

When Bianca was undressed, and drowsing, Goki drew Sher Khan to the window. 'Lord, there are some matters I would speak about—'

Sher Khan, with a glance at the sleeping girl, nodded to the door, and they went out, and into the anteroom. There they found the children once more curled in sleep, on a divan, Muna's hand clasped close in Sara's hand.

'Lord of the Hills—the hakim must come. The Khanum bleeds badly, all is not right with her, and I cannot tell what it is. She is feverish.'

Sher Khan remembered Reiss saying, 'Do not allow your hakims to give her any of their insanitary treatments—'

'Which of our hakims is the best?' he enquired, mentally calculating how long it would take to get Reiss down from the mountains. The weather was dry—say two days—Goki broke into his calculations.

'I do not give a fig for any of these hakims. Better that you get that white hakim from Sadara. Now, Lord, there is another matter, touching the Khanum very closely. Your child, Sara.' Goki drew a deep breath, like a prayer for strength, and watching Sher Khan's face, said, 'You know Kurmilla, curses on her, swore to give the child to the Temple if she was a girl—they will come for her very soon, you know. They take them at six, and she is nearly that age now.'

'She cannot go.'

Bianca would break her heart, and in any case, he wanted no daughter of his house sent down to the priests for training.

'Lord of the Hills—you cannot rob the Temple. No good can come of that, and also, imagine to yourself the trouble it will cause among the people. Every bad harvest, every death or misfortune will be laid at your door. There will be dissension and disaster—'

Her voice stopped, and they stood looking down at the sleeping children. Sara had moved, and was lying on her back, one arm flung up over her head, the tiger's claw birthmark clear on her chest. Muna, her eyelashes thick black semicircles on her white skin, lay curled against Sara's side.

'In the name of Allah—' said Sher Khan, the fact that he had to keep his voice low making it all the more violent. 'Am I never to have respite from that bitch Kurmilla? Since she entered this State she has caused nothing but disaster and pain.'

As he spoke, there was a sharp clatter of horses outside, and he heard the gate keeper's challenge, and hurried out to find

Kassim stripping off his fur-lined poshteen, his face a mask of worry.

'Sher Khan—how is Bianca?'

'Not well. I have sent for Reiss.'

'Then there is no good news. Someone has been stirring up trouble in Palgaon—our men have been fighting there, against some who crossed the river from the empty territory. Have I your permission to go up there at once, before the dedication ceremony?'

'You will have to go before the dedication ceremony. There is no possibility that we can take our vows. Bianca cannot be moved. As soon as Reiss comes, I shall leave her with him and join you.'

'But it is a risk to leave Lambagh, just now, without a Ruler—it only needs that damned Lungri Pass to be taken, and we could have a crowd of disaffected, lying trouble-makers in here from the lower villages. The people are already in great distress and uncertainty after the disaster in Madore—'

'The people will stand steady for me. I do not fear any treachery here. But up there, Palgaon, and the northern borders—take all the men you need from Lambagh, I will move the garrison at Sattagaon down to Lungri, and they will hold it fast.'

Kassim leaned forward, and touched Sher Khan's hands in the old gesture of fealty. 'My life for yours, Sher Khan—and please do not ride all our best horses to death sending out your various messengers—'

'You grudge a horse ridden to death for Bianca's sake?'

Kassim stared at him. Where was Sher Khan's sense of humour? Then he saw the desperate worry on his uncle's face, and said quickly, 'Sher Khan Bahadur—forgive me—I was jesting at a stupid time. I shall await your coming, and good news about Bianca and if I have to fight, I am fighting not only for the State, as you know, but for you—'

This time Sher Khan was able to smile at him, but the smile quickly faded as Kassim said, 'There is another matter. The head priest from the Temple has a visitor—a holy man, from the Temple of Surrendra Nath. He has come to take the child, Sara—'

He stopped, astonished at the anger that Sher Khan displayed. 'The child does not go—she is my daughter. She bears the mark—I was not told of it. But she is indeed my child. No daughter of mine goes into the Temple. I did not give my consent in any case.'

No, thought Kassim, you did not give your consent. But you denied that the child was yours, and made no objection when Kurmilla vowed her to the Temple. He thought of the trouble that would be caused among the Temple priests if a Muslim Ruler went against their customs, and broke a vow, and felt that nothing was ever going to come right again. He looked at his uncle, and decided that this was not a time for argument—he made his farewells, and went off down the hill to his men with his head full of apprehensions and worries, feeling that he had never been young, or unworried, and that he never would be again.

Bianca had not heard his arrival, and did not hear the clatter of his departure. The next two days passed in a blur of feverish pain. She slept and woke, and slept again, without any desire to move, or indeed to see anybody.

It was late on the evening of the third day that Reiss came riding through the falling snow to the Chotamahal. He had ridden all day, and was exhausted, but Sher Khan gave him no chance to rest. After he had drunk a glass of pale tea with lime that he asked for, he was led into the room where Goki was sponging Bianca's body, now so thin that red marks showed where her bones made pressure points. Reiss bent over the bed, and then straightened, and said, 'I must clean myself, and examine her at once—you did right to send for me. I presume that one of your hakims has already seen her—yes?'

He went into the bathroom, Goki with him, and when he came back, his shirt was off and he was angry. 'Your servant tells me that one of the hakims was called when she had her miscarriage. God alone knows what he did. Now, Lord of the Hills, you go. There is nothing for you to do in here just now.'

Outside the room, Sara came to him, and took his hand. 'Is my mother better?'

'No—but she will be soon. This white hakim is clever.'

He looked down at the glowing little face raised so confidently to him, and thought of the frightened little waif that Bianca had brought back from the Lalkoti. 'Do you like living here, Sarajan?'

'I like it very much. Is that my new name?'

'I think it must be—does it please you?'

'Does Sara still mean bitter?'

'In our language Sara has never meant bitter—it has *never* meant bitter.'

'Strange—my name has always meant bitter—and it was all lies—I do not understand. But it does not matter. My name is Sarajan—Muna, Munabhen! Come here—I have a new name. Muna is my new sister, you know.' She took Muna's hand. 'She has no mother or father, they were killed by soldiers. So she has no family but us.'

Muna looked up at Sher Khan with great dark eyes. Of the two children, she was much the darker—her hair was black, her eyes very dark brown—beside her, Sara was fair, and could very easily have been Bianca's own child. A bitter and stupid regret seized on Sher Khan, and putting the children gently to one side, he stood up. How foolish to regret what could not be undone. There would be other children, born of his love for Bianca. At least no lasting wrong had been done to Sara—she was happy and would be safe, and cared for now, for ever. That ridiculous vow of her mother's, taken in a rage against him, must be forgotten. He would pay them in gold, and all would be well.

When Goki came to call him, she found him standing out on the steps, regardless of the snow and the cold wind. He came back into the hall, and found Reiss waiting for him, obviously in a towering rage.

'Prince—I warned you. Keep your hakims with their filthy ways and hands off that girl. But it seems you did not listen. She is very ill—there has been a severe inflammation in her womb, a very severe infection. Only because she is young, and strong, and very clean-blooded is she alive now. But—Lord of the Hills, I do not think she will ever bear children now.'

Sher Khan looked at him in white faced silence. 'The hakim was called by Ragni, who knew no better. The Begum was miscarrying.'

Reiss listened to the story of the rescue of Sara, and Bianca's terrible experiences in the Lalkoti in silence. Then he said, 'Well, it is a desperate tragedy. She is sixteen and, as far as I can tell, she will be barren. Are you going to put her away?'

'Never.'

Reiss nodded. 'The State is fortunate. You already have a good heir in Kassim Khan Bahadur. But my grief for you is great. All men want a son of their own—' and on his words, Sher Khan turned his head away, and looked out at the lake.

'All I want is to get my hands on those who caused this. Then I can live quietly with Bianca—'

'I grieve for her too. She loves you very much. She will want your children.'

'She will want nothing but me. If she longs for a child—well, she already loves Sara as her own, and there is also the child that Goki brought from the plains. We have all the children we need. But—I need one more thing. Vengeance for my unborn sons.'

Reiss nodded. 'I understand. Now, Lord of the Hills, come and listen to me. I think there is very little time for you to waste, waiting for vengeance. It appears to me that the trouble up in the northern passes is due to Kurmilla, and I think two men who came up from the south. Do not ask me how they got in through your guarded passes. But the poison they brought with them is spreading; their story of the fleeing whites, and the end of all tyrannical Rulers. You and your uncle accused me of inflaming the people against you! You should hear the stories these creatures are telling. No one would listen to them here, but on the northern borders, they listen. Kurmilla has much gold. She buys men, who are in any case always ready to be bought. They are very poor up there, where the rocks yield poor pasture, and the winters are long and cruel. The river narrows there, and you know who waits in hope of disaffection in this State, as they have always waited. You will have to get up there, Lord, and quickly.'

'Kassim has already gone—I only waited for you.'

'If I may suggest that because you are not yet sworn, you declare a longer period of mourning for the late Ruler, before you go—and also, Goki has spoken to me of the child Sara. The priest has already come from Surrendra Nath—'

'I know. She is not going anywhere. She is my child, and I made no vow. I will buy her back. Gold always satisfies the gods of those priests—'

Reiss shrugged. 'You know your own people very little, Lord, if you think gold will help to break a vow. But there is no time now for this. Leave the Begum Sahiba, and the child to me. I will hold all safe until you return. And—Lord—let *me* tell the Begum—do not tell her now.'

'I may say goodbye to her?'

'Of course—she is waiting for you. But let her think you return soon.'

Bianca lay, as white and frail as the jasmine flowers she loved so much. Sher Khan, bending to kiss her, was made afraid by her pallor, and her weakness. But she raised her arms and clasped them firmly round his neck—her smile for him was gay, her lips as clinging as her arms. '*Where* are you going?'

'I go to see what is happening on our northern borders.'

'Sher Khan—you promised me I could come with you—to see the northern passes and the bridge of snow—'

'I did—and you will. But are you going to tell me that you are fit to ride now? Do not be foolish, my love, we will go again when you are stronger.'

It was hard for Sher Khan to put up his hands and break her grip. She whispered, as he loosened her arms, 'Oh come soon—I shall be waiting, and I shall be well—I swear I shall be well—' and with her kiss still burning on his mouth, Sher Khan walked out of the room, his eyes full of tears. He was sure that Bianca knew that she would not see him for some time, and that he was going to fight—what else had she guessed?

He looked at Reiss who was waiting for him outside. 'You will not have to tell her anything—she knows already, I think. May it please Allah that I find those creatures that did her this harm, and that they live long after I find them, for they are going to suffer very much. My wife is breaking her heart.'

'Well—their suffering will not help the Khanum—or you. But you are the Lord of the Hills. Let it be as you wish. Go safely, and return safely, and leave the rest to your God, and my God, and all the other Gods—who are in fact, all one great being. In the name of that unknown Greatness, worshipped in different ways by all of us, I bless you, Maharaj. Go in that blessing.' He went into Bianca's room, his tall body briefly outlined against the rosy light from her door as he opened and closed it again behind him.

As Sher Khan was buckling his *poshteen* close about him, Goki came out, and stooped to touch his feet. 'My life for yours, and for hers, Lord—go without fear. The Khanum lives, and will live.'

Oddly comforted, Sher Khan turned to go, when Sara came from behind Goki, and hurled herself into his arms. 'You are going away, and not saying goodbye to me. I would have died if you had left me without saying goodbye—' Sher Khan groaned and, picking her up, held her tightly. 'Say anything but that, Sarajan. Goodbye, my daughter—be good. I will be back soon.'

Sara, back on the floor, pulled his arm. 'And Muna? Say goodbye to Munabhen—' Muna in turn was lifted and kissed. She looked gravely at Sher Khan, and said, 'My life for yours—and for the Khanum—and for Sarajan—Lord.' Sher Khan, on his way out, stopped, arrested by her words. 'Where did you learn to say that Muna?'

'I heard my mother say it to my father often—and then Goki says it—and so I say it to you, whom I love also. Is it wrong?' Sher Khan shook his head, and kissed both children again, and rode off down the hill.

It was late when he rode into the village, but there were lamps burning still, and smoke and flame, and the sound of hammers—the weapon-makers were hard at work, sharpening and tempering old swords and spear heads, and hammering and riveting the body armour that had been rusting in chests in the valley houses. The small raids and quarrels that had so often broken out between village and village had not needed armour. This was different. This time they were going with their Ruler, to defend their borders, and all other feuds were forgotten. Kassim Khan had done his work well—the men were all alerted, and ready.

The sight of all this activity, heartened Sher Khan as nothing else could have done. Bianca must be put out of his thoughts now—nothing must remain but the struggle for the safety of the States, and the arrangements for the coming journey.

It was a wonderful release for him to lose himself in his preparations, and in planning each stage of what must be a very speedy journey over bad terrain, to the northern borders.

They went, Sher Khan and his picked men, by short cuts, goat paths and scrambling climbs up seemingly impossible mountain cliffs. The little hill ponies climbed like cats, and were as sure-footed. They came up with Kassim's men on the third day—Kassim was delighted to see them, because he had not expected Sher Khan to be able to get to him so quickly.

17

There was no pitched battle. It was mountain fighting, a series of running engagements. Sher Khan and Kassim and their men had had much practice at this type of warfare, and the country lent itself to it.

The men from the south were used to fighting in the open, and would have done better to have listened to the Lambaghi officers and men whom they had bribed into fighting for them. Instead they tried to make a stand in any open field that they could find, but there would be no enemy to fight. Then, proceeding among rocks and deep defiles and gullies, Sher Khan and his men would fall on them, howling like devils, and Kassim would leap on them with his men, and cut them to bits when they tried to take cover.

Sher Khan's men enjoyed themselves. Their casualties were few, and as the days went on, they found themselves opposed by a half-hearted army. Men slipped out of the rebel camp by night, and came, asking for Sher Khan, standing with bowed, shamed heads before him.

'Lord of the Hills—we were told that we were to fight against a foreign invader, an army of foreigners, who were coming to impose their religion on us, to take our land, and desecrate our Temples. Instead, we find that we fight our own people, led by our own Ruler—and our leaders are foreigners.'

'Who are these leaders?'

'Lord, there are two black men from the south, and a European—but he does not resemble any European that we have seen before.'

'You took gold.'

'Lord, we were promised much gold. More than we have ever dreamed of. We saw much gold. But we have not been given any—we had promises, but no gold. Indeed, we are fools.'

'So—now you come back to me, because you were not given gold, and you hope that perhaps I will get it for you.'

'Nay—we ask you only for one thing. Let us come back to you and fight with you—give us our lives.'

Sher Khan's army increased. There were many of these men, and they all told the same story—promised gold, and foreign leaders.

'Well—we already knew our enemy. But who is the foreigner—the European?'

'Russian—what else?'

'Yes. I suppose, Russian—to observe, and see how close to breaking we are—'

'I am not interested in the Russian, Kassim. But those two men—the men from the south. Let it be known in the ranks that they are to be taken alive. I will kill the man who touches one of them. I want them.'

Something in his voice made Kassim look across at him. Ever since Sher Khan had joined him, Kassim had seen a strangeness in him—a new hardness, and strain, a constant sense of waiting, as of one who anticipated a pleasure for which he could barely wait. Kassim did not feel that it was Sher Khan's return to Bianca that he waited for with such strained impatience. This was a darker longing, a frightening desire. Kassim did not recognise this new side of Sher Khan, and watched him with anxiety. He tried to speak to his uncle of the two men from the south—

'Hardyal's men, no doubt about it—he must have more influence than we thought, for them to have got up here so quickly.'

'Not more influence. More gold. Do not forget, he now has all my uncle's possessions, and also Khanzada took him a rich dowry—and he was rich before that. Money can lend wings to men's feet. I could never understand why my uncle chose that family to join to us in marriage.'

'But there was always an association—Hardyal's father and mother were great friends of your uncle's—'

'Well—the old man was a good old man—God knows what devil was at Hardyal's birth. As for Kurmilla—'

Sher Khan fell silent. He recalled with pain Kurmilla, when he first raised her veil to look at his new bride's face—the soft eyes, the curved seductive mouth with its full scarlet lips—and her body, rich and so excitingly formed, promising fulfilment in every way—as did her eyes, and her smile. He had thought himself so fortunate in his beautiful passionate wife; he had burned for her, could never have enough of her skilled love-making, until he returned home unexpectedly and had found how she learned her skills. He was appalled by her deception and his own naïveté. She was so beautiful and yet so evil, like a cobra. He would have put her away at once, but she had skills. She made him drunk, and was pregnant again, swearing that it was he who had taken her and drugged and drunken for three days, as he had been, he knew that he must have taken her—Sara was the proof. And yet he had never really been able to believe that she was his own daughter. And when Kassim's mother told him that his wife was in any case a half-caste, and had been the talk of Calcutta, this strengthened his suspicion. Kurmilla had been divorced at once and Kassim's mother had suffered the fate of all those who bring bad news. Sher Khan could not bear to look at her. He must heal that breach—he needed Mumtaz, and her kind wisdom, for Bianca—and it was not fair to Kassim.

Kassim, watching his face, wondered what paths of memory he was treading and regretted ever mentioning Hardyal.

Sher Khan came out of his reverie, and smiled at Kassim. 'You look as worried as a man of eighty with five young wives. Come, Kassim, we are doing well.'

'God knows what lies ahead of us through the passes—but we know how the trouble started. And yet, not a sign of a southerner among any dead we have seen—these sons of swine keep themselves well back.'

The moon was rising, and Sher Khan looked round him from the cleft of rock where he lay. Not a man of his but was in good cover, lying close under rocks, and in folds of the rough rocky country, weapons at hand. He felt an enormous pride in his army—it had grown from nothing into a well-trained fighting band, and he knew how pleased his uncle would have been.

A shadow fell across a rock, shifted, and was gone. Both Sher Khan and Kassim sat rigid and alert—then Kassim sighed, and they both relaxed.

'Habib, you fool—we nearly killed you. Do the houris in paradise beckon that you are in such a hurry to leave us?'

'I have news, Lord. The last two men who defected say that

the rebels are camping for the night in the old fort above Landi. Hardyal is with them.'

Sher Khan raised his eyebrows. 'They have chosen well—that cliff is impregnable—I do not know of anyone who has climbed it from this side. I wonder how much he paid for news of that stronghold. From here, I do not think we can do anything—and by the time we get up to the plateau, where I know there is little cover, they could be anywhere. They must be stopped before they cross that plateau to the river—because once they get to the river, where it narrows, they can be across and gone before we can do anything to them.'

'Lord—I have a man here who says that he knows a way up the cliff—he used to go up to get eggs from the eagles' nest on the ruined wall, and he used a way that he swears we can all use.'

'He must be mad—'

'Nay, Heaven born. He says that if the Lord Kassim comes with him first, he will show him, and of course myself—and then I will come back and lead you up.'

Sher Khan smiled at him. 'Habib, you have all the virtues—but I do not think that silence and an ability to climb like a goat are among them. Bring the man here—and avoid rousing the whole camp while you do it.'

When Habib came back with a very young soldier, Sher Khan looked closely at him in the moonlight, and then burst out laughing, stifling his laughter with his hand.

'Rama—I should have known it would be you. Kassim—this man is a shepherd, employed by the State. He has lost more sheep in these hills than any other man I know, but he knows the mountains as he knows the lines on his own hand. If he says he can get us up, he can. But Habib stays here. Separate the men into two groups—those who can climb, and those who cannot. Send the non-climbers up the other way, with all the weapons, to the plateau. They will wait there until they see a fire lit on the top of the old tower, then they come in to the attack, and fast. The climbers carry nothing and wear as little as possible. They may each have a knife, but nothing more. I will send Rama back to tell you when to start. Habib, my splendid bull, you go to the plateau and watch for the fire. Is all understood?'

It was early dawn when they set off. In the clear pearly light,

Kassim watched them go, and settled himself, with what patience he could, to wait.

He had changed the sentries thrice, and it was growing dark, and no one had returned. Kassim was about to send scouts to the cliff foot, when he saw two figures approaching.

'In Allah's name—what have you been doing? Where is the Ruler?'

'He is at the top of the cliff. We have been watching the enemy. If you are ready, Lord, I will take you now, it will take us some time to reach the beginning of the climb—'

When they reached the Landi cliff, it looked huge, black and threatening. Kassim was awed by its height; the great ruined fort on its summit was lost in darkness. The night was thinning—soon it would be dawn, and too late to climb.

The climb was in fact almost impossible. In places, clinging with fingers and toes on what seemed to be a flat, perpendicular surface, Kassim wondered how many of the men would make it to the top. Two were lost—falling, brave to the last, in silence, to their deaths. Every now and then a bit of rock, displaced, would rattle down the cliff side, sounding like an avalanche in the silent night. Then the men would cling flat against the mountain, tense and waiting with held breath for the first shots. But there was no shooting, no cry of warning. Kassim, pulling himself up over the lip of the last crag, was met by a grinning Sher Khan, who took his arm, and hauled him to safety.

Each man who reached the cliff top turned and took the hand of the man behind him and helped him up and over. Soon they were all lying, regaining their breath, behind rocks that rose in a natural wall about three hundred yards from the fort, stark in splendid ruin, with one tower still intact.

There were fires outside the fort, and the smell of cooking, and a great deal of noise round the fires. The ground was rough, with boulders and bushes, and shallow gullies.

'There is plenty of cover, should we need it.' Sher Khan speaking to Kassim, barely lowered his voice.

'They have no sentries on this side at all. What they have on the plateau side, according to Rama who worked his way round there with no trouble, is a small collection of extremely drunk soldiers, supposedly on sentry duty. Most of the officers are drunk as well. We take no prisoners of rank, Kassim. They are disloyal indeed, and I do not want them, but the rank and file—well, we know they were bribed, and they are not rich people. I wonder if they have been paid at all yet, except in drink and women!' He laughed unpleasantly.

'What a campaign! There are women here as well. Rama says they are whores from the taverns, but some are wives of our men here. Kurmilla and that bitch servant of hers are here somewhere. Do not forget, Kurmilla, Kusma, and Hardyal are to be taken alive. Are our men ready?'

It was obvious that they were. Knives were out, and the men were as tense as cats waiting at a mousehole.

'Pass the word, Kassim. They are to make no noise until they are well in amongst the enemy. The first man into the fort lights a fire on the roof of the old tower.'

He paused to run a considering eye down the group of his men, then stood up and climbed casually over the barrier of rocks, and walked forward, like a man who had every right to be there. His men, scattering among boulders and bushes followed him, and unnoticed, were among the fires, and the men who stood and lay, laughing and talking around them, waiting for their food to be ready.

Kassim kept his eyes on Sher Khan, and followed him as closely as he could. He saw him glance round, check that his men were ready, and then, with a cry as piercing as the call of a hunting eagle, Sher Khan leapt straight into the thick of the crowd round the largest fire. Kassim followed him, his knife flashing, and heard the roar of the fighting break out behind him, like the sound of the surf on a reef.

The mêlée was sharp, and brief. The men, already fuddled by drink, confronted by grinning enemies who had apparently fallen out of the sky, put up little opposition. Their own fires were against them. Men rolled, screaming among the embers, their clothes catching, so that human torches were leaping and shrieking among those who did fight, causing horror and disorder in their own ranks. Men who had climbed, armed only with knives, found it easy to snatch up swords forgotten by drunken and startled opponents.

Kassim saw that Sher Khan was running from one fire to

another, killing swiftly, and moving on, like a man searching. Kassim rushed after him, determined to guard his back, but was himself suddenly attacked by a man who sprang on him. Sher Khan turned, in time, and knifed Kassim's attacker, taking his sword as the man fell, and proceeding to cut a swathe round himself and Kassim until he saw that Kassim was on his feet again, and armed. Then he forged on, the deadly cut and thrust of his knife and sword never halting, his arm, it appeared, tireless.

'Prisoners!' thought Kassim breathlessly. 'Prisoners—he has not taken one, that I can see—' He then set to himself, still vainly trying to keep Sher Khan in sight.

The fires, sputtering, lit up a disorderly fight, which was rapidly becoming a rout. The fire on the tower was lit and Kassim heard scattered musket fire, but the fight was over. Men, those on their feet, were throwing down their arms, shouting for mercy, and already Sher Khan's soldiers were beginning to lower their swords, and collecting the prisoners. Sher Khan himself was nowhere to be seen.

Going rapidly in search of him, Kassim saw that it was growing light—the night was over.

Sher Khan was looking for him. They met in the big roofless hall of the fort, with its crumbling, cracking walls, and stood looking at each other. Sher Khan had a cut on his cheekbone, and his eyes were sparking like witch fire with the excitement of the fight.

'Well, Kassim Khan Bahadur! That was a short fight. We have not lost a man, I am told—there are some bad burns, and some wounded—but nothing serious. Where are our prisoners?'

Kassim pointed to a depressed group, huddled against the farther wall. There were several women, Kusma amongst them—and a dark-skinned man who stood apart from the others.

'And?' Sher Khan raised questioning eyebrows.

'There is no trace of Kurmilla, or of Hardyal, her cousin—nor the Russian.'

'When did they leave?' Sher Khan was suddenly tense, his voice almost a whisper.

'Lord of the Hills—' Kassim, who never called Sher Khan anything but by his name, cleared his throat, and spoke as quietly as Sher Khan had, with the same apprehension on his face. 'They left three days ago. They have gone in the direction of Lambagh—and the Russian was not with them. He left the fort before they did and went back over the river, saying that he knew a beaten army when he saw one. Sher Khan—I think we must leave our men to follow us, and go with speed—I am very afraid.'

Sher Khan did not answer him. He walked over to the group of prisoners, and ordered the guard to take Kusma and the southerner to one side. Then he spoke to Habib, who was in charge of the men guarding the prisoners. 'These men, if they can prove to your satisfaction that they were bribed, can be put to work rebuilding this fort, and then return to their villages. The women—well, if they are whores, they have but practised their profession, and go free. Some may be wives who followed traitorous husbands. But if any here are unfaithful wives, then let their husbands deal with them as they wish. Now—'

He walked over to Kusma, and her companion, and as he approached them, Kusma started to scream, like a rabbit screams, trapped by a stoat. The man said nothing—it seemed as if he was not there, as if his mind had taken him out of surroundings that he found unpleasant, to a place where he wished to be. His face wore an expression of peace, and he did not move, nor appear to notice Kusma when she flung herself grovelling on the floor before Sher Khan. Sher Khan nodded to one of the guards.

'Make that noise to cease—I wish to speak—'

The guard did not have to do anything; Sher Khan's tone had been enough. Kusma lay, silent, her face hidden in her hands, and Sher Khan said, looking over her head to where a ruined window opened on to the steep side of the cliff, 'You die for only one reason—because of what you helped to do to the Begum Sahiba. I have no time, which is fortunate for you—you die more easily than I intended.'

He turned away, and spoke to Habib, and Kassim, watching him with horror, saw Kusma and the southerner tied back to back, and then raised and swung like a bundle of dirty clothes out through the broken window, and down into the great drop from the cliff. He heard the woman's scream die slowly away—

but there was only one voice screaming. The man had fallen as silently as his own men had died when they fell down the cliff.

Sher Khan came over to him. 'Kassim, can you ride with me? We must go at once—and the men must follow as quickly as they can. I fear very much what we may find, and I cannot live until I get to Lambagh.' Kassim was astonished by the change in his uncle's face. For the first time he was conscious of the difference in their age, and his own inexperience. Sher Khan looked as if everything in him was now concentrated in one thought—and it was obvious that the couple who had just died had affected him not at all—nor did the slowly rising screams from the group of women who had been separated from the rest, and were now confronting their own husbands, who had accompanied Sher Khan. Kassim was glad to follow Sher Khan out into the light of the rising sun, and find their horses ready saddled and waiting for them.

Once they had passed over the very difficult twisting road from the plateau down to their last camp, they began to ride as Sher Khan had come originally—by every short cut he knew. At the last minute, the boy Rama had asked to come with them. He led them by paths that even Sher Khan had not known, and by the evening of the second day after their departure from the fort they were within sight of the lights of Lambagh. It was dusk as they came over the Pass at Akhsi, and looked down. The lake lay dark in the gathering shadows of night. Beside it glimmered the lights of the Chotamahal, and then, further on, the lights of the village.

There was no sign of anything being wrong—Kassim heaved a great sigh, and felt all his muscles slacken with relief.

'See—Sher Khan. All is well, all as we left it—Allah be praised. I have been so afraid, for no reason—' He broke off, trying to see his uncle's face in the fast gathering dusk.

'Allah be praised indeed—if all is well. It is not always possible to be sure that all is well, from outward appearances. A snake leaves no trace on the grass—' The silence that fell between them then was for Kassim full of a terrible fear and he could not understand why he felt so afraid, and then knew that fear had spread to him from Sher Khan. Rama rode down ahead of them, to give news of their arrival. Sher Khan and Kassim followed slowly, which was in itself strange; after all the haste, it was as if Sher Khan feared to face the end of his journey, feared his homecoming.

18

Bianca had taken time to recover.

After Sher Khan left, she did everything she was told by Reiss, meek and obedient in her desperate desire to grow strong again. He watched her with pity, and said nothing to her. After all, he reasoned with himself, I am only a man—I cannot tell for sure that this child is barren now. I will leave it, and time will show one way, or the other. He was ashamed of his cowardice, but he could not bring himself to confirm the fear that he saw sometimes in her eyes as she looked at him.

She grew stronger, and her face began to regain its bloom. Her body, always slender, but of late emaciated, began to curve again, and her hair grew glossy with health under Goki's unremitting care.

The children were Bianca's greatest solace. As soon as she was able to go out, they spent much time on the lakeside, muffled in furs, for although it was spring, and the sun was growing warmer, it was still bitterly cold when the spring winds blew down from the snowy peaks.

One day, Sara and Muna found a vixen and her cubs in the base of a hollow tree, and were with difficulty dissuaded from taking the cubs, with their bright eyes, thick furry little bodies and questing pointed ears. On another day, a bird sang on a bare black branch, and the next day when they went down they found that, as if the bird had woken the sap in the tree, the branch had pale green buds all along it. The streams, frozen and silent for so long, began to melt and run again—everywhere there was the sound of water beginning to free itself from the hard hand of winter. Bianca began to turn her eyes more and more to the mountains of the north—surely Sher Khan must come soon?

In the evenings, in her lamplit room, with a great fire in the hearth making the carved figures on the walls leap and dance as the shadows moved, Bianca would sit and dream of Sher Khan's return. Like the dark frozen branch of the tree, her body was waking to the spring. She put her secret fear behind her, and waited with impatience for Sher Khan's return.

The evening of the battle for Landi Fort was a peaceful one in Lambagh. Goki had taken Sara and Muna off to their bed. Their goodnights had been prolonged, and they went reluctant, begging for another story, another song—anything, in order to be allowed to stay up. Bianca laughed at the last dragging little figure, more than half asleep, and still fighting to stay. Then, as the door closed, she stretched out in the alcove and, watching the firelight, from one minute to the next was asleep herself.

She slept, and dreamed that Sher Khan was back, calling to her.

She woke suddenly to a dark room, and dimly seen against the firelight, a man was bending over her. The darkness did not matter. Still held in the magic of her dream, with a little sound of pleasure, she put up her arms, and he said softly, his voice muffled against her hair, 'My heart—you welcome me so sweetly. Drink with me, here is our loving cup, drink.'

It had been so long, and now, at last the waiting was over. The blurred magic of her dream all about her, Bianca, feeling the edge of the goblet against her mouth, put her hand up and holding his hand in hers, tilted the goblet and drank deeply, of wine that ran through her veins like fire.

She felt his arms tighten round her as he lifted her up. Her head reeled, the darkness was full of strange shapes and sounds, and as she felt herself beginning to fall into whirling blackness, she knew, beyond all doubt, that the arms holding her were strange, this was not Sher Khan, and her voice would not obey her. Black night and silence closed round her, as she was carried from the room.

She woke slowly, and in great distress, both physical and mental. The place where she lay was uncomfortable—it seemed as if she lay on a bare rope bed, in stifling darkness. Her whole body ached—every limb seemed bruised, and a more agonising, intimate pain forced a moan through her bitten lips. As she tried to see through the darkness, she heard laughter somewhere, and knew at once who laughed. She covered her mouth with her hands, to smother the groans that she could not stop. A man's voice, slow and silky, said something, and Kurmilla laughed again.

Bianca, moving as slowly and quietly as a chameleon, investigated her hurts. She had many—her breasts ached, and when she touched one nipple, her hand came away, wet and sticky with blood. She found blood drying on her thighs, and then the voices outside sounded nearer, and she lay paralysed. Closer and closer came the voices and the footsteps, and Bianca lay, naked and defenceless and terrified.

A door opened on light, and Kurmilla stood looking down at her, a lamp in her hand, and laughed her harsh grating laugh.

'At last—you wake at last! We thought we would have to carry you back still sleeping—'

'You are taking me back?' Bianca spoke with difficulty, her throat was so dry it seemed it was full of sand.

'Taking you back? Of course—or did you enjoy your hours with Hardyal so much that you wish to stay longer?'

'Hardyal?'

'Yes—Hardyal. My cousin. A mighty man in love, and war—and you seemed to appreciate his prowess in love very much. You whisper now, but you screamed like a mating cat when he took you—screamed and begged for more. I had no idea your little body could be so insatiable. You were mad for loving—'

Bianca stared at her, a slow cold horror creeping like a tide all over her body. 'What—what have you done, Kurmilla?'

'Done? I? *I* did nothing. But I watched. It was greatly amusing, I assure you. You obviously have a taste for the bizarre—you complied with skill and pleasure with every desire Hardyal expressed—and he is noted for the diversity of his desires—'

'You drugged me—'

'You did not seem to me to be asleep,' interrupted a man's voice, 'and I am sure that it was no unconscious body I held in my arms, little Begum. You are the most accommodating partner I have ever had—do not say you cannot recall any of our hours together? Perhaps we should try again—'

The silky voice of the tall man who stood with Kurmilla startled a flight of evil echoes in Bianca's brain, as vultures disturbed will rise from their prey. In her mind, half seen, were pictures—memories of what, she did not know—but surely they could not be memories, these blurred pictures, they were just the smoky remnants of a drugged nightmare.

Kurmilla put her hand on the man's arm. 'Do not be foolish, Hardyal. Thou and I must be far from here by nightfall. Come—call the palanquin. It will be light in an hour.'

Bianca dragged on the clothes they threw to her with shaking, fumbling fingers. She lay in the palanquin, her body wincing at every movement, and wondered desperately how they would get her back unseen. For that was all she wanted—to be safely back, in her own room, hidden away.

No one came out to the gate when the two men, faceless in the dark, lowered the palanquin to the ground. Hardyal was riding. He dismounted, and picked Bianca up and carried her past the sleeping gate keeper, and into her room, as brazenly as if he had every right to be there. He even laughed under his breath at her shrinking withdrawal from his arms.

'Indeed and indeed Kurmilla found a wonderful drug. You certainly did not wear that face last night, Khanum, you came to me like a harlot to her favourite customer—'

He stood for a moment, looking at her, and then left her, moving as quietly as a shadow—one minute his figure showed against the light from the last of the dying fire, then he had gone, and the room was empty.

Dawn light was grey in the room, where the curtains had not been drawn for the night, when Goki came in, dishevelled and distraught.

'Bianca—I do not know what happened to me last night. I do not think that I am well. I beg your leave to go to my room, and I will send one of the girls to look after the children today, so that Ragni will be free to do your work. I know not what I ate or drank, but I feel death has looked at me.'

There was no reply from Bianca, and Goki was suddenly afraid. 'Bianca—you do not speak—are you also ill? Did we all fall sick?'

She hurried to the bed, and what she saw when she looked at Bianca made her cry out, a wild wailing cry that echoed back from the walls of the beautiful room. Then, for the first time, Bianca moved, and speaking barely above her breath, told Goki to be quiet.

'Goki—I was drugged and taken away last night. No one must

know. Keep Ragni away, let her see to the children—are they all well? For I know that the gate keeper was drugged. I must have Reiss quickly, and first let him look at the children. But for your life's sake, do it all as privately as possible.'

With no more words, Goki went. Bianca lay, not moving, her eyes wide open—she dared not shut them, for then terrible pictures danced on her eyelids.

Reiss came, and Goki, with shaking hands opened Bianca's robes. He looked at the girl's body in horror, and went himself to get cloths and water, and helped Goki to clean her. Her body was bruised and torn in a way he had only once seen before—when he had been learning to be a healer, taught by monks in a monastery in his own country. A harlot, brutally beaten and raped by two soldiers, had been brought in for treatment, and he remembered her wounds now as he helped Goki. As he bent over his work, he could smell an unmistakable odour.

'Khanum—who drugged you?'

'Kurmilla, I think. She was there—all the time. Doctor Reiss—I was drugged as you say. I thought I slept, and I—I woke. But every now and then, I seem to recall things—cannot remember well even the things that happened after terrible things. Do you think I had nightmares, while I was drugged?'

With compassion, he assured her that she had dreamed. Poor child, he knew what a clever combination of drugs and certain aphrodisiacs could do, and he hoped that her memory of the night would quickly fade. Bianca was watching his face.

'Doctor Reiss—must Sher Khan be told?'

'Yes. He must.'

'I did not mean to do anything to dishonour him. But I do not know—I cannot be sure of what happened.'

'Khanum—I must tell you. You were raped—'

With difficulty, through her swollen lips, she said, 'Perhaps, after all I am fortunate if I am barren. Oh yes, I knew that I was barren. But as I say—I am fortunate. At least there will be no results of my shame. Will everyone know what has happened?'

'No one will know,' said Reiss, lying with conviction. He was sure, in fact, that Kurmilla would make every detail public. He had already started a hunt for Kurmilla, but so far there had been no trace of her, or her companion.

He did what he could for Bianca, sent Goki away to sleep, and himself sat in the alcove in case Bianca needed anything. But she did not speak to him for a long time. She was fighting to stay awake, dreading the pictures that floated into her mind when she closed her eyes. Her body ached and throbbed and smarted as if she had been severely beaten, and there was a terrible tearing pain between her legs, as if she were on fire. The pit of despair into which she fell seemed to be bottomless—she lay and suffered in every way known to women, and Reiss sat and helpless, watched her, and suffered with her.

At last she spoke. Like a child begging for a favour, she said, 'Must my lord know?'

Reiss did not know how to answer her, and it took all his will to look at her pleading distorted face and say, 'Yes—you know he must be told.'

'But at once? Could I not—could we not at least have three days together, and be happy as we used to be? Just three days?'

'Bianca, no—he must be told at once. If you do not let me tell him, someone else may, or rumours may be started, and that would be very bad for you—if it were told about the village that you went willingly with them—rumour, once started, feeds on itself, and God only knows what would be said.'

'Sher Khan will put me away—'

'That is not so—he will not, if you tell him the truth at once, and he can see you as you are—also there is the Dedication Ceremony, he must be told before that.'

'I only want three days—if I promise I will tell him myself before the Dedication?'

The bruises, the cuts, the swollen lips, the scarred, torn breasts—how did she think Sher Khan would be able to ignore them?

'I could say I had a bad fall riding—I fell into thorns, because I rode too soon—in any case, I do not intend to lie with him—how could I, defiled as I am?' Bianca's eyes were full of tears. 'I only want to be at peace with him for three days—to have three beautiful days to remember—I beg you, as I would not beg for my life—'

Reiss was only a man. He could stand no more. 'Very well. But you swear that he will be told before the Dedication Ceremonies?'

'I swear. You will be silent?'

'I will say nothing—'

Bianca turned her head away, and was instantly asleep, a sleep in which she twisted and moaned and cried out—and Reiss, after watching her and listening to her, went away and woke Goki, and finally, risking much, he made a concoction of opium and herbs, and waking Bianca, made her drink it. She fell at once into a deep quiet sleep, and Goki and Reiss looked at each other in relief.

'Thank God—but she can only have that mixture for a week—or she will become addicted. Listen Goki—'

Goki, when she heard that Bianca did not want Sher Khan told for three days, agreed with Reiss that it was most dangerous.

'It will be bad if she tells him—terrible. But if she does not tell him, and others do—'

Sher Khan's most precious possession, his perfect companion, defiled and dishonoured—bad enough indeed if it had been proved that she went unwillingly. But if it could be made to look as if she had gone happily with a lover—Goki shuddered. She knew all about the violence that lay beneath Sher Khan's controlled and trained self-discipline. She could guess what Bianca feared.

It was dark, and a new moon was setting through the smoke of the village cooking fires, as Sher Khan and Kassim rode up to the Chotamahal. Kassim said goodbye to Sher Khan there, and rode on to start with his men on the search for Kurmilla and her cousin.

The gate keeper, calling out in greeting, was the first notice that Bianca and Reiss had of Sher Khan's arrival. Bianca heard Sher Khan's voice, heard his booted feet running up the steps, and then the door opened, and he was there. Reiss went out of the room at once, and left them alone.

Out of a long silence, as Bianca looked up at Sher Khan, she said, 'Lord of the Hills—' for this was neither her lover, nor her husband, this stern faced man who looked down at her, his face etched with new lines, his hair glinting with grey at the temples. Bianca knew at once that Reiss was right—she should have let him tell Sher Khan immediately. This was not a man to deceive in any way. She stared, one hand to her cheek—here was a man of command, with no tenderness or love showing in his face. Where was she going to find the courage, or the words, to tell him that her body and her spirit had been mauled and debauched, even though she was innocent of intent? She tried to speak, to tell him, and her breath was shallow with fear.

Sher Khan said slowly, 'Is this your greeting, Bianca? Lord of the Hills? I thought I was lord of your heart, my bird—'

His smile was the same, the arms that went round her, bruising her already sore body, were known—her beloved was back, and she felt her whole self, body and soul, clenching and straining away from him, his every touch brought back terrible memories, blurred horrors that she was trying to forget. He held her away from him, saying, 'Bianca what is wrong? You are changed—tell me—'

She could have told him, but her courage failed. She stopped his questions with kisses, and felt a terrifying revulsion rising in her at every kiss.

They had two days together. They sat talking, and Bianca felt no joy in their companionship—she was unbearably conscious of his nearness, terrified of his love-making.

They walked by the lake, with the children riding ahead of them. Bianca walked slowly, and could not ride, saying that she was not yet ready as she still felt weak after her fall—and hoped that neither Sara nor Muna heard her lie. It was terrible to be lying to Sher Khan.

Reiss, questioned closely by Sher Khan, said that her recovery had been very slow, and speaking, was afraid to turn his eyes away from Sher Khan's searching stare. It was very plain that Sher Khan was worried and suspicious, but could not sense what was worrying him. He had thrown every available man he had into the search for Hardyal and Kurmilla. He spoke to Reiss about the search, and Reiss was afraid that his suspicions had been roused by the fact that Reiss had already started searching for these two—with no apparent reason for doing so, for he was not supposed to know anything about the campaign until Sher Khan's return.

But Sher Khan did not appear to know that Kurmilla and Hardyal were already being hunted. He told Reiss about his expedition, and about the Russian who had left very early in the campaign, before the real fighting had begun. 'He vanished like a snake into a hole—he left the fort before we even thought it was possible to take it. They are not fools, these Russians. It must have been plain to him that he was with a defeated army—so. For the next two or three generations at least, our passes to the north will be safe, except for the usual small forays, the autumn skirmishes, when the harvest is in, and young men are bored. The Russians know now that there is no easy way through our country to the plains—and I think they have found out that the English armies are not defeated, but that this mutiny has only strengthened their hold on India. For a century perhaps, we can live in peace. But all this is dust in my mouth so long as the Begum is as she is now. She is changed so terribly—'

'It takes time—' said Reiss helplessly.

'Time! As you say, hakim, it appears to take time. Well, the priests have settled on tomorrow as an auspicious day for the Dedication, and—'

'Tomorrow!' Reiss did not know what to do or say. 'Tomorrow—I had thought—the Begum is far from well, you know.'

'I know. I know indeed. But the day is right, the priests have consulted together, and as soon as the ceremony is over, I will take the Begum away—just the two of us, we will be alone and quiet together. She is so nervous and in such distress—she does not sleep at all, and is like a little collection of bones—somehow, I must find peace for her, and I cannot leave here now until the Dedication is over. So—tomorrow, and then we will go. I know she will recover alone with me—she has always wanted to go up into the mountains.'

Reiss was silent. If he told the truth now, when the priests had already chosen a day as being auspicious, it would cause terrible disruption, not only in Sher Khan's life, but also among the people, because of the ceremony. He realised that in his preoccupation he had not noticed all the preparations. He had seen the Temple precincts gradually filling with priests from other villages, had seen without any intelligence, the priests and the Moulvi from the Mosque conferring together and the silks and finery being brought out in all their brilliance, shaking in scarlet and gold and silver magnificence over every balcony and from every doorway, as the women prepared their best clothes, had seen all this, and had registered nothing. This ceremony of Dedicating a Ruler only happened once in a lifetime, all being well—and was of tremendous importance in the lives of these hill people. If Kurmilla was going to make trouble, she would certainly choose the time of the Dedication, when all the people were gathered in one place.

But there had been no sign of Kurmilla, or her companion. Bianca had told Reiss that she could remember Kurmilla saying to Hardyal that they must be far away by that night. Perhaps they had slipped through the passes, and gone south and there might be no need, God willing, to tell Sher Khan anything. Reiss turned away, and spent a miserable day, as usual, wondering where that evil couple were.

These nights, Sher Khan slept in the alcove, on the wide alcove seat, while Bianca lay, feigning sleep in her bed. Once he went over, and lay beside her, holding her close, whispering, 'Beloved—it has been so long. I know you cannot love me yet with your body, but let us lie close here together, and talk, until we fall asleep. I have missed you as I would miss water in the desert—' and he had felt her stiffen and shudder, and force herself to turn to him, pillowing her head on his shoulder with a catch of her breath, as if she could hardly bear to touch him. He did not stay with her long after that, but kissed her gently, covered her with blankets, and returned to lie wakeful through the night, full of unhappy questions, but hopeful for the future. Bianca was ill, very ill, that was plain, but she would get better once they were alone. He would take her to the shrine by the lake, and they would stay there quietly, together, until she had recovered her health. She was so young, and had suffered so much—he put her present withdrawn state down to her discovery that she was barren. She had not mentioned it to him, but Reis had thought it best to at least tell him that she knew that she could never have children. Surely the shock of that knowledge was enough to make her remove herself from all bodily contact. But she would return to him, once she knew that it made no difference to him. He heard her stirring in her bed, and held his breath, praying that she would call to him as she had so often in the past. But there was no sound but the wind outside, and the call of a night bird.

19

Before dawn the next day the drums and Temple bells and the priests blowing the conch shell had disturbed all the birds who nested in the trees around the Temple, and the dark sky was filled with the sound of their disturbed calling, and the clap of their wings. The people from all the villages of the valley had come in: the *serais* were full, and the *chaikhanas* round the square of beaten earth before the old palace did good trade in steaming bowls of tea, the steam from their great copper samovars misting the little lamps that hung over each booth. In brilliant silks and brocaded padded robes, the people were in holiday mood—this was a day of days. Beneath all the other noises was the deep continual hum, the sound of a crowd of happy, expectant people. The bowl of the slowly lightening sky seemed to echo with sound, as if a gong had been struck, and was still vibrating.

The morning was still young when the chief priest of the Temple, and the Moulvi from the Mosque came to take their places on the stone dais at the end of the square. At once the people began to gather, crowding on to the square, as many of them as could get on—the rest spilled over on to the village streets, and hung out of the tilting curved balconies. In front of the dais the priests of the Temples of other villages made a brilliant patch of colour in their orange robes, and between them and the dais was the royal guard, the troops in brilliant emerald turbans, each man holding his burnished sword and spear with the peacock emblem fluttering at its point.

Kassim stood at the head of the royal guard, facing the crowded square. His eyes were constantly seeking among the crowd and he knew that not all his men were standing behind him. Many of them were moving through the crowd, or standing on the outskirts, looking and listening. Kassim had spent two days and nights without sleep, going from one place to another, seeking information. He had immediately discovered that another search was already in progress, instigated by Reiss and had sent for Reiss, who had, with Goki, told him the whole story of the attack on Bianca. He had intensified the search, and had found nothing. No one had seen Kurmilla or her companion, no one knew anything about her—and he could find no trace of the men who had carried the palanquin.

Reiss's account of Bianca's condition was terrible to him—he felt that his youth and inexperience were a crime, that he should be able to advise and guide, and could not. In the end he went with Goki to his mother, and told her the story, and took her advice.

'Say nothing now. It is too late. Why did that fool Reiss not call me? Goki, you have been very foolish for the first time in your life—now all we can do is try to prevent a terrible scandal. I am afraid of that woman Kurmilla. She did not only wish to harm the Begum bodily. This is a much more serious matter than that. Sher Khan is already a man who expects the worst of women. Bianca was a miracle to him, and he loves her with all his heart and strength—but that does not mean that he will ever trust a woman again. I think Bianca, with all her youth, has already guessed this—and do not forget, she saw what he was like when she wanted to bring his own child to live with them. She is afraid to speak, because with her loving heart, she knows what he could be like. No, Kassim. Say nothing, and search for that devil and Kurmilla with every man you have. I will start enquiries among the women—but all must be done so carefully, and with such discretion—our every question could be all that is needed to bring down the disaster we fear.'

Goki spoke of the peaceful evening they had spent on that dreadful day, of the drugged gate keeper and guards who had taken twenty-four hours to recover, and who all thought they had been smitten with some terrible illness. 'I too—I took my usual milk with cinnamon and herbs infused in it—and thought, when I woke up, that I was dying. Someone who knew all our habits did the drugging.'

'Ragni?'

'Never. Ragni is loyal, even if a fool. But Kusma—now she was Kurmilla's creature, she lived here, she knew every door and window, every move we made—'

'Kusma is dead. I saw her die.'

'Kusma spent her days going from the Chotamahal to the Lalkoti. She was Kurmilla's spy. She told Kurmilla everything that happened in the Chotamahal, from the moment that Bianca came. I have talked with Kurmilla's ayah, who hates her, and with a very little money has opened her mouth very wide. I know enough now about Kurmilla to have her killed—but not enough to find her. The ayah would tell me if she knew where Kurmilla was—she does not know.'

Begum Mumtaz nodded. 'You are right, Goki—that ayah did hate Kurmilla—so it appears she has left, if the ayah cannot tell you where she is. But—I wonder. Kassim, my son, set your men everywhere because she must be found. There is this other matter also, you remember Kurmilla's vow to give Sara to the priests, for the Temple? Well, the chief priest from Surrendra Nath is here to take her. I spoke with Sher Khan at the time of the vow, telling him to repudiate it at once—but at that time all he would do was to repudiate the child. Now, of course, he has seen the mark on Sara, accepts her as his own, and says that she is not going to the Temple. Kassim, these are heavy matters for you, but there is no other man in our family now. You must go and see the priest.'

Kassim, quaking inwardly, went. He found the priest to be a gentle, elderly man, who was waiting for permission to take Sara for her long training as a temple dancer. The vow had been made, the child belonged now to the gods. He expressed surprised offence when Kassim bluntly told him that Sher Khan wished to break the vow, and buy Sara back.

'He offers a golden ransom to the Temple instead.'

'The gods do not need gold,' the priest said stiffly. 'The old Ruler would never have dishonoured a vow made to the gods. Is Sher Khan Bahadur so young and foolish that he thinks the gods forget? The child was given to them at birth.'

'Sher Khan made no vow. The vow was made by Kurmilla, not out of respect for the gods, but out of malice.'

'It does not matter why the vow was made. The gods see into the hearts of men. Sher Khan did not refuse at her birth. Why now?'

'Because he did not know that she was in truth his daughter.' Kassim's patience was beginning to run out. 'Holy one, you will have heard, even in your mountain Temple, of Kurmilla and what she was like. It was not possible for Sher Khan to believe that any child born to that strumpet could be his—and for her own evil reasons, Kurmilla did not tell him of the birthmark that all our family bear. When he saw that Sara had the mark—'

The priest's face changed. 'I understand my son, better than I did. But the vow was made. Gold will not placate the gods.'

It was plainly hopeless to go on arguing and Kassim had no time. He asked for leave to go and discuss the matter, and left the old man seated peacefully on a bit of matting in the shade of the Temple wall, his carved beads slipping softly through his fingers, his lips already moving in prayer.

After all this, as Kassim stood in his brocade coat and jewelled turban, watching the shifting, laughing crowd, he had so much to worry him that he found it hard to be still. Where *was* that bitch Kurmilla hiding? He was convinced that she was still in the State, waiting to strike, like a coiled cobra in a basket. He saw, among the priests before the dais, the old man from Surrendra Nath—Bianca, who loved Sara as her own child, would surely die if she lost her now. He stood there, his hand resting on his sword hilt, his face impassive, and his heart felt like a stone, as the people round him in their brilliant best clothes laughed and talked, their voices rising, as the holiday mood grew in them from minute to minute.

When Bianca and Sher Khan came, they were greeted by a great shout of pleasure. Bianca looked like a beautiful dream of mist and pearl in her delicate creamy silks, her hair dressed with pearls and diamonds, and one great emerald falling from her headdress to lie between her brows, her only touch of colour, green fire against the cream of her skin. Sher Khan was dressed in cream brocade, bare-headed, his only jewellery the emerald buttons that closed his long close-fitting coat. Behind Bianca and Sher Khan came the children, Sara and Muna, bright as butterflies in scarlet and gold. There was a vague murmuring of pleasure from the crowd as the two little girls went hand in hand to sit on the steps of the dais. Bianca and Sher Khan went up the steps, and the crowd fell silent then, as the ceremony began.

It was not a long or complicated ceremony. It had come down from priest to priest, since the days when the old Temple had been built centuries before by the dark little people who lived in the valleys long before the Aryan peoples had come down from the mountains to conquer and destroy the aboriginal dwellers. The old Ruler, Sher Khan's uncle, had kept the ceremony in its original form when he took the two States of Jindbagh and Diwarbagh, and joined them to his own State of Lambagh. The language of the Dedication and the prayers had changed, otherwise it was the same simple ceremony, the Dedication of a Ruler to his people.

The priests prayed, their voices blending together like the humming of bees in summer. Drums throbbed, the conch shell roared, and the Muslim priest, his voice trained to sound from the minaret in the thrice daily call to prayer, raised his hands and his voice was clear above all the other sounds. Sher Khan stood forward, confronting the people, and made his vow of service to them, ending with the words so often used by the hill people themselves when they spoke to their Ruler—'My life for yours, now and always.' Bianca, as the Ruler's wife, made the same vow, her voice soft, but so clear that they all heard her words—but as she spoke, she looked only at Sher Khan.

The priests stepped forward, and the eldest, a very old man indeed, who had been present at the Dedication of the old Ruler, turned to the crowd, holding up the twisted coruscating chain of gold and emeralds. He blessed the new Ruler in the old language, the language of the little dark peoples, long forgotten. This blessing, and the emerald chain were completely unchanged since those long ago days, and were the most important part of the ceremony. The old priest put the chain, with the great central emerald carved into the rough similitude of a peacock with spread tail, round Sher Khan's neck, and shouted to the people, his old voice cracking, 'Behold your Ruler, O people of the hills and valleys!'

The roar from the crowd as they acclaimed Sher Khan beat against the dais like a wave roaring in from the ocean, frightening in its power and intensity. Bianca caught her lip between her teeth, Sara and Muna flinched, and leaned close to Goki.

The ceremony was over, except for the granting of the three ritual boons. An old farmer asked for a grant of land, and was given it in perpetuity. A very young soldier, scarlet-cheeked under his tan, asked for a village head man's daughter in marriage—she was brought to him, unable to hide her happy smiles, and given to him, while the crowd shouted.

As the third petitioner, an old woman, came forward, there was a sudden upheaval in the crowd, a voice cried out, and heads began to turn, as the people tried to see what the disturbance was.

Kassim, pressing forward, saw a heavily veiled woman pushing her way through the laughing crowd. Behind her were three men, one of them magnificently dressed in pearl-embroidered brocade, bare-headed, walking with an insolent swagger, as he looked towards the dais, a small smile that was almost a snarl, twisting his mouth.

Kurmilla did not need to show her face. Her walk, and her figure, were unmistakable, the crowd had already recognised her, and were muttering and staring. But as she and her companions reached the steps of the dais, she threw back her veil, and raising her arrogant, beautiful face, called, 'I have a boon, O Lord of the Hills—'

The old priests on the dais were confused. The third petitioner fell back, staring, and Kurmilla repeated her cry, adding, 'Do you answer me, Lord of the Hills?'

'I answer you—' Sher Khan's voice was so roughened that it was a growl more than words. Bianca looked once at Kurmilla, and then, her face grey white, looked down at her hands. At the man standing beside Kurmilla she did not look at all.

Kassim felt the helpless horror of one who sees from a distance a disaster that he cannot prevent. He could not seize Kurmilla now, she had made herself part of the ritual. He stood, desperate, not knowing what to do, and his men stood irresolute behind him.

'I ask this boon for myself, and for his honour the priest of Surrendra Nath Temple. He does not need, in fact, to ask any boon. He came here to take, as had been promised to him that he could, the right of his Temple—my daughter Sara. I now ask that my vow is not dishonoured, and that my daughter is given to the Temple.'

On the steps, Goki was standing, looking towards Sher Khan. Sara had not moved. She looked at her mother, and then looked away, up to Bianca, a perfect trust on her face. Muna, sitting beside her, gripped her hand, and stared round-eyed at Kurmilla.

'My daughter goes nowhere,' said Sher Khan.

As if his voice had roused Bianca from some terrible dream, she looked at Kurmilla again, and past her, to the tall man, who smiled and bowed. Bianca's face looked as if it had been carved in ivory. She moved swiftly down the steps and stood between Sara and Kurmilla. Behind her, Goki, as if at a sign, took the children away, unnoticed by anyone except the priests, who did nothing, though they watched them go.

Sher Khan stood firmly where he was, and repeated clearly, 'My daughter goes nowhere. She stays with me and my wife, the Begum Bianca, in Lambagh.' The peacock chain glittered and burned with green fire on his chest as he spoke.

'So *ho*—she is *your* daughter now, after so many years of being the daughter of a groom. Strange—for the daughter you have so long denied, you are willing to risk the anger of the gods, not only for yourself but for all your people. "My life for yours", you have just taken that oath—but already you are forsworn. Your promises were never to be trusted, were they, oh Sher Khan Bahadur, Ruler of the Hills—a man who runs away and leaves his own kin to be slaughtered, because he covets an emerald chain—or was it that you lusted for that white girl, daughter of a hated race, barren and eaten by unhealthy lusts? Oh people of Lambagh, look at your Ruler, and his Begum—look, and take pride in them. Forsworn and dissolute, who will protect you from the anger of the gods, which will surely fall on you with such Rulers. Who will help you, if he breaks a vow made to the Temple?'

Sher Khan was moving towards the steps, when Bianca stood forward. She faced Kurmilla, and for a moment the woman was silent. Then she laughed, the screech of laughter that Bianca would remember all her life.

'Have you come to ask me a favour—O Begum Sahiba? What boon do I have to grant you? Would you beg something from me? I have heard you beg before, do not forget—but then you were begging for something I could not give you—it was Hardyal from whom you begged, was it not?'

'It was you who drugged me,' said Bianca quietly.

'Oh—so you were drugged—wait, I wonder if you are trying

to tell us that the night you took so much pleasure in was forced on you—do not lie, little Begum—'

'I do not lie.'

'No—it would be unwise. You see—there are witnesses. Mangalbhai—Randhal—come, tell us all of the night the Begum came to the house where I was staying with my cousin—come, do not be afraid. You speak under the protection of the ritual—none shall harm you. Now—how did the Begum come?'

'She was carried in our palanquin.'

'Was she drugged?'

'Nay—she was laughing. She walked into your house.'

'And then?'

The man who was speaking lowered his eyes in what appeared to be embarrassment.

'Speak, Randhal—speak. Say what you heard—'

'I heard—we heard the Begum and your cousin laughing together, and then we heard the sounds of love.'

'Mangalbhai—you looked through the window—what did you see? Was the Begum Sahiba drugged and helpless?'

'Nay, Lady—she was very active. She loved as a tigress loves, with a fierce lust, she was not drugged.'

Kurmilla looked up at the dais, where Sher Khan stood, like a figure of stone. Then she turned back to Bianca. 'Well, little Begum. Is that enough? Do you still say you were drugged?'

'I say nothing.'

'Oh? Then why do you look at me so? What do you ask from me?'

The blade in Bianca's hand was slim, the hilt set with turquoise and corals. Above it, her eyes were steady, cold and calm.

'I ask your life,' said Bianca quietly, and drove the blade home, pushing until her hand was flat against Kurmilla's body.

Kurmilla fell, very slowly it seemed, to lie, staring up at the sky, with no sight in her eyes, and blood embroidering a strange pattern on the dusty ground on which she lay.

Hardyal looked down at her, and then, before any of the staring onlookers could move, had slipped through the crowd and gone. The palanquin-bearers were easy to capture—they did not move—like puppets when the puppet master has dropped the strings, they stood, staring, almost lifeless and were dragged away. The crowd parted to let them and their captors through, and then turned back to the dais again. Sher Khan had not moved—he stood, and looked at nothing, and the only live thing about him was the emerald chain, flaring green fire with his every breath. Bianca looked up at him for a second, and then, no one preventing her, she went quietly away, taking the path that Goki and the children had taken earlier. Then, at last, Sher Khan moved. Without a backward look, he walked from the dais and followed Bianca, and Kassim was left alone, facing the silent crowd.

The silence of the crowd was as frightening as their previous shouts had been. They did not look at each other—they did not have to. They were as one person, all of them, one person, watching and listening, and waiting—and they would not, Kassim felt, wait very long. Their precious ritual had been broken, murder had been done before their eyes—he could feel the tension in the crowd mounting, and stepping forward he began to talk to them.

Kassim spoke to the crowd as a man telling a story to children. As the story began to unfold, told slowly in his clear voice so that everyone could hear, his audience began to relax, and listen in a different way. They listened as they had used to listen to the travellers' tales brought back by the visitors to the plains in the old days.

This was a splendid tale—heroes and villains, plots and disasters, courage and love and murder—and all the characters were known to them. Painted by that quiet clear voice, they saw pictures: Khanzada, known to them as a beautiful child, the youngest sister of their new Ruler. They saw her dying, and they saw the old Ruler fall before his time, through the treachery of Hardyal. They saw the young white Begum they had come to love, risking her life, and losing her son, to save the little girl Sara, whose paternity had always been whispered about. They raged when they heard that the young Begum had been brutally mistreated by Hardyal and his cousin, the woman they had always thought of as being a witch, Kurmilla of the Lalkoti. Some of them were loosening their weapons, and would have gone off there and then to start a search for Hardyal—but a new voice held them still.

With a long sigh of relief, Kassim looked behind him, and stopped speaking. Sher Khan had returned, and was in command of himself again. But when Sher Khan began to speak, Kassim would have stopped him, for what he said seemed terrible.

'Kassim Khan Bahadur has not told you all the story—and that is well, for this part of the story I must tell you myself. In saving my daughter Sara, the Begum lost our child and is now barren. She can never give me the son that every man hopes for. It does not concern you, my people, for you have the Yuvraj, Kassim Khan Bahadur, a young man in the full strength of his youth, who, if Allah so wills, will take the throne after me. But I can never forget that I can have no son—and nor can the Begum.'

There was no sound from the crowd—they stood, mesmerised, one great listening ear. Sher Khan paused, and looked down at all the staring faces upturned to him.

'My Begum, who is a brave girl, sends you a message. She regrets that it was necessary to defile the Dedication Ceremony by killing Kurmilla before you all. She is sure that by doing this, she has brought dishonour to my reign, and to the gods of the hills and valleys that she loves. I was in time, thanks be to Allah, to stop her taking her own life—but she will not accept the honour of being your Begum. She says that she is unworthy, and has, before the priests, revoked her vow of Dedication. She sends you, instead, a guiltless child—the child she bought with the loss of her own children—the price of her barren body. My daughter Sara.'

There was, for the first time since he had begun to speak, a murmuring among the crowd. Sher Khan paused again, until they were quiet, and then went on speaking. 'I know that you have had knowledge of all the trouble and disaster that Kurmilla brought to this State. This has now been wiped away in blood—the blood of my son, and the blood you saw shed. Not only has shame been taken from the State, but Sara, my daughter, has been twice bought, and no one can take her from us now. You have heard all the doubts expressed about her not being my child. I tell you now—she is my child. She bears the mark of our family—and I have the three priests here to vouch for this—'

He turned aside, and spoke to someone Kassim could not see,

and when he turned back, Sher Khan had Sara in his arms. She was frightened, Kassim could see her great wide-eyed stare, as the three old priests stepped up to the dais. The chief priest of the Temple spoke first.

'The child bears the mark of the tiger's claw—she is the true daughter of our Ruler, a child of the blood.'

Beside him, the old priest from the Temple of Surrendra Nath nodded. 'Yea—it is so. But she was vowed to our Temple—this is a hard matter—I know not how to proceed—' Sher Khan interrupted him.

'This is your new Begum, bought for you by blood, and by the bravery of my wife. I now dedicate her to your service. Sara, can you say the words?'

'Now?' questioned the child.

'Now.'

Sara turned in his arms, so that she faced the packed square. 'My life for your lives—now, and always—'

Her words fell into a pool of silence, and then the crowd went collectively mad, shouting itself hoarse, acclaiming their Ruler, his wife, his daughter, and his heirs, mad with a sudden unreasoning joy. Kassim heard his own name being shouted, as he stood beside his uncle and the little girl, and his eyes pricked with sudden tears. These people were not easily turned from their loyalties. He knew how superstitious they were—and that they must be terrified of what would, they imagined, come to their State if the Ruler went against the priests. But still, in their hearts, Sher Khan and his family were their choice, their protection, and their loved and honoured Rulers.

Sher Khan bowed deeply, first to the people, and then to the Moulvi and the two old priests. Sara still held close in his arms, he walked down the steps, and into the old palace, and the people began to disperse.

The Moulvi and the old chief priest were both of an age. They could remember the old Ruler being proclaimed, and the festivities that followed—but this time it was obvious that although the people of the States were loyal to Sher Khan, they were disturbed and worried. They dispersed quietly, and the stalls set up round the square, stalls selling hot cooked food and breads, and the *chaikhana*, the tea house, were not doing good business. The people were leaving, going to their own homes, not stopping to celebrate round the stalls. Already the shadow of the anger of the gods seemed to hang over Lambagh.

Kassim took Sara back to the Chotamahal, very tired and over-bright of eye. Goki took her off to bed with Muna at once.

They lay, the two children, holding hands and talking, until Sara fell suddenly asleep, her grip slackening on Muna's hand. But Goki saw that Muna was awake, her wide eyes staring up at the ceiling.

'What is it child? Why do you not sleep?'

Muna turned her head and looked at Goki, and her eyes were full of fear.

'Tell me, old one—will they take Sara—the priests?'

Goki shook her head. 'Nay, never, the Ruler has dedicated her as Begum of the State. They cannot touch her now.'

'Then—what will happen? Will the gods be angry? My mother was very afraid of the gods—there was a shrine near our house, and she used to take butter and marigolds there nearly every day, and pray for good fortune—'

Goki shook her head again, with a deep sigh. 'The gods are—the gods. The Great Ones. No one can tell what they will do. It was an evil vow, made by an evil woman, but it was a vow to the gods themselves—may they show mercy and understanding. Now child, sleep—this does not concern you—'

But Muna still looked at her beseechingly. 'Please, old one—leave the lamp, and do not go yet. I would know something. If the priests took Sara, what would they do? Would they kill her?' Her eyes were full of frightened tears.

'Oh child! What foolishness. Sara is not a lamb to be sacrificed on an altar before Kali! No indeed. If they took her, she would be treated with great care and kindness, and taught her trade well, so that she would earn much money for the Temple. She would wear silks and jewels, and be loved and respected all her days—'

'What would they teach her?'

'To sing, and play musical instruments, to dance, and every art there is to please men. Now, for the sake of all the gods, both great and small, sleep, Muna. Sara will not leave you, so put your mind at rest, and close those eyes. I will put the lamp here, so—

and I will come back and sit with you as soon as I have seen that all is well with the Begum—sleep, Muna, and sleep without fear.'

Goki was gone a long time, but Muna did not sleep. She lay, staring at the lamp. Once Sara stirred, and murmured in her sleep, and Muna rose on her elbow, and looked down at her, the envy, and the love on her child's face making it look older than her years. Then she lay down again, her eyes following the shadows the lamp threw on the wall, her hand still firmly clasping Sara's hand.

20

In her quiet room in the Chotamahal, Bianca sat, in fresh robes, her hair combed out about her shoulders, looking at the evening shadows closing over the lake, and waiting for Sher Khan. When he came, he stood for a minute looking at her, and she looked back at him in silence. He had changed his clothes, as she had, and was bare-headed. Bianca held his look, and he spoke first.

'It is done, as you wished.'

'That is good. There was no other way, Sher Khan. I wish that you had let me follow Kurmilla into the shadows of death. It would have been better.'

'Bianca—' At her raised hand, he stopped.

'Lord of the Hills—are you free now to speak with me?'

'Bianca—I am free. But before you speak, there are two things I must say. My name is Sher Khan.' He stopped speaking, and moving forward stood leaning against the arch of the alcove, as she had seen him do so often in their happy days together. 'Have I your permission to sit, Bianca?'

As she nodded, he sat down, his back against the opposite side of the alcove, his eyes turned to her. 'The second thing I would say is this. The people accepted Sara with joy—but they called your name too. They love you Bianca—as I do. Bianca—'

'Wait, Sher Khan. I have a great deal to say. When I have finished, you may take me in your arms—if you still wish to do so—'

'Bianca!'

He got up and went over to her, and taking her in his arms, began to cover her face with kisses, his whole body shaking with the intensity of his passionate longing. Then her stillness stopped him, and he looked down at her face, feeling as if he held an ivory figure in his arms. 'Beloved—' his voice was barely above a whisper, 'Bianca—what is it? Am I repulsive to you? For I cannot bear this—you turn to stone when I touch you, and shudder as if I were a snake—look, it is I, Sher Khan who loves you—not that monster who maltreated you.'

Bianca nodded at him. 'I know who you are. But how can you say you love me—you heard the story that woman told. She was not lying you know—she spoke the truth. I can remember more every day. Do you want to hear?'

Sher Khan drew a deep torn breath, and put out a hand to her. Then as she involuntarily flinched away he said, 'But do you not know—I love you forever. I could no more put you away than I could take my own life—in fact it would be easier to take my life. You are my spirit and my soul as well as my beloved bedfellow. Nothing else matters to me—even if you had gone willingly, I would not have been able to tear you from my heart. But you were drugged.'

'So you could take me now, and make love to me, even after what you heard—and all that I could tell you?'

'Let me show you,' said Sher Khan, and lifting her in his arms, carried her over to the bed. But as with gentle amorous hands and lips he began to make love with her, he saw she was weeping, and raising himself, stopped at once, and said, 'Oh God, Bianca, what is it? Do I hurt you?'

'In a thousand ways that you do not know of. You and I must part, Sher Khan—and as you have said to me, I say to you—you are my spirit and my soul. My bedfellow I think no one can ever be again. My body is not the only thing they defiled. They have imprinted filth on my mind, and I am lost.'

He got up, and covered her, and sat beside her on the bed. 'Tell me, Bianca, tell me all that you have not told me.'

Slowly, as she talked, he began to see with horror, that she had learned a concept of evil that far transcended all hope of comfort. No revenge that he could think of could return to her her lovely purity, her gentle pleasure in his love, her innocent, ardent lust and passion. She had looked at the face of evil, and it was not going to be easy—or perhaps, even possible—to uproot from her mind, her horror of herself. She was remembering more clearly every day scenes from that terrible night—and his every touch, his loving words and actions, his passion, only made it worse for her, as she recalled with revulsion her own reactions in the arms of a stranger.

Sher Khan turned away, and wept, and Bianca wept with him,

but could not bring herself even to touch his hand.

Presently, Sher Khan went through into the bathroom, and she heard him bathing—when he came back, he was dressed again, although his hair was still wet and tousled.

'I go, my dear love, to speak to Reiss and Kassim. Rest—and try to find peace. Be very sure that I will give you nothing that you do not want, and never forget how much I love you. It is your essence, your very self that I love, quite apart from your beautiful body. Promise me you will do nothing foolish to break my heart—promise me?'

Bianca lifted heavy eyes. 'There is nothing more I can do, Sher Khan. I will wait here for you, but as to resting—will I rest again?

Sher Khan looked down at her, bit his lip on something he would have said, and left her.

Reiss and Kassim had a blistering hour with him.

Strangely enough, he did not ask that the search for Hardyal be continued. He showed no pleasure when he was told that Hardyal was known to have left the valley by the Lungri Pass, and that the two men who carried the palanquin had been found with their throats cut, hanging like vermin in a tree by the main village street, a warning to all.

'Let Hardyal go—the British will deal with him in due course. But you—you two—I cannot trust either of you again. Kassim, stay away from me, for I am afraid of what I may do. You knew you should have told me. You wronged me deeply by keeping this terrible thing from me. As for you, Reiss, you stay, because I need you for the Begum. Now, send Goki to me.'

But there was no need to send for Goki. As he spoke, she was there, wild-eyed, her head cloth flying in haste, calling for Sher Khan. 'Lord of the Hills, Muna is gone—'

Sher Khan only said, 'And Sara?'

'She is there, asleep—but I left Muna with her, and she is gone. I cannot find her anywhere.'

Sher Khan turned to Kassim. 'Like a stone thrown into a pool, this stupid secrecy of yours has started to spread in ripples that will end God knows where. Let a search be mounted. Goki, you have something more to say?'

'Lord, she questioned me last night about the Temple priests. She was distressed believing that Sara was to be sacrificed. I wonder—'

But Kassim, raging, was already gone on his way to the Temple, and Sher Khan went with Reiss to Bianca's room.

The old priest from the Surrendra Nath Temple had always wakened before dawn to say his morning prayers. He had washed himself, gasping at the cold of the water from the well, robed himself in his orange robes, and was seated on his mat under the tree in the courtyard, going deeper and deeper in contemplation, his brown carved beads idle in his hands, when he was brought back to earth by a gentle plucking at his robe. He opened his eyes to see a very small girl looking at him. Her face was terrified, and she looked as if she might turn and run, but the old man had a gentle smile, and loved children.

'What is it child?'

'I am Muna. I come from the Chotamahal—I am the adopted daughter of the Ruler. I come to ask if it would be well if I came with you for the gods, instead of Sara—she cannot come, she is the real daughter of the Ruler, and she is also the Begum of the State. Would the gods be satisfied and forget to be angry, if I came instead?'

The priest considered her seriously. 'A willing sacrifice, made for a whole State's good, and for love of another? Yes, my child. The gods would be very pleased, and you would gain great merit. Are you sure you wish to come?'

The word sacrifice had made Muna very frightened—sacrifice, to her, meant the bleating of a dying kid on a bloodstained stone. So Goki had not told the truth about all the teaching and the dancing and music. But she set her will, and said firmly, 'I am sure. I wish to come with you instead of Sara.'

'It is hard work learning to be a servant of the Temple—'

'Hard work? But you said sacrifice—'

The priest took her hand into both of his. 'Tell me, child—were you willing to come when you thought a knife was to be your fate?' His voice was very gentle. Her eyes full of tears, Muna nodded.

'Then indeed the gods will be pleased. You have already

gained merit, and you will be remembered for ever in the hills and valleys of the three States. There is no blood, child. You will learn many things, and I hope that you will be fortunate and come to enjoy your life. Let us take this matter to the priests of this Temple.'

When Kassim came to the Temple, he was met by the old chief priest.

'The child came to the Holy One of Surrendra Nath, before the birds had begun their morning song. She has taken Sara's vow on herself—to remove the anger of the gods from the valley, and to save Sara from having to fulfil Kurmilla's vow. It is very well so, Kassim Khan Bahadur—the child has come willingly—and she came, believing that she would be sacrificed on the altar of the Temple. Truly, she is a brave and beautiful child. I will tell Muna's story all about the valleys, and her name will live here, with honour, as long as there are our people in this valley.' Looking at Kassim's worried face, he laid a gentle hand on the young man's shoulder. 'She will have a good life, Lord. You know how she will be treated, and what she will become, because she is so beautiful. Here, she would have always been the adopted one, the unknown child from the plains. Now she has a future, and will be honoured. It is better thus. Tell the Ruler—and tell him also that the gods will smile on his reign, and the people will prosper. He is of another faith, but like his uncle, he has to please all his people, and protect their worship.'

Only Goki saw Muna before she left. No one was present at the meeting between the old woman and the child she had saved. Goki came back, dry-eyed, and her old face was as expressionless as always. Sara was told that Muna had gone to Surrendra Nath to learn many things, and at once demanded to go too.

'But you have many things to learn here—besides, how can you speak of leaving your beloved new mother, who needs you? Sara, have you so quickly forgotten her? You cannot go. You are the Begum of Lambagh, and must stay here and do your learning, as Muna does hers in Surrendra Nath.'

'But will I never see her again? She is my sister—I want her here—'

It was impossible to explain to Sara that the paths of a Temple dancer, a trained and very expensive prostitute, and a Begum were unlikely to cross—so Goki said no more, but took Sara to Bianca, who held her close while she wept, and said nothing. Later, when the tempest of tears was over, Sher Khan took his daughter out riding, and expressed himself dumb with admiration at her prowess in the saddle—and in two days, a small well-behaved pony, with a mouth like silk, and a scarlet saddle and scarlet and silver reins, was produced for Sara—and she rode every day with the Guard Commander's youngest son, who was not much older than herself, and she seemed to grow more reconciled to Muna's absence. But at night she often woke Goki, weeping in her sleep, and she did not eat as much as she should have done.

Bianca herself was skin and bone. Her eyes were large in a small white face. Reiss had stopped the opium mixture, and she was now either sleepless, or else had the terrible sleep of those who have a constant nightmare. Sher Khan watched her twist and turn, and heard her cries, and grew thin himself, and the frown between his eyes was permanent.

After a night when he had watched her lie, desperately trying to keep awake to avoid her dreams, he went to Reiss, and asked that the opium be given to her again.

'No, Lord. Not unless you wish to add an addiction to her other troubles. She will have to fight her way through this. No one can help her.'

Sher Khan said, with difficulty, 'It is my name she calls in all her nightmares—yet she wakes screaming if I touch her. Can you not help us, Reiss? I cannot bear any more of this.'

Reiss had never heard Sher Khan speak like this before. There was a plea in his proud, desperate eyes. 'Lord of the Hills, indeed and indeed, if I had any skills to minister to the mind, I would help you. This evil is not in her body, it is deep within her brain—and I know nothing of such things. I am not a healer of the soul, Lord. Let me go to the priests of the Temple, and speak with them. I think they have many skills that I have not—'

Sher Khan was willing for any kind of help to be called on. 'Bring in the devil himself if it will help—'

Reiss shook his head. 'No, Lord. The devil is what we fight—and one of the strongest weapons we have is that child Sara.'

This was true. Sara gave Bianca so much pleasure. It was as if the two comforted each other for their losses—Bianca for the loss of her innocence and her peace—Sara for the loss of her sister and beloved playmate. The hours she spent with the child were the hours that kept Bianca alive, Sher Khan was convinced of this.

Before Reiss went to the priests, he said, watching Sher Khan's face, 'Lord—Kassim would speak with you—' and saw, as he had feared, Sher Khan's face grow hard and cold.

'I have nothing to say to him. I can forgive you, for Bianca has told me how she prevailed on you to be silent. But Kassim should have told me, instead of leaving me to face that terrible disclosure before the people.'

'Lord, you cannot be at odds with Kassim. He is your heir—'

'So. He is my heir. When I die, he will be Lord of the Hills. But while I live, I have nothing to say to him.'

Reiss went away, and before he went to the Temple, he called at the house of Kassim's mother.

When Sher Khan came out of Bianca's room later that day, he found the Begum Mumtaz waiting for him, her veil thrown back and her beautiful eyes, so like his own, blazing with anger.

'Listen you to me, O little brother—Lord of the Hills you may be, but to me you are still my brother, the scrubby little boy who used to run to me with every cut or bruise he had—what are you doing to my son? He was chosen as your heir by the old Ruler himself and you treat him as a dog, passing him in the street as if he was not there, and refusing to see him. He mopes, and grows thin and wishes to leave the State. You are doing well, are you not? You know that if you had listened to me you would have had none of this trouble, for you would never have married Kurmilla—'

'Mumtaz—this is old history you are repeating to me—'

'This history of Kassim my son is not old.'

'Mumtaz—you know how much trouble I already have—do you wish to add to it?'

'I do not come to add to it. I come again, to warn you. Kassim will leave you. He will do what he has longed to do—go and join the army. Is that what you want?'

'Mumtaz—sister. I can think of nothing but Bianca—you know how things are with her.'

'I know everything. Nay, then, Sher Khan. I love my brother. But do not destroy everything around you in your pain. You have held off from me for so long—are you going to treat Kassim in the same way?'

Sher Khan went over to her and took her face in his hands. 'Mumtaz—you once told me the bitter truth. No man wishes to be told the truth when he is newly married. But you were right—and I was wrong. Perhaps you are right again. Bring Kassim in—indeed, I need my family, I need your help.'

Kassim, when he came, was a very angry young man. No longer a boy, he found it hard to face his uncle. His pride had been hurt, and he could not forget Sher Khan's words—'I cannot trust you again.' No matter how much oil was poured on troubled waters by his mother, the words remained, sticking like a thorn in his mind. He spoke coldly to Sher Khan standing stiffly in front of him.

'I have news. You were of course, right. I sent a man to follow Hardyal, and he has now returned. Hardyal was taken by the British just outside Multan and is now imprisoned, I understand for life. It seems that among other crimes, he murdered an English colonel, and his wife, and three children, and witnesses have come forward—the servants of the colonel. Hardyal killed two of them also, but the cook remained.'

'So—the snake is trapped, but not killed. I do not understand the British.'

In his state of angry hurt, Kassim took this as a veiled insult to his British father. He stood more stiffly, and said, 'He was of royal stock—so was not killed. Lord of the Hills, I have a request.'

Sher Khan looked at him wearily. 'Kassim—must you stand there like a wooden man? Sit, boy, for God's sake—I have many things to ask you.'

'As you will not believe any of my answers, I see no point in you asking any questions. I repeat, I have a request. I would leave Lambagh and go down to Madore, and join the Lancers there. Have I your leave to go?'

'Will you stay if I refuse it?'

'No. I will renounce my rights if you refuse to let me go.'

'And if I die, you will be happy to know that the States will be in the hands of a child—a girl.'

Kassim preserved a cold silence. Sher Khan looked at him, and said, 'Very well. I give you leave on one condition. You do not renounce your rights—you do not marry—and you return here, at once if I die, in ten years from now if I live. Is that understood?'

Kassim, astonished, not only at the conditions his uncle had laid down, but also at having got his way so easily, bowed, and stepped back.

'It is understood, Lord of the Hills. Do you want my written promise?'

'Kassim, I have your word. Do not make me angry.'

Kassim bowed again, his hand on his heart, and then on his lips, and from there to his head in the old salutation, and saying quietly, 'My life for yours, Lord,' left Sher Khan alone.

Shortly, Mumtaz Begum came to Sher Khan. 'Well?'

'You were right. I have lost him.'

'Not quite. He loves you. He will not desert you—but he needs to go away. He will learn much, and become a man of authority—as you did. He has always admired and loved you, and tried to emulate you. But now you have hurt him badly. He will heal his hurts, trying to become a man like you.'

'A better man than I am, I hope, Mumtaz. Now, will you come with me and see Bianca—she is waiting for you.'

Late that evening, when Bianca was lying on her bed, with Sher Khan talking to her, Goki came in to say that Reiss was outside, asking to speak to the Ruler.

Outside, in the anteroom, Reiss was waiting with the chief priest of the Temple, and the Moulvi from the Mosque.

The old priest was the spokesman. 'Lord, we have come to a decision after much prayer, and thought, and after consulting the Koran, and our holy books, and the Christian bible. All these sacred writings teach us that there is, within each of us, a creative power, a sleeping serpent, that can be used for great good, or great evil. Those wicked ones who took the Begum on that ill-starred night, and drugged her, by their evil doing, roused the sleeping serpent within her, and misdirected it into her lower nature, where it has coiled and now brings only the knowledge of evil to her. Until that serpent moves upwards again, towards her head and her heart, she can find no peace.'

Sher Khan looked from one to the other, a cold fear invading his mind. 'So—you have brought a remedy, I trust, as well as telling me the cause of her illness?'

'Lord, the remedy is a hard one. The Begum must go from this place. Everything here now recalls that terrible night. She must go away, and live where she only knew happiness.'

'Do I go with her?'

'Nay, Lord of the Hills. For you only remind her, and your presence and your touch keep the serpent awake. She needs no man now. She needs to be alone. But the child must go with her—for without each other, those two will surely die. Truly a child can belong to a woman, without the accident of birth. In some other life, Sara was your Begum's child, and they have recognised each other. The bond is very close, thus.'

'And I live here alone?'

'Lord, we said it was hard.'

'It is not hard—it is impossible. I am not a god—I am a man, I want my wife, and my child with me—'

Reiss spoke then, for the first time. 'Lord—the Begum is very near to death. One can die of a broken heart and mind, as easily as one dies from a broken body. The Begum Sahiba has her hand on the latch of the door of death, even now.'

Sher Khan left them, and went into Bianca's room, and found her lying as he had left her, in her beautiful bed with its silver lamp, that now showed no beauty in her face, but made her look all bones and hollows.

'My love, if you wish to leave me where will you go?'

'Sher Khan, I do not wish to leave you. I would give all the years of my life to stay with you for one day as we used to be together. But I must go. I would like to go to the Madoremahal. Perhaps I will find myself there, as I was when you first met me. If not, and I die, will you bury me in that garden? But Sara—oh Sher Khan, look after Sara—'

Her face twisted into an ugly mask of pain, and Sher Khan said swiftly, 'Sara goes with you—no one else can care for her, and bring her up as you will be able to. I will tell you our plans tomorrow—or later tonight, if you prefer. Rest now, my soul, even if you cannot sleep.'

He joined the men waiting in the anteroom.

'She goes. You are right. Kassim Khan Bahadur will be her escort, with twenty men of the Guard. She will live in the Madoremahal, and she must have every comfort. Goki and Sara go with her. Reiss, I would like you to go.'

'Lord of the Hills, no. I stay here with you. She will not need me there. There are many skilled doctors in Madore. I will be here, with you.'

'In case my heart breaks?'

'Men do not have broken hearts. There is much for you to do in this country of yours, Lord. In these years, you can make it a land of great ease and civilisation, and be the envy of your neighbouring States.'

'In how many years? Am I to be alone for perhaps ten years? I shall be an old broken man.'

'If it is ten years Lord, you will be thirty-eight. The Begum Sahiba will be twenty-six—and Sara will be nearly sixteen. Then, when they return you can begin your lives again and you will find many consolations within the next years. It may not be so long.'

Sher Khan stared at him like a man who had just been given a death sentence. The old priest and the Moulvi each blessed him in their different ways, and left. Reiss stayed, and watched a strong young man fight his way through a storm of grief and pain that he would never forget. Then, calm again, Sher Khan went back to Bianca.